THE POWER OF
Yesterday's Tears

Gloria F. Martin

iUniverse, Inc.
New York Bloomington

The Power of Yesterday's Tears

Copyright © 2010 Gloria F. Martin

This is a work of fiction. All of the characters, names, incidents, organizations, and dialogue in this novel are either the products of the author's imagination or are used fictitiously.

iUniverse books may be ordered through booksellers or by contacting:

iUniverse
1663 Liberty Drive
Bloomington, IN 47403
www.iuniverse.com
1-800-Authors (1-800-288-4677)

Because of the dynamic nature of the Internet, any Web addresses or links contained in this book may have changed since publication and may no longer be valid. The views expressed in this work are solely those of the author and do not necessarily reflect the views of the publisher, and the publisher hereby disclaims any responsibility for them.

ISBN: 978-1-4502-3707-9 (pbk)
ISBN: 978-1-4502-3708-6 (cloth)
ISBN: 978-1-4502-3709-3 (ebk)

Printed in the United States of America

iUniverse rev. date: 8/4/2010

Dedications & Acknowledgements

I would like to delicate The Power of Yesterday's Tears to the people who provided the most encouragement: my intelligent and handsome son, Howard Javar Martin and my wonderful and caring mother, Dorothy Mae Rowden. I would also like to extend a special dedication to the loving memory of my daddy, the late John H. Rowden. First, I would like to thank my Heavenly Father because without Him I am nobody and can do nothing. I wish to acknowledge the following people for their loyal and unrelenting assistance in the editing process: Talena Kimble, Adrina Beaumont, Suzel Woods, Randall Johnson, and all of my coworkers of FloriMed Medical Clinic. A special thanks to the two men in my life, Joseph Franklin and Howard J. Martin for their unwavering efforts and support in the creation of my book cover.

PART I
JACKSONVILLE, NORTH CAROLINA

Chapter 1

1991: Henry dropped us off at the Jacksonville bus station and couldn't even wait until we got on the bus before driving away. Me and Li'l Henry sat there for about 30 minutes before the bus finally arrived. Yes, Henry knew what time that bus was due in, because he was the one who called the station to schedule it. I remember feeling as though he had someone else on his mind other than me; especially after that morning at the hotel room, when he received a telephone invitation to a cookout that his friends were having. I didn't really concern myself with it, because I felt he did all he could in trying to keep us here in Jacksonville. We couldn't find an affordable and decent place to live, and when the money ran out, Li'l Henry and I had to go.

After about three hours of nonstop riding, the passengers on the bus grew quiet. I looked over at Li'l Henry, and he was sound asleep. He resembled his father so much with his Chinese slanted eyes, bushy eyebrows, and dark complexion. My family joked about how his father could never deny that Li'l Henry was his child. He was my little bundle of joy who made the idea of meeting Henry seem worthwhile.

Henry and I were high school sweethearts. We met when I was in tenth grade and he was in twelfth. Everyone thought that we were the perfect couple, and we did look good together. He was medium built and stood a little over six feet tall. He had very dark skin that was flawless, and his wavy hair was always cut in a short, tapered style. He had slanted eyes, bushy eyebrows, and was a very handsome man. I had a light-skinned complexion and was supermodel thin. My dark brown hair hung to my shoulders and was always curled in a nice, conservative style. I was on the high school pom-pom team and was known for my big, pretty legs. Because we were so in love, it was inevitable that we would get married one day.

1983: Henry enlisted in the Marines during my twelfth grade year. After I graduated, and when he had served almost three years, Henry asked me to marry him. I can still remember it so vividly. I had

1

arranged all of the wedding plans: where we would get married, have the reception, the color scheme, who would be the bridesmaids and groomsmen, etc. In Saginaw, Michigan, there was a place called the Rose Garden, and it was absolutely beautiful in the summertime. Even though it was called the Rose Garden, it had other types of flowers, such as annuals, water lilies, and perennials, that were all in those soft, pastel colors that released an aroma of fresh, floral scents. These flowers were in full bloom and superbly situated around a setting that was perfect for a wedding. The Garden had a waterfall at the end of the walkway that could be viewed by everyone in the guest seating area. It created a relaxed and serene atmosphere that could serve as entertainment during the candle-lighting portion of the ceremony. At the end of the walkway stood a big jacaranda tree that bloomed violet-blue flowers and left its reflection in the waves of the pond created by the waterfall directly behind it. Under this tree was where the preacher, Henry, and I would stand for the union of our lives together.

The guesthouse of the apartments where I lived was reserved for the reception. I bought and mailed the invitations, purchased all the decorations, and ordered the cake. I put the deposit down on the Rose Garden, the photographer, and the catering company. I was so excited about my accomplishments and couldn't wait until Henry got home. So you can imagine my disappointment when, upon his arrival, he went to his mother's house before seeing his fiancée, but I didn't make a big deal about it. After all, I was going to be his wife, the woman he would come home to everyday.

When he called, I updated him on all I had accomplished with the wedding since we last spoke. I could sense some hesitation on his part, but I was too excited to address it. At first he didn't come straight out and say it; he beat around the bush by talking about things that happened while on his drive home.

Finally, after what may have been careful consideration, Henry said, "I don't want to get married." I heard the words loud and clear, but I hoped I didn't hear what I thought I did. However, shortly thereafter in the pit of my gut I knew for sure exactly what he had said. After about a minute or so of complete silence, I was able to speak and calmly asked, "Why?"

"I'm just not ready to get married," he said. I looked down at the engagement ring that I had worn on my finger for the past four months and thought about how happy we both were when he gave it to me. I started crying, a small whimper at first; and then, after he said nothing else, I hysterically began pleading with him. "Don't do this Henry, please don't do this!"

He finally said, in a harsh and cold voice, "This is my final decision, and please don't try to change my mind, Gwen."

When I realized he meant what he said and there was nothing I could do or say, I grew angry and vindictive. I wanted to hurt him now; I wanted to make him experience the pain I was feeling, so I cursed at him! I said words he had never heard me say—that anyone had never heard me say before. After I released all of my energy, hostility, and frustration out on him, I slammed the phone down, went to my room, and cried my eyes out.

I didn't hear a word from Henry until the next day. He called and asked if I was okay, and by that time I had cooled off. He finally got me to agree to wait by assuring me we would get married, but just not now. We made plans to cancel and return everything we could and call all of our friends to inform them of the cancellation. As I agreed to everything, I plotted in the back of my mind that as soon as he went back to Jacksonville, I was going to enlist in the Army and he would never see me again. No way was I going to marry this man after he had humiliated me.

Henry started behaving like the sweet and kind gentleman that he was when I first met him. He was home on a one-month leave from the Marines, and he spent most of the remainder of his time with me. He took me to dinner and to the movies, held my hand, told me I was beautiful, and just showered me with attention. He even stayed in Lansing with me instead of in Saginaw with his mother, which made me finally believe I was someone significant in his life. So naturally when he said, "Let's get married now, before I go back," I quickly agreed, "Yes!" Before he left, we ended up getting married at the courthouse, three days after that originally scheduled wedding date. My friend Alice and his friend Kenneth were our witnesses.

When Henry got back to Jacksonville, he was supposed to search for a place for us to live and then send for me. Every time we talked, it was this and that excuse. Finally I got fed up and wasn't taking any more of his lame excuses. I told him I had saved some money and was coming there whether he had an apartment or not. I told him we could look for one together, and he basically had to agree with me because he didn't have any other choice. About a week later he called and said he had been scheduled to go on a six-month float. That's when the Marines go out on a ship for six months, just sailing around and stopping at ports from time to time. Of course that destroyed my plans to come, which was what I believe he had wanted to do all along.

It had been about three weeks since he had supposedly gone, and I hadn't heard from him. Prior to leaving Henry, promised to write and also call when they made port stops. One day I thought I'd call his unit to get the address to write him, because I was missing my husband. Someone answered the phone and I babbled on about how I wanted to get an address to write my husband who was out at sea. I was sort of embarrassed that I had to ask someone for information I should have already known. "Are you talking about Corporal Miller? Wait a second, Ma'am, he's right here." He then placed me on hold. While I waited I could feel the rate of my breathing speed up and my heart began pumping twice as fast and ten times as hard. As I tried to think of what I would say, I became convinced that if I had waited on hold another minute longer, I would hyperventilate. Henry finally got to the phone and in the middle of saying hello, I screamed. "What the hell are you doing there?" He concocted some cockamamie story about returning early. "Gwen, I was going to call you today, honest I was!" I was so angry that I didn't just hang up but slammed the phone down. I could not believe this man. No one had to beat me across the head for me to realize he did not want me there.

Once again, my idea to enlist in the regular Army resurfaced. It was always my plan B and my way out. I wouldn't completely call it my revenge tactic, because I had been considering enlisting ever since I completed basic training. I was in the Army Reserve at the time and was told I had to work at least a year for them before I could enlist in the regular Army. The Reserve had to get a little of their invested money out of me. However, the advantage of being in the Army Reserve gave me the choice of being stationed wherever I chose. Normally, a person chooses three preferred permanent duty places, and the military tries to station him or her at one of their choices. The twist to this was the Army doesn't really have to secure the permanent choice until after the person completes basic training and a specialty school. There's a chance of not getting any of the choice places, especially since nothing is guaranteed prior to the start of basic training.

In my situation, I would be going straight to my permanent duty station, so if I couldn't get North Carolina then I didn't have to enlist, and of course the Army wanted me to do that. Even though I was mad as hell at my husband, I was a levelheaded person, and I wanted my marriage to work. So making a decision like stationing myself somewhere other than close to where he was, just to play some type of revenge game, would be foolish.

A couple of months later I got stationed at Fort Bragg, a post that was situated in the heart of Fayetteville, North Carolina, and two hours away from Jacksonville. I kept Henry informed of my whereabouts even though we were still not on good speaking terms.

1991: After 48 hours, the bus made its last stop. When Li'l Henry and I arrived in Saginaw, I didn't call my husband, because I didn't think he could be reached at the barracks. There was only one telephone on the floor, and half of the time no one answered it. I was also having mixed emotions about his lack of concern that we couldn't be together. Besides, he said he would call and give me a better number to reach him.

After one week of not hearing from him, I decided I would contact his job at the Marine Corps Base Camp Lejeune to see why he hadn't called. "Your husband was admitted to the Naval Hospital, Ma'am," said the corporal who answered the telephone. "What happened?" I somehow choked out. I was told Henry had been stabbed, and my eyes almost popped out of my head. I immediately asked for the telephone and room number of the hospital, which the corporal quickly provided.

Henry sounded a little muffled when he answered the telephone. "What happened, Baby?" I asked. He told me he got into an argument with a woman at the cookout the day Li'l Henry and I left Jacksonville, and she ended up stabbing him. "What the hell were you arguing about?" I asked in my scrutinizing voice. He explained how this woman wanted him, but he didn't want anything to do with her. As a matter of fact, he tried to avoid her at the cookout, but she was determined to get his attention. She kept playing and joking around until finally he got fed up and told her to leave him the hell alone. When she realized he was serious, she started an argument, which ended with him being stabbed in the stomach.

Of course, there are always two sides to a story and I didn't believe his, but I didn't say anything as I continued to listen. His story sounded so far-fetched, and even I knew that if a female stabbed him, there was definitely something going on between them. The bottom line was I was committed to making my marriage work this time, so I chose to believe he was telling the truth, and I tried very hard not to think otherwise.

Chapter 2

1992: This is my third time relocating to Jacksonville. In 1987 Henry had completed his first enlistment in the Marines, and the plan was for him to relocate to Fayetteville, where I was stationed at the time, and enlist in the Army so we could be together. After Henry couldn't get into the Army and I had orders to go to Germany, we packed everything and moved to Jacksonville. Henry reenlisted in the Marines, I went overseas, and Li'l Henry stayed in Jacksonville with Henry. Shortly thereafter, I got out of the Army on a hardship and joined my family back in Jacksonville.

To be granted a hardship discharge is very difficult in the military. However, Henry was given orders to go on TDY (temporary duty) in California for three months and my sister who was currently living with them could not continue to care for my son. Since we did not have anyone assigned as Lil' Henry's legal guardian, the discharge was granted. When Henry returned from TDY we lasted about six months before I walk out on him and took Li'l Henry home to Saginaw to live with my mother.

The second time I moved to Jacksonville was in 1991 after living in Saginaw for a year. Henry came and got us after he and I agreed to try and make our marriage work. We stayed in a hotel for two weeks, and since we couldn't find a place to live, Li'l Henry and I ended up going right back to Saginaw on a bus. Now we are here for the third time; they say it's a charm.

"Gwen, are you listening to me?" Sheila asked while I was deep in thought. Sheila is a friend of mine from when I previously lived here in Jacksonville, and we met through our husbands. She is a beautiful dark-skinned girl with a slim physique. She dresses nice all the time and wears different types of hats. I swear she has a different hat for every day of the month. I don't understand why she wears them, because she has nice long, black hair. Sheila's husband, Marcus, who is about a foot shorter than she, is also a Marine and in the same unit as Henry. They didn't have any kids back when I lived here, but now they have a little girl who is almost two years old.

So Sheila and Marcus were at our apartment last night, and we were all having a good time reminiscing about how they used to come over and play cards. We were some serious card players back in the day, and we would play until the wee hours of the morning. Henry and I teamed up against them, and we spanked their butts every single time. They would beg for rematches, but of course the couple from Saginaw was undefeatable.

While we were laughing, Sheila leaned over and whispered to Marcus to take her over to Lynn's house to get a hat she had previously loaned her. Everybody heard her, grew very quiet, and started looking around, which made me feel there was something I should know. However, I didn't say anything, because I learned a long time ago it's best to listen, observe, and learn. I was also sure that since my recent return, I would be faced with some uncomfortable situations, since my husband had been here in Jacksonville alone for over two years. Anyhow, Henry boldly suggested we all go. He asked me to get Li'l Henry ready, which I did, and we all drove over there together. But only Sheila got out.

When she returned to the car, Henry asked her, "What did she have to say about me?" He seemed pretty confident she had at least said something about him, and Sheila replied, "Nothing." He began calling Lynn offensive names while demeaning her personal hygiene and physical appearance. It seemed to me to be an attempt to confuse me or maybe give me the impression she was someone he was not interested in.

Today is my day off work, and Sheila came by to sit with me as she often did. We didn't keep in contact after I left Henry, so I valued our private girl talk. She didn't have a job, and her daughter was living in

Texas with her mother because Sheila had recently left Marcus. When I got back, I learned they had gone through some difficult times, and Sheila took their daughter and moved to Texas, which was where they both were originally from. Marcus had convinced her to come back, but she didn't bring her daughter with her because she wasn't sure it was going to work out. Anyhow, this was her chance to enlighten me about Lynn, since Henry was away at work. She thought I knew about Lynn, especially after Henry spoke of her so candidly last night.

Sheila explained, "Lynn and I used to hang out together, but now we barely speak."Lynn was a manipulator, and Henry had fallen head over heels in love with her while I was gone for those two years. They'd had a relationship, and my husband still cared for this woman; even I could sense that.

Henry and Lynn met right before he and Marcus had to go to Saudi Arabia for the Gulf War and shortly after I'd left him. The four of them used to hang out together often. Lynn was also in the Marines and had a little girl, whom Henry would babysit while Lynn and Sheila went to the club together. That made me recall the many times Henry shoved in my face the fact that if I wanted to go anywhere when he also had plans, I had to be the one responsible for getting a babysitter. How dare this Negro babysit for someone else's child!

"Girl, Henry and Lynn had knock-out, drag-down fights all the time because he was so jealous of her," Sheila said.

1987: I wanted to hear all of the juicy gossip about my husband and his so-called other woman, but I couldn't help reminiscing about the time when Henry and I got into our first fight in Fayetteville. It was after I had joined the Army and Henry had gotten out of the Marines and was living there with me. He had been talking long-distance to Tyrone, a friend from Saginaw, our hometown. Tyrone told Henry that he and I had engaged in sex back when we were in high school. He was obviously joking around, because it was a straight-out lie, but Tyrone never told Henry otherwise. Henry got off the phone believing it. When he questioned me about it, I joked as well and answered, "Yeah," not thinking he would take me seriously. I can't remember how we started arguing, but I yelled out, "Its a lie! Its a lie!" when I noticed Henry wasn't joking. He didn't believe me, so we started fighting—despite the fact that I was about five months pregnant at the time. Somehow I always managed to end up on the floor when we fought, and this time he rammed the back of my head into the cement so hard I saw stars. I always fought back, but he was much stronger than I was. I had a cut in the back of my head and a headache that lasted an entire week.

1990: Sheila continued, "After Henry and Marcus left for Saudi Arabia, they called all the time. After a while, Lynn didn't want anything to do with Henry, so she wouldn't take his calls anymore."

Now I'm feeling like a complete fool because I can recall that time, too, and Henry was also calling me in Saginaw. This was after I'd left him here in Jacksonville and moved back home. I had enrolled in community college, thinking I was going to get on with my life without him. When the Persian Gulf War had started, I became so upset I couldn't concentrate on school anymore and ended up dropping out. I would sit in front of that TV day and night trying to learn all I could about Desert Storm, because I knew Henry was there. That thought made me forget about the problems we'd had and even the reason why I'd left him. All I could think about was my husband could die in Kuwait, and how much I wanted him back in my life.

So I got his address and began to write, hoping we could reconcile. His return letters never reflected that he wanted to get back together, but he never denied me hope. When he would call, I'd be so happy to hear from him I felt that if I brought it up it would jeopardize the nice conversations we would have. He would only tell me how much he loved and missed Li'l Henry and me, which is the reality I clung to.

Finally, out of the clear blue sky, I received a letter saying he indeed wanted his wife and son back into his life again. He professed how he'd changed his ways and wanted another chance to make us happy. The war was over by this time, and I figured maybe that had something to do with his abrupt decision. Maybe he thought just as I did that something might happen to him, but unlike me he pulled away. Nevertheless, I was happy he had decided to give our marriage another chance, and I really didn't care why nor did I question it.

Now I'm hearing from Sheila that the real reason why I was chosen back then was because Lynn didn't want him! It doesn't surprise me, because it seems as though I'm always his second choice.

1987: I remember when he completed his first enlistment in the Marines and was supposed to come live with me in Fayetteville, which was where I was stationed in the Army at the time. We had never lived together, nor had Li'l Henry been born yet. Henry called one day saying he'd changed his mind and was moving to Georgia instead, because there was a post office job awaiting him there. Of course I was heartbroken but could understand that a post office job would pay far more than he could ever earn off post in Fayetteville. Besides, we had already been living apart since the day we were married, so I was used to it. However, I unenthusiastically went along with the decision and tried to recondition my mind, because I was so happy when I thought we were going to finally live together as man and wife.

He out-processed from the Marines and moved to Georgia, only to call two weeks later saying he had changed his mind, sincerely missed his wife, and was indeed coming to live with me. I was happy once again, because I was living in the barracks at the time; and more so because of the fact that I wanted to finally live as man and wife and get the hell out of there. I later discovered while we were living in Fayetteville that he was initially moving to Georgia to live with his baby's mother. A child I didn't know anything about at the time. Hell, I hadn't even had Li'l Henry yet. That post office job was just a crock of bull he'd conjured up because he'd rather be with his baby's mother than to be with me, his own wife!

So, again, I found out I was second best. If Lynn had wanted his punk butt back then, I wouldn't be standing here in Jacksonville today. That also holds true if I hadn't given up my lost love to be with Henry. I met him after high school when Henry was stationed in Japan. It was only supposed to be a fling but I developed some strong feelings for him. Of course, Henry was the chosen one after his return from Japan.

"Gwen? Gwen!" Sheila said, as she shook me back into reality. "Girl, if you're not going to listen to me, I might as well just shut up!"

"I'm sorry Sheila, I was just thinking about all that I've put up with while dealing with this husband of mine."

"Promise me you won't say anything to him," she asked sternly after seeing the anger in my eyes. "I don't want to start anything between you two." I finally promised I wouldn't say anything, but boy, I really did want to! Sheila began to tell me side number two of the cookout story when Henry was stabbed.

1991: "Lynn didn't want anything to do with Henry," she began again. "She and I were in the kitchen, and Henry kept going in and out of there trying to spark up a conversation with her." Lynn wouldn't give him the time of day, according to Sheila, so Henry eventually got upset. I imagine that was a strike against his ego, because he's forever assuming all females want him like he's God's gift to women. She said he had been drinking a lot that night. Henry has a drinking problem, and in the past he would drink so much that when he talked, he slurred. He really was, if not already, turning into an alcoholic, in my opinion.

Lynn tried to walk away from Henry, but he grabbed her and that's how the fight began. "Lynn was hanging in there with him, too," Sheila said. "You know she's been through all of that hard-core Marines training, too, so she gave him a run for his money. They were tussling all over the house until some of the guys finally broke it up, but before we all knew it they were at it again. That's when she stabbed him in the stomach. He didn't even know he was stabbed until he saw the blood, because he was so drunk. Afterward he passed out. One of the guys at the cookout called an ambulance, and he was taken to the hospital."

I thought about that cookout all day, and I wanted to say something to Henry so very badly, but I knew I had to honor my promise to Sheila. I had to suck it up, so that night I didn't talk much to him. He said something to me and I couldn't help but snap, "What the hell do you want?" like I wanted to bite his head off. He asked with a confused look on his face, "What's wrong with you?" I looked at him for about five seconds with my most defiant stare. Then I softened my face, walked up the stairs, and didn't utter another word.

Henry and I were invited for dinner over to the house of another one of his Marine friends. There were two other couples over there, and everyone was introduced to one another. We played cards and dominos, and it was as if everyone had known each other forever because we got along so well. I love meeting down-to-earth people who I can just be myself with. Tammy, who was one of the wives, and I hit it off pretty good. She picked me up one day to go shopping. She doesn't have any kids but is crazy about Li'l Henry.

We were talking, and Lynn's name came up yet again. I was surprised that Tammy, too, had known Lynn, but I played it as it I knew all about her so maybe I could get more information. Tammy talked about her, her husband's, Lynn's, and Henry's basketball game outings and just went on and on about how much fun they used to have. After she finished her story, I revealed to her that I had just recently found out about Lynn. Tammy's husband had told her that I knew all about Lynn. Tammy thought Henry and I had an understanding that when we were separated, we would date other people. I found out that Henry didn't tell anyone I'd left him. He had everybody thinking I just went away for a little while and was coming back. Even Sheila thought it until I told her differently.

After listening to Tammy talk about Henry and Lynn as a couple, I became very jealous. I realized he must have really cared about her, especially after all they had done together. He flaunted their relationship as if they were the ones who were married. It made me wonder how she looked, especially after knowing she was able to make my husband act like a complete fool. Despite the feeling of disloyalty, I had to take into account that I had left him, so the last thing I could do was get upset about it. However, I recalled him telling me he would never fool around with a Marine woman, explaining that they were as hard as men. Lynn is the second one I have discovered so far. The first Marine woman he was involved with was, of course, his baby's mother.

Since Tammy had brought up Lynn's name, I felt that was the perfect opportunity to reveal what I had discovered to Henry and maybe get some answers. I could keep my word with Sheila as well as ease my mind by learning what really went on right from the horse's mouth. I needed to make sure it was over between Henry and Lynn so he and I could put it behind us once and for all.

When Tammy dropped me off at home, my intention was to stay calm as I nonchalantly asked Henry about Lynn. He told me she was someone he dated after I'd left him and they broke up a long time ago. I reminded him about the way he behaved the other night when we went over to her house and how it made me feel he still had feelings for her. "And if you do, you had better tell me right now, because I can go right back home from where I came from." Out went the calm and I began yelling, "Tell the truth—she's the one who stabbed you, right?"

No reply, so I repeated, "Is . . . she . . . the . . . one . . . who . . . stabbed . . . you?"

"Yes, Gwen, she's the one who stabbed me, and it was because I broke it off with her."

I looked at him in disgust, shook my head, and walked upstairs because I should have known I couldn't trust him to tell the complete truth.

Chapter 3

1992: It's only been a few months now since Li'l Henry and I returned from Saginaw. It had only been eight months prior, when we lived in a hotel room for two weeks here before Henry put us on a bus back to Saginaw because we couldn't find a place to live. At the bus station Henry promised to come get us before Christmas but changed the date several times because he still hadn't found a place to live.

January is when he finally came to get us. The first month's rent was already paid on the triplex townhouse where we were to live. Only stopping to gas up, it took Henry 15 hours to drive from Saginaw back to Jacksonville. That was always something that I admired about him, because it reminded me of my stepfather, who did all the driving whenever we went on family road trips.

To me, it represented a strong man, because I remember as a child waking up in the middle of the night, discovering that everyone had fallen asleep except my stepfather. I would start asking questions, feeling compelled to do something to keep him awake. He would answer a few and then eventually tell me to go back to sleep. As I sat quietly in the back seat I prayed he wouldn't fall asleep, because how could anyone possibly stay awake all night long? Sure enough, he got us safely to our destination every time without stopping to rest. Slowly my fear of him falling asleep vanished and was replaced with a strong sense of his protection, and I knew from that point on that I could always count on it.

Although I will never condemn a man if he needs my help when driving on road trips, I do know that subconsciously I will always compare him to my stepfather.

When I walked into the townhouse, I instantly fell in love with it. Right inside the door was a stairway to the upper level, and the living room was to the right. There was a half bathroom off the left side of the living area underneath the staircase. The kitchen and dining rooms were situated in the back of the townhouse. Upstairs there were two bedrooms and one full bathroom, all separated by a long hallway. It was completely unfurnished but definitely a place that I could call home. I was impressed that Henry was able to find something so nice without my help.

I applied for a housekeeping position at the Hampton Inn. The manager hired me on the spot, because she remembered the many calls that I'd made from Saginaw asking about a transfer. She expressed how impressed she was that I wanted to continue working for the Hampton Inn chain and at how determined I was to find out how to make it happen. After I got the job, Henry and I immediately applied to get Li'l Henry into daycare on the base. However, when we registered him we were told they had a one-month waiting list. Fortunately, Henry asked around, and the wife of a fellow Marine, Kim, agreed to babysit until on-base daycare was available. After talking with Kim, I felt really comfortable leaving my baby who was only three years old at the time in her care. Without me having to ask, she showed me around her apartment and assured me that Li'l Henry would be well fed and cared for.

Everything was working out okay, even though our finances were extremely tight at first. We spent all the money we had trying to get things that we lacked for the apartment. My paycheck was about $200, which I brought with me when Henry came to get us, and he had less than that after paying for gas all the way back. We didn't have anything because when I'd left Henry, I sold everything and had no intention of coming back. In addition to food, we had to buy towels, linens, and household supplies. We had sheets covering the windows and eventually had to buy new blinds to replace them. We also had to make sure that we saved enough for gas to get back and forth to work until either I received my last paycheck or Henry got his, which was two weeks away.

Our refrigerator was completely empty the day Henry got paid. I couldn't believe how we stretched that food so far; but we did, and we made it through. When I finally got a chance to go food shopping, I damn near bought out the entire store. After that, we were doing fine; no arguing at all, and Henry really was trying to do right by me. But then I discovered he was paying child support. I wasn't trying to be nosey, but I noticed a $100 difference in his paycheck and I questioned it. "Babe, why is there $100 being deducted from your paycheck?"

"I'm paying child support," he said nonchalantly.

"What … what! For a child who you denied all the way until

the bitter end and still yet to this day have not confessed that she is yours?"

Henry grew totally silent after he heard the boldness in my voice. I didn't care and I continued to talk. "You love it when I talk junk to you, don't you? That's why you always do things so butt backwards; always trying to keep me in the dark about everything. What, you didn't think I knew she was your child? I knew all along, even if you couldn't bring your sorry self to confess. Tell me, Henry, before something else slaps me in the face. Is there anything else I should know?"

I waited on an answer as I rolled my neck as hard as I could.

"I'm so sorry Gwen, I couldn't tell you, and that's why I hoped you'd notice it on the paycheck. We both know she's my child, and this happened a long time ago. Do you remember our agreement to start brand new? Let's not give the past a chance to mess up our future, okay?" he said, shaking his head as if answering no. I didn't say anything else after that, because I primarily wanted him to guess about what I was thinking, and I needed to think about the best way to behave after agreeing to give our marriage another try. I didn't want to say anything I might regret later like the fact that I dated someone while I was in Saginaw who Henry knew nothing about. Besides, I could see he was trying really hard this time, especially as far as prioritizing when it came down to paying bills, which was one of the reasons why I'd left him in the first place. However, I was glad he chose to do the right thing and support his child instead of denying she even existed.

Chapter 4

1989: When I first found out about Charkeshia, Li'l Henry and I were living in Fayetteville and Henry had already reenlisted in the Marines. I talked with Charkeshia's mother, Valerie, and she revealed all the lies Henry had told about me before we got married. How he had only married me to get the BAQ—the basic allowance for quarters—which is an extra $250 or more a month depending on your rank that the military pays soldiers for their dependents. He said it was an agreement between him and me in order to split the money. That's ludicrous, because if I was going to marry for money, it definitely would be for a hell of a lot more than $250! He also told her he was staying with a friend when we were in fact living together in Fayetteville.

Prior to Henry and I getting married, he had dated and impregnated this girl named Valerie who was in the Marines and stationed in Jacksonville. She was in the same unit as Henry, and that's where they met. I had already enlisted in the Army, relocated to Fort Bragg, and he was dealing with the both of us at the same time. She got out of the military and moved back to her hometown in Georgia after she had their baby. Then about a year later, Henry got out of the Marines and instead of coming to Fayetteville to be with me, his wife, he went to Georgia claiming to have a post office job. I never found out why, after two weeks of living in Georgia, he changed his mind and decided to come live with me instead. But he and Valerie never stopped communicating. They conversed through letters, telephone calls, and Henry even drove there on two occasions to visit her during the time he was living with me. Of course I wasn't aware of them communicating or that a baby even existed at the time, but I did know about Valerie. She had co-signed for the very car Henry and I were driving when we were living in Fayetteville. I discovered that secret by mistake way before we even lived together

1986: It was when I first enlisted in the military after being so disgusted with my conniving husband who lied about going on a six-month float to keep me away from Jacksonville. I was stationed at Fort Bragg, and after things had gotten better between us I came to visit him one weekend as I often did. I went through the glove compartment and discovered Valerie's name on all of the paperwork. I asked about it, and he portrayed her as a real cool friend who only helped him out in purchasing his car. He had messed up his credit so bad he needed a co-signer.

It really was a big mess when we first got together in Fayetteville. After his unemployment ran out, he didn't work for about a month. Every time the phone bill came, we argued over why he kept running it up with calls to Georgia. Henry wasn't working, and he didn't have anything else to do with his time. At one point I got so fed up with paying the bills alone that I filled out an application at a gas station near the apartment where we were living, signed his name to it, and, believe it or not, they hired him.

He was always the one getting the mail from the mailbox, but once he started working I was able to get it for a change. One day a letter from Valerie came, and I, trying to believe that they were just friends, gave it to him without giving it a second thought. About a week later and after he'd gotten his first paycheck, he told me Valerie's brother was getting married and Henry was invited to the wedding. He was going away for the weekend and taking his car, which was our only vehicle at the time. I was a little naive, trusting soul, and since he said he would return in enough time to take me to work that Monday morning, I didn't question the fact that I wasn't asked to come along. He even called when he got there, trying to play the faithful husband; collect, of course. I don't know what compelled me, but I started searching through his things. I have no idea what I was looking for, but when I reached the bottom of the duffel bag, I found that letter. The very one that I'd handed to Henry only a week ago. I knew something was going on when the letter began, "Dear Sweetheart." She told him how much she missed him, how much she loved him, and how she longed for him to come to Georgia to visit her. At the end of the letter it read, "Charkeshia says hello."

When he returned on Sunday night I had the letter right in my hand and immediately started asking questions. Instead of answering, he wanted to know why I had searched through his things. I replied, "Look, you cheating son of a bitch, I'm asking the damn questions here." When he realized I wasn't playing, he revealed how he and Valerie had been in a relationship, but he broke it off when he went down there for the post office job. He told her he wanted to be faithful to me, and they agreed to remain friends. The mysterious question of why Henry initially called off our wedding was finally revealed to me. Henry was also involved with Valerie at that time, and couldn't decide between the two of us who he wanted to be with. As a matter of fact, when he came home to marry me, some of his friends had made wagers on the chances of him going through with the wedding.

"Who is Charkeshia?" I asked.

"She is Valerie's baby," he answered. He also assured me that Valerie and her brother did not live together, and he had spent the weekend with him. I just let it rest because what else could I say? He had an excuse for it all. When the next phone bill came, I noticed the number he'd called collect from was the same as the one on the previous statements. I didn't say anything to him but I thought to myself, This man is so devious. He had to know I would realize that he called from the same number. I can't believe he thinks I'm that shallow! Then again, he is such a liar that he won't tell the truth even when he knows there is a loophole with a chance of me finding out. I suppose he thinks that from the time it takes me to discover the truth he can probably concoct another lie even more convincing.

Even knowing that Henry was a lying cheat, I still wanted our marriage to work and I loved him so very much. Besides, I didn't want change, and if I kicked him out, how would I get back and forth to the post to go to work? To set my mind at ease, I placed a block on the phone where no one could call long distance or accept collect calls.

1989: I didn't find out about the baby until much later. We lived together in Fayetteville almost two years before Henry reenlisted in the Marines. He requested to be stationed in Jacksonville again. It was nice because he would come home every weekend, and he seemed to appreciate Li'l Henry and me more. We would have a family night on Saturdays when Henry would take us to dinner or to the park and give us lots of attention. I felt we were a happy family because finally everyone did what they were supposed to do. However, reality always seems to find its way back in, because one night Henry called and we got into this big argument. We hung up and the phone immediately began to ring. I picked it up thinking he was calling back to apologize, but it was the operator asking if I would allow Henry to charge a call to my line. I said yes thinking maybe he was calling his family or friends from back home. A few weeks later I got the phone bill, and guess whose number was on it? Valerie's!

My usual way of handling confrontation was not to. I was always the type of person who kept to herself and never bothered anyone. If I thought a person didn't want to be bothered, they didn't have to worry about me approaching them. For the most part, I was typically not a person who looked for trouble. However, once trouble found me, it took an army plus some to shut me up from defending my honor. I really wanted to know what was going on, but I just couldn't find the nerves to make the call. Cheryl said, "Give me that phone; I'll do it."

I met my girlfriend Cheryl through Pam, after I moved out of the barracks. Pam was my roommate when I lived in the barracks. Cheryl was a civilian who was married to an Army man, and Pam and her boyfriend were both in the military. When Henry came to live in Fayetteville, all six of us would get together at our apartment or at Cheryl's house for dinner. We all got along pretty well. The men would do their thing, and Pam, Cheryl, and I would do ours. Pam received orders for Korea so she had to leave, and Cheryl and I remained very close friends. Cheryl stood about 5'0" and weighed about 180 pounds. She loved to cook but enjoyed eating more, and her protruding stomach revealed her secret. She and her husband had two kids, a girl who was five and a son who was a toddler. Cheryl suggested I call Valerie's number and get to the bottom of it.

The call was placed, and an older woman answered the phone. Cheryl asked, "Ma'am, do you know a man by the name of Henry Moore?" The lady hesitated and then answered, "Yes I do, and he has a child here." Cheryl could sense that the lady didn't care much for Henry by the snickering bitterness in her voice. After some careful probing, Cheryl found out that this woman was Valerie's mother, and Henry wasn't financially doing anything for the child. Of course he wasn't, I thought. Before Henry reenlisted in the Marines, he hadn't worked in the last three or four months. Maybe this little girl was the reason he was in such a big hurry to go back into the Marines. Before I could elaborate on that thought, Cheryl said something that took my breath away. She asked the grandmother when was the child born and what was her name. I stared at Cheryl as she listened to the grandmother's reply, and I studied every move she made. I saw Cheryl's eyes widen as she placed her hand over her mouth as if to say, "Oh My God." It seemed like time was standing still as Cheryl listened without interrupting. Finally she repeated the birth date out loud. This little girl was born after Henry and I were married but conceived before, and her name was Charkeshia.

After Cheryl hung up the phone and conveyed the contents of the conversation to me, my heart felt like it was jumping out of my body onto the floor and Henry was stomping it into mush. Cheryl knew exactly how I felt, and she tried to console me by telling me some conniving things her husband had done. I couldn't listen to what she was saying. My mind immediately went into reverse, and all I could think about was that first letter I found, all the phone calls to Georgia I had to pay for, the two trips that Henry made there, and that second letter.

1988: I found that letter in his coat pocket one day when he was at work, much later after finding the first letter. This letter wasn't dated, and there was no envelope for me to establish a time line. Fortunately, I still had the old telephone bill with her number on it, but the block was still on the phone. Even though confrontation was not my usual way of handling things, I just could not allow two letters from this same mystery woman to enter my household without addressing both parties involved. So I picked up the phone and dialed the number from the bill; I called collect. I disguised my voice by making it sound deep and husky, and I said my name was Henry when the operator asked. A lady picked up and the operator asked would she accept a collect call from Henry? It may have been Valerie's mother. She yelled to Valerie, "Do you want to accept a collect call from Henry?" I could hear Valerie's distant voice in the background saying, "Yes!" She was now much closer to the phone, and I could hear the excitement in her voice. She probably hadn't talked to Henry in a long time, since I had put the block on the phone. After she said hello, I hesitated for a second and almost hung up, but then I regained my courage and said, "This is not Henry. This is Henry's wife." She instantly became very quiet, but I knew she was still on the line because I could hear the quiver in her breathing. I told her I had found the letter she wrote to Henry. "Is my husband going to leave me for you?" I asked. "No," she replied sharply after a slight hesitation. I then asked her if she was aware Henry had a son. She said she did not know, and after her response I became speechless. I had expected someone to get on the phone and talk smack to me. The woman on the phone didn't have any arguments for me at all, and she was kindly answering all of my questions while the charges were on her end. So I just said, "Well, when Henry gets home, he and I will discuss this and look for us to call you back together." She just said okay and we said good-bye. When I got off the phone I was mad and confused. Hell, I was not used to confronting strangers, nor did I have any experience on how to handle a cheating husband.

There is a phrase that people say: sitting on pins and needles. Well, I could not sit down to save my soul. I paced the floor up and down until he finally got home, which was normally around 12:30 AM because he worked second shift. I had to get up at 6:00 AM to do PT, as the Army calls physical training, but I didn't give a darn how sleepy I would be.

When he walked in, I immediately asked, "What the hell is this? Are you supposed to, what, leave me?"

He looked dumbfounded until he spotted the letter in my hand. He snatched it away from me and looked at it. "Look, Gwen, this letter is old as dirt," he replied. "I have not called Valerie, I have not written to Valerie, and I have not heard from nor seen Valerie since I don't know how long." He then firmly stated, "Gwen, don't mess up what we have over this old shit. I'm still here and I'm not going anywhere."

He kept trying to display a pitiful look on his face. I ignored it and looked him directly in the eye as my eyebrows raised and my lips formed a straight line and I said, "We are going to call Valerie together and we will get this straight once and for all. You are going to tell the both of us who the hell you want."

"Gwen, why do you want me to call that woman? I haven't talked to her in God knows how long. It will only stir things up, do you understand? I'm not calling her."

I said through clenched teeth, "Call her or get the hell out of my apartment."

He looked at me for the longest time, picked up the receiver, and then he dialed. He called collect and she accepted the charges once again. He began asking how was she doing and he inquired about Charkeshia. He told her how much he loved his wife, that he wasn't going to leave me, and that there was never going to be anything between the two of them. I had the other receiver to my ear listening to everything as I watched him fidget at the predicament he was now in. Valerie said okay and nothing else. They both said good-bye and that was it. Even though I knew that was the first time those words had ever been spoken to her, I took comfort in knowing that for once I was his choice.

After I had found out about Charkeshia and Cheryl had left, I was a total mess. I didn't call Henry because I wanted to figure out first how I would handle it and what choices I should make. I couldn't sleep at all that night, and I kept thinking what a fool I'd been. After all I have been through and endured from this man, thinking every unfaithful act would be his last one, this had to be the ultimate heartbreaker. Henry had a daughter older than my son yet younger than the day we were married. All this time I thought Li'l Henry was his only child. I felt that fate had singled me out for cruel and unusual punishment.

The next day at work, I made up my mind to call Valerie. I rehearsed all day what I would say to her. I didn't want to argue, I just wanted to understand; I needed to know everything. That's when she told me all the lies Henry made up. She also told me her daughter was handicapped. Charkeshia couldn't walk or talk. I thought about her handicap being a punishment for Henry's and Valerie's wrongdoing, yet I had compassion for her because she really didn't have to tell me anything. Besides, she was as much in the dark as I was. She told me Charkeshia was born well over a year ago in November, which made her child two years old which was one year and three months older than my son. That was also the time when Henry first got out of the Marines, and that had to be the reason why he was going to live with Valerie instead of me. After our friendly chat, we both agreed that we would meet up in Jacksonville with our children and confront Henry, but we didn't set a date.

After I got off the phone, I thought to myself, How stupid I am to not see this coming! All the clues were right in my face, and I ignored them. All the while, I'd thought he was in love with another woman so much so that he would risk his marriage time and time again when all along it was for a baby. I understood because when Li'l Henry was born, I remember becoming overwhelmed with jealousy when Henry showered all of his attention on him. It was the baby this and the baby that, and of course my twenty-three year old hormones were so out of whack that I was feeling embarrassed and jealous all at the same time. At that point I could also somewhat understand him jeopardizing our marriage to become a part of his child's life, but he had handled the situation all wrong.

The time had finally come to confront Henry with my newly found enlightenment. When I called to ask him about Charkeshia, I threw in his face all the phone calls, the letters, the trips, the lies, lies, and more lies, as well as the fact that it was all confirmed by Valerie. "Charkeshia ain't my child," was Henry's only reply.

Chapter 5

1992: I had gotten up early this morning to take Li'l Henry to daycare and just nestled down to complete the dream I was having. A knock on the door followed by a persistent roll of doorbell pongs interrupted my presleep rituals. I jumped up, put on my robe, and ran downstairs. Before I could completely open the door, Sheila pushed her way inside. "Henry and Marcus have been arrested! They were picked up at the base by the police, and Marcus just called from the jail."

"For what?" I asked.

"Hurry and get dressed, and I'll fill you in with everything Marcus told me on the ride there."

"One night before you returned," Sheila said when we were underway, "Henry and Marcus went to Raleigh to a car dealership to check out some rims. Henry saw some that he really liked and decided to come back later that night to steal them. They drove around Raleigh until Henry thought the place was closed. Marcus didn't want anything to do with it and demanded Henry drop him off somewhere when he realized he was really going through with it. Henry dropped him off at a corner and said he would return afterward. When Henry was removing the third rim from the car, a security guard approached him. Henry quickly got into his car and drove away and left all the rims behind. The security guard got the make, model, and tag number of Henry's car. Henry picked Marcus up and they were on their way back home when they were stopped by a policeman. Henry, being the slick talker that he is, lied his way out of it. Now everything has caught up with him."

When we got to the jail, we were allowed to visit with them. They were behind a glass window, and we had to pick up a telephone in order to communicate. They were in some type of holding cage where prisoners are placed before they are sent to their cells. I saw a row of telephones through the glass window, so they were able to call out at will. Henry was trying to explain what happened, and he told me he tried to call his father, but his dad's telephone service did not receive collect calls. He asked me to call and ask his father to wire some money to bail them out. Marcus was also asking Sheila to call his mother.

When Sheila and I walked from the holding cell, she shared with me what Marcus had confided to her. He said if he wasn't released before the next morning, he was going to tell the truth. Henry had asked him to lie and say they were somewhere else that night, and Marcus had agreed to the story. "Baby I didn't have anything to do with this," Marcus told Sheila again. "I'll be damned if I spend the night in jail for this punk. I'll tell on his ass first."

The bail was set at $500 apiece, and together Sheila and I only had $600. We couldn't get in touch with anyone. Finally we called Tammy's husband, Tony, and he came up with the rest of the money to bail them out. When Marcus and Henry walked out, we could tell Marcus was some kind of mad. They looked like Laurel and Hardy by the height Henry had over Marcus. Henry had a big smile on his face trying to cover up his shame. I looked at him with disgust, because even though he denied it to me, I believed he was guilty.

1989: As I continued to stare at him talking to Tony and Marcus, I remembered a time when we were living in Fayetteville. Henry had been drinking with a couple of his buddies. He took the car and didn't come home all night. The next morning I'd waited and waited until finally I had to call my Noncommissioned Officer in Charge (NCOIC in Army terms) and tell her what happened, and that I would probably be late coming into work. After I hung up the phone, there was a knock at the door. One of the guys who had left with Henry the night before had come to bring the car keys and to tell me Henry was in jail.

I'd dropped my son off at the babysitter's house and gone to work as if nothing was wrong. I felt that it was no better for him, because he'd promised he would never drink and drive again. I let him stay in jail for the entire weekend and didn't bail him out until Monday.

That night as I lay in bed next to Henry, I asked him if he'd stolen the rims. He looked me straight in the eye and answered, "No."

I often wonder why I endure so much from Henry. There are times when things are going really good between us. We joke and laugh and can have a good time together. Our sex life is normal; his drive is always greater than mine. Sometimes I may not be in the mood when we make love, but I enjoy being close to him. I love having his undivided attention, which is something I don't often get enough of throughout the day. He seldom takes me to the club, but when he does he treats me like a lady. He walks close by my side and keeps his arm around my waist or holds my hand. He pulls out my chair when I sit and asks if I want something to drink. He moves his chair next to mine and wraps his arms around me and just makes me feel secure. He is so attentive in every way to what I need at that moment that I fall in love with him again every single time we go out. It really doesn't take much to please me, and it must be something about nightclubs that brings out the gentleman in him. However, the reality is he is twenty-nine years old and very immature when it comes to life, family, and responsibility. I am not second in his life after God. God is not even first in his life; Henry is. I believe one day he has to grow up and be the man he should be. I just hope I'll be able to stick it out and see it happen.

Henry wasn't always a liar and a cheat like he is now, and he used to be an all-American ladies' man. When I first met him, he was chivalrous. He used to open the car door for me and light my cigarettes; a real gentleman, and it didn't have to be on a special occasion like going to the nightclub. He was attentive all the time, and that's how he was able to reel me in. One time he bought me a trophy that read, "Girlfriend of the Year." It wasn't my birthday or any special day; it was just because. I do love him very much despite all the mess he's made and continues to put me through. I also have this insecurity of not being able to make it on my own if I were to leave him again. I don't really know which of the two reasons keeps me here, but I continue to stay despite all the bad treatment. I wonder what it would be like if I had the total package. I would love to have a husband who loves and adores me, respects me, provides for me, and wants to protect me. I imagine him hanging with the boys and always bringing my name up so much that his friends would have to tell him to stop talking about me. He would always put me first in his life before himself, but never before God. He would strive to make a better life for us and always, always want to keep a smile on my face. Of course, as long as I have a smile on my face, I will make sure my husband stays happy as well. Unfortunately, I gave up that exact type of relationship when I left Saginaw in order to try and make my marriage work.

The reality was I only had a portion of that good life, and most times it was only when Henry and I had a night out. Even though I thought I found what I was looking for while I was in Saginaw, I wasn't willing to give up my marriage in order to pursue it. I still think about him a lot. Women always want what we can't have, and the grass always seems greener on the other side. I must admit that Henry wasn't the only one unfaithful in this marriage. I have done my share of dirt in the past, and at the same time I found ways to justify it. I cheated simply because I was lonely and my husband wouldn't give me the attention I needed.

Chapter 6

1986: Like I said before, when I first enlisted and moved to Fort Bragg, I was mad at Henry for lying about going on the six-month float. He knew I had enlisted, but I wasn't about to call him to let him know I had arrived. I wasn't sure if he even cared, but if he did, I was going to make him sweat. There were two girls, Lucy and Kellie, whom I'd gotten pretty close to. Kellie was a bright-skinned, chubby-faced girl with short, brownish-red hair, and she lived in the barracks with me. Lucy was dark-skinned, thin, and had a nice, toned body. She was divorced and lived off post with her five-year-old daughter. Lucy and Kellie would sometimes drive to Jacksonville on the weekends. When I met them, I shared with them where my husband was stationed, and one weekend about two weeks after I had arrived, they asked me to go along. I said yes. I didn't call Henry to let him know I was coming. As a matter of fact, I had not contacted him since my arrival at Fort Bragg.

We got to Jacksonville around 8:00 Saturday night, and we were stopped at the gate by a Marine who was on guard. He directed us to the Welcome Station when we asked how to locate a Marine. The Marine on duty provided us with a pass and a map that showed exactly where the barracks were that Henry lived in. We had to pass the gate again after leaving the Welcome Station, and I marveled at the different gestures the guardsman made with his hands. He was trained to look for the stickers on the cars that identified who was driving. If it was an officer, he immediately stood at attention and saluted. If it was a fellow Marine, he made a certain hand movement to motion him or her through. If the car didn't have a sticker at all, he would motion them to stop by raising one hand while the other one was held behind his back. He stood in the middle of what looked like a median, and there were about four lanes of incoming traffic. He was working his hands nonstop, and the stopped cars would move forward only at his command. He had on white gloves and was clothed in those sharp Marine dress blues. I was so fascinated by his swift and sharp movements and how disciplined he was that I watched him until I couldn't see him anymore.

Henry wasn't home when we got there, but his roommate was kind enough to let us wait for him. Lucy and Kellie waited a little while and then decided to leave. They promised to pick me up the next day and provided a number to call if I needed them sooner. As I sat there watching TV, I spotted Henry's photo album. I couldn't believe there was a picture of Ava in there. Ava was a girl from high school who was sweet on Henry, and obviously Henry liked her too because he had a big 8×10 photo of her. She used to stir up a lot of trouble with me when Henry was stationed in Japan. She would spread rumors at school about Henry writing her saying he and I were not a couple anymore and that he was going to marry her when he got back to the States. Henry denied it all when I wrote and questioned him about it. Ava and I almost fought at a party one night, because she kept talking a lot of trash. She got kicked out of the party for stirring up trouble. He had several pictures of me as well as some of his family in the album also.

His roommate asked if I was hungry, and I said, "Yes." He took me to Burger King to get something to eat, and he also treated, which was nice of him. We arrived back at the barracks as Henry was pulling up. It was about midnight, and I looked to see who might have been in the car with him, but no one else got out. He looked in my direction for the longest time when I got out of his roommate's vehicle. It was dark and I was at a distance, but he knew who I was. He was shocked to see me standing there. I hadn't seen my husband since we were married five-and-a-half months ago. Instantly I forgot about being upset, because I was so happy to see him again. We hugged and he asked, "How did you get here?"

I told him I had driven down with my new friends.

"How long have you been waiting?"

"Three-and-a-half hours. Where were you?"

"At the movies with a friend," he answered. I found out later that the friend was Valerie.

We went to a hotel that night and everything was good between us again, or so I thought. It seemed as though every time he saw me, he wanted to be a good husband. He acted as though he missed me, treated me special, and made me feel he loved me. However, once I was out of his sight, the problems would always begin again. I wouldn't hear from him for long durations, and my attempts to contact him were a waste of time. When I was able to reach him by phone, he would have an excuse about why he never called and why we couldn't be together that weekend.

The next morning we went to breakfast and then back to the barracks. Kellie and Lucy came to pick me up, but I wasn't ready to go. My husband said he would drive me back to Fort Bragg, so Kellie and Lucy left. Henry and I had a hard time finding the barracks where I lived, because I've always had a poor sense of direction. On a piece of paper I wrote my work and barracks numbers, and I handed it to him before I got out of the car. We agreed to see each other every weekend, and I was happy and willing to let the past be just that—the past.

The following weekend, Lucy was invited to a party in Jacksonville, and she asked Kellie and me to come along. "I'll ride to Jacksonville, but I'm not going to the party because I want to spend time with my husband," I said. I enjoyed referring to Henry as my husband, and I said it all the time. When I called to let him know I was coming down, he told me he and the guys were going to play basketball at Cherry Point, which was a small military base close to Camp Lejeune. When I told Kellie and Lucy why I decided not to go, Kellie said, "Now, you know darn well he ain't going to play no basketball. That man is going to be with some woman. Explain to me what man would choose basketball over spending time with his wife when he only gets to see her on the weekends?"

They continued asking me to come to the party until eventually I said yes. There was this new girl named Tracy who had just gotten to Fort Bragg that week, and she turned out to be pretty cool. She was in the Army Reserve but had missed the training that her unit in Virginia routinely completed once a year. She had come to Fort Bragg to complete that two-week training.

The four of us, Kellie, Lucy, Tracy and I, set out for Jacksonville that Saturday evening. It was a two-hour drive and the party was at Keith's house. Keith, Lucy's boyfriend, was a Marine who was stationed at Camp Lejeune but lived off base in a two-bedroom townhouse.

Brian, Kellie's boyfriend who was also a Marine, was going to meet her there. When we arrived, the party hadn't started yet, so we just sat around and talked until people began to arrive. I asked Keith if I could use his phone to call the barracks where Henry lived, in hopes that maybe he would be there, but to no avail. I didn't really want to be at that stupid party; I didn't talk much and sort of moped around.

Two guys walked in, and I noticed one was very good-looking. I kept my eye on him as they walked and mingled. He stood about six feet tall with a dark-skinned complexion and a muscular build. He dressed really nice, and his confidence was apparent from the way he held out his chest while maintaining his upright posture. I was sitting alone on the couch, and the guy I wasn't attracted to came and sat beside me. He asked my name and told me his. We engaged in some small talk, and I suspected he could sense I didn't particularly want to be bothered. I avoided direct eye contact and wasn't paying attention, so he had to repeat himself whenever he said something. He finally got the message and got up. I continued looking at the other guy through my peripheral vision, and I noticed that he, from time to time, would glance over at me. Of course I pretended I wasn't looking whenever he looked my way.

As this continued, I thought to myself, If he comes over here and says something to me, I'm going to talk to him. Sure enough, he came right over and started conversing. His name was Jody. He asked was I married and since my wedding band wasn't in plain view I said, "No" and slipped it into my pocket when I had a chance. After we got pass the formalities and started laughing and talking comfortably, I could see Kellie and Lucy teasing me through my peripheral vision. Kellie came and whispered into my ear, "See there, I knew you were going to have a good time."

Kellie wanted to go to the club, so the four of us, Kellie, Lucy, Tracy and I left the party and I told Jody I would be back. On the way, they all asked questions about Jody and saying how cute he was. "Give me high five girl; you landed a hunk!" Lucy said. I hesitated for a moment and then the biggest grin appeared on my face as I gave them all a high five.

The club was jammed and there were Marine men everywhere. I think the ratio was five men to every woman. I don't think I'd ever stayed on a dance floor so long. I was introduced to this drink called

Kahlua and Cream, and it tasted like chocolate milk. It was so good, I gulped it down and boy, did I feel dizzy afterward! It was a rather nice feeling of dizziness, I might add. We only stayed for about an hour, but I really enjoyed myself.

When we returned to Lucy's boyfriend's house, Jody was right there waiting for me. Tracy hooked up with Mark, Jody's friend, and the eight of us were left after the party was over. Lucy and her boyfriend went into his bedroom while Kellie and her boyfriend were in the living room on the sofa bed. Tracy, Mark, Jody, and I were all left to share the spare bedroom. Tracy and Mark were already lying across the bed, so I looked in the closet and found a blanket. Jody and I cuddled up with the blanket on the recliner that was also in the guest room. I didn't object to sleeping in the room with Jody while Mark and Tracy were there, because I had no intentions of having sex with this guy, especially after just meeting him. I did kiss him, though, and he was a great kisser. I played hard to get, but I wasn't playing. I was hard to get, and believe me when I say he tried all night long.

The next morning, Jody and I were the first to wake up. After leaving the kitchen when we couldn't find anything to eat, we discovered we were locked out of the bedroom. We returned to the kitchen and began talking about our jobs in the military. Jody had been in the Marines for six years. He wasn't married (so he said, just like I wasn't married, either), but he did have a four-year-old son. I guess we got a little too loud when we started laughing at the fact that I couldn't shoot an M16 rifle. I had shared with him the time when I was in basic training and had to qualify shooting the pop-up targets. In order to qualify, I had to shoot 23 pop-up targets out of 40. Needless to say, I couldn't qualify and the Army only gave two tries. I was on my second try, and if I failed I would have to take basic training all over again. The reward of qualifying was getting to wear a camouflage cover over your helmet. Otherwise you had to continue to sport the hard shell; and because it was green and round, you were called "turtle" by everyone, including the drill sergeants. I hated being called turtle, and I was so happy when I finally qualified that last time, thank God.

Jody couldn't stop laughing at my story, and he was so loud he woke up Kellie and her boyfriend. I was glad because then we were able to sit in the living room and watch TV. Everybody finally got up and began taking showers with their partners. Lucy and her boyfriend went first, and then Kellie and hers. I couldn't believe it when Tracy took a shower with Mark. All the while they were in there I kept thinking to myself, What am I going to do? I didn't want Jody to feel left out, but my goodness I'd just met him!

"Gwen, I guess it's our turn," said Jody, breaking my concentration. I gazed at him with a perplexed look, shook my head, and said, "Okay, let's go." I really didn't want to do it, but I knew everyone expected me to. I guess I didn't want to be the oddball, and I really didn't want to appear immature. My heart was pounding as I gathered my clothes and walked toward the bathroom. This pounding did not represent love as it normally would, but fear of what was to happen next.

Jody was already in the shower when I got undressed. When I stepped in he immediately grabbed me and told me how nice my body looked. I thought he was just trying to butter me up so I said thank you, turned around, and began to lather up my washcloth. My back was turned to him and he started passionately kissing down my neck and around my ears. He grabbed my soapy washcloth and started washing my breasts and stomach. After he got my front side nice and soapy, he dropped the towel and started using his hands. He softly encircled my nipples with his pointer fingers, and I could not resist anymore. I turned around toward him and he kissed me ever so tender and with so much passion. I was able to fight the feeling all night long, but he made me so weak that I couldn't help but to let down my guards and surrender.

Everybody finally got dressed and the guys treated us to lunch. I kept looking around in the restaurant, worried that Henry would walk in. That would have been a hell of a coincidence for him to step into the very restaurant that I would be dining at.

After we left the restaurant, we went back to Lucy's boyfriend's house to gather up our things for the long drive back. Jody said he would call me, and Mark got Tracy's number at Fort Bragg as well as her home number in Virginia. We talked about that night all the way home. Everybody was very shocked to learn what happened between Jody and me while we were in the shower. We all definitely had a good time, and it was a weekend I will never forget. I wanted to see Jody again but I never did, and I assumed it was because he thought I was easy. Maybe he thought that I did that sort of thing all the time. Little did he know that was the first time I had ever met someone and had sex with him the very next day. I was ashamed for being weak and giving in to what was totally out of my character. It was disappointing that he would never know the real Gwen.

Chapter 7

Weekends would come and go without a word from Henry, and I just sat in the barracks alone. I became fed up and refused to allow myself to continue to be a hermit, waiting for a telephone call I was never going to get. I started going out with Kellie and Lucy to this club at Pope Air Force Base, which was also located in Fayetteville. Fort Bragg was an open post so there weren't any guards or gates like there were at Camp Lejeune. Pope, however, did have a gate, which separated it from Fort Bragg. I had never seen anything like it.

Right before the club was about to end men would assemble outside the door like a soul-train line and try to talk to every female who didn't have an escort. I didn't like that at all, because it made me feel like I was fair game.

One night we went to a civilian club off post, and this really nice-looking guy asked me to dance. While we were dancing, he asked my name and told me his. When the song ended, he thanked me for the dance and just left. When I got back to my table and sat down, I wondered why he didn't try to talk to me. Maybe he was married or didn't find me attractive. Maybe he felt I should make the first move, or what if he simply wanted to dance. He was definitely my type, because I love a slim physique. The more I rationalized his lack of interest, the more attractive he became to me. I decided to write my name and number on a napkin, and I searched the club to give it to him, but to no avail. Finally, when we were walking toward the door to leave, I saw him. I tucked the napkin in his hand and whispered in his ear, "Call me." I was nervous as hell because I had never approached a man in this way before, and there was the possibility that he wasn't interested.

He did call, and we got together. He was attracted to me after all, and I thought that was a cleaver way to act because it got my full attention. We spent a lot of time together until one weekend, out of the blue, Henry called and said he was coming up. Whenever he called or came to Fort Bragg, it didn't matter who I was dating or befriending. Henry came first in my life, and others were kicked to the curb. I loved my husband, and I wanted to be with him so very badly, but if he didn't want the same, I wasn't going to sit around the barracks waiting for him anymore.

Christmas came and I rode the bus home to Saginaw, only to discover that Henry was already there. I didn't know he was going home, because, of course, we weren't communicating. I decided one day to go to his family's house to visit, and he answered the door. "What are you doing here?" I asked. He said he decided at the last minute to come home for Christmas. He said it as if my not knowing he was there was perfectly fine. He said it like we weren't husband and wife, and I didn't have the right to know. I stood there speechless, because I did not know what to say. What I wanted to tell him was he was a sorry excuse for a husband. What I wanted him to explain was why we couldn't have a normal and good marriage. I also wanted to know what would we tell everyone: Were we a couple or not?

He broke the silence by grabbing me, pulling me close to him, and holding me. It felt so good being in his arms again, and I still loved him beyond a doubt. We spent time together in Saginaw, and neither our families nor friends knew of our actual circumstance. I thought Henry would volunteer to drive his wife back to Fort Bragg, but I ended up catching a ride with Larry. He was my high school classmate, whom I bumped into at a party I attended one night. Larry was also in the Marines and stationed at Camp Lejeune.

While we were in Saginaw, Henry filled me with hope again, making me believe that when we got back to North Carolina, the situation would be better between us. I got back before Henry, and when he returned, once again no calls and no visits. I waited and waited until one weekend I decided I would rent a car and drive to Jacksonville to find out what the problem was. When I arrived, I couldn't remember my way to Henry's barracks, so I stopped at the Welcome Station and called him. Thank God I was able to reach him! I waited for what seemed an eternity before he finally drove up. He got into the car with me and immediately started asking questions about Larry. I skeptically answered, wondering where he was going with his line of questioning. Then he told me that my riding back with Larry didn't sit well with him. "You are my wife, and you didn't have any business coming back with some dude."

Total silence filled the air. He broke the silence and said, "You shouldn't have wasted your time driving here, Gwen, because I don't want anything else to do with you."

I looked at him for the longest time through squinted eyes. I felt like cursing at him, because I shouldn't have had to catch a ride back with anyone. Hell, I shouldn't have even had to ride that darn bus home when I had a husband who owned a car and was in fact going to the same place. I spent all day Christmas Eve on that stupid bus and didn't get home until 7:30 PM Christmas Day. Henry had been well aware that I was going to ride back with Larry, and he didn't get upset when I told him nor did he volunteer to take me himself. Since I had driven down here to find out what was going on and to get things right between us, if at all possible, I said, "It's too late to drive back, so I am going to get a room at the hotel where we usually stay. Come with me and let's talk about this, Henry, please?"

He refused to go, got out of the car, and left. After he drove away, I just sat there as tears filled my eyes. Oh, how badly I wanted my marriage to work, but I just couldn't do it alone.

After awhile, and when I was convinced that he was not coming back, I regained my composure and drove to the hotel. I took a shower and got in bed, but I couldn't sleep. I kept hoping and praying he would come, and finally he did. I heard the knock and jumped up and ran to the door. My heart was beating so fast I had to hesitate before opening the door. I extended my hand in front of me with palm facing downward, and I could see the slight tremble. I don't know why I was so nervous, but I began taking deep breaths trying to relax myself, thinking, Get a grip on yourself, Gwen; that is your husband out there.

I took one more deep breath, grabbed the handle, and opened the door. Henry came inside, looked around, and then said, "I wanted to make sure you knew how to get back to Fort Bragg from the hotel."

"I do," I said, disappointed yet hopeful. He told me to drive safely, turned around, and left as quickly as he came. Even though I waited half the night, he did not come back again.

The next morning, I got up in a different frame of mind. I was convinced that Henry couldn't love me, and he'd only come to the room last night to find out if I was alone. Once again I decided that if he didn't want anything to do with me, I would reclaim my single life. I called Larry and told him that I was in town, and he gave me directions to his barracks. We had exchanged telephone numbers when he drove me back to Fort Bragg after Christmas. I had no intentions of ever using his, even though his appearance had taken a 360-degree turn since high school. He had been a little scrawny kid with two missing front teeth. Now, after some dental work and some training in the military, he was a new man. The muscles in his chest and arms were so perfectly toned; it was difficult for me to avoid stealing a glance every now and then when we'd driven back together. He was a good-looking, light-skinned black man with what appeared to be very strong legs; wow!

I drove over there and visited him for a little while, and I didn't tell him what had happened between Henry and me the night before. Larry kept saying that he knew I drove down to see Henry even after I denied it several times.

When Larry and I first saw each other at home at a Christmas party, he'd asked if I was married. "I married Henry," I'd replied. " Do you remember him?"

"Yeah I remember him. He graduated before us, right?"

"Yes, but we're not together anymore." This was before I'd discovered that Henry was also home on leave, which is what the military calls a vacation. Larry asked me to slow dance, and I could sense he wanted to hit on me. He was holding me very close and singing in my ear. Even on the 12-hour drive home from Saginaw, our silences spoke loud and clear the attraction we shared. He never pursued me, and this was our first time talking since the drive back.

While I was there Larry, introduced me to a couple of his friends. I visited for a few hours then Larry trailed me back to Fort Bragg, because he had made plans to visit his sister in Durham, a city nearby. I invited him up to my room, as I had when he dropped me off after Christmas. Once again nothing happened between us. He said he was tired, so I offered him my bed to lie down. He closed his eyes, and I left the room for about an hour to give him some peace and quiet. When I returned, there was a note saying he had to go.

Larry came to Fort Bragg again to bring his friend Calvin to catch a military hop home. A hop is a $10 flight that's available to active-duty personnel if there is room available. The flight was full, and Calvin needed to stay the night so he could try and catch one the following day.

Douglas, another classmate of ours, was also there visiting his sister, who happened to be stationed at Fort Bragg, too. He found my number through the Post Locator, which is the same as the 4-1-1 information line or an operator you would call to get a telephone number. He called to see if we could meet someplace. Larry called shortly thereafter, and I told him that Douglas was in town. Larry came to the barracks and trailed me to pick up Douglas. My mom had brought my old, beat-up Dodge Omni to me about a month prior. It was my first car, and before I'd left to come here, I gave it to my sister, who said she would continue the payments. She got behind, so I took back the car.

We all drove back to the guest house where Calvin was going to spend the night. It is an inexpensive lodging place for military personnel and their dependents during the time right before they get ready to leave for a permanent change of station, or when they're arriving at Fort Bragg for the first time to await on-post housing. Luckily, Calvin got a room to spend the night in because they are usually hard to get.

We were all there talking and reminiscing about our high school days. Both Larry and Douglas began discussing how attractive I was back then. "You still are," said Douglas as Larry agreed, and it made me blush. Calvin didn't say much, because he wasn't from Saginaw and didn't attend high school with us. I was attracted to Douglas when we were in junior high. I remembered when we were in seventh grade and in Mrs. Newman's class, he shouted across the room to me, "Do you want to go with me?" I said, "No," because I was embarrassed that everybody had heard him ask. I really liked him then and my feelings continued on well into high school, but we never got together. He started dating someone else, and then I met Henry. We all finally left Calvin's room late that night. I dropped Douglas off at his sister's house, and Larry drove back to Jacksonville.

When I got home from work the following day, there was a message on my door to call Calvin. I called, and he had gotten bumped from the plane again and would have to stay another night. He said he had called Larry, who in turn told him to call me. I asked if he wanted me to drive him to get something to eat, knowing that I really didn't want to. Of course he said yes, so I picked him up and we went to eat.

Calvin was the same age as I, 22 years old, and he was single with no kids. He joined the Marines straight out of high school and was working on his third year. He was originally from Chicago, and Jacksonville was his only duty station so far. I told him that I was married but separated, and my husband was also stationed at Jacksonville. Afterward, I drove him back to his room, and he asked me to come in. I answered, "No." Then out of nowhere he asked for a hug. With a semi puzzled look on my face, I hesitated. I thought it through for a moment and couldn't see a reason not to. So I did, during which time he tried to kiss me. I immediately turned my head and his lips landed on my cheek. I gave him the funniest look, because I didn't see this coming. I had no idea he was attracted to me. Then, for the first time I noticed those beautiful hazel eyes. Calvin was about 5'6", only two inches taller than me, and he had a small build with definition in his arms and legs. He had smooth, caramel-brown skin with straight hair that was fine and closely cut. "Have a safe flight home," I said; and as I turned and walked away, I thought about Larry. I was confused now because I really thought that he and I were making a connection, but obviously it wasn't communicated to Calvin.

The next day was a replica of the day before. After I arrived home from work, Calvin called and again had been bumped from his flight. However, this time I was somewhat happy. I picked him up and drove him to my room to wait while I took a shower. It was Friday night, so I asked if he wanted to go to the club, and he answered yes. We picked up Douglas, and the three of us went together. While we were there, it seemed as though Douglas tried to compete against Calvin for my attention. Douglas would try to hold my hand and be the first to ask me to dance whenever a slow song came on. I allowed him to do this, but I didn't like it much because I was beginning to fall for Calvin. I guess Douglas's final attempt at letting Calvin know "hands off" was when he sat in the front seat on the way home and kissed me on the lips when I dropped him off. Calvin was quiet and soft spoken; of course he didn't let any of it bother him at all, and I found that very attractive. Since he wasn't able to keep the room at the guest house, we set out to find a cheap hotel.

When we found one, he asked me to come in, and I did. We talked some more, and he revealed how he was attracted to me when Larry first introduced us in Jacksonville. I wasn't aware that Calvin was one of the two men Larry had introduced me to that day. The slight glance that I had given him revealed a man wearing a shirt with a connecting hood that was pulled over his face. He had come out from underneath the car that he was working on just long enough to say hi. I spend the night with Calvin, and he was a perfect gentleman. He held me all night long and did not try or ask for anything except a kiss, which I willingly gave.

Calvin never did get to go home that weekend, and we spent the entire time together. I really enjoyed him, and all it took was four days for him to win me over. From then on he came to see me every weekend, and we grew fond of one another. There was one weekend he called and said he couldn't make it because he had car trouble. I asked a girlfriend to take me to get him. He was the first guy who ever took me to a carnival and won a big stuffed animal and gave it to me. That was a childhood fantasy, and he fulfilled it.

Everything was going real good between Calvin and me when Henry called. He told me that he was in Saginaw and that his mother had taken a turn for the worse. His mother had cancer, which I was aware of before I enlisted in the Army. His family tried to keep it hidden from Henry, so I don't know when he actually found out about it, but I wasn't going to tell him.

I caught a flight home, and three days after my arrival she passed away. Henry really took it hard, and I was hurting for him. I had never seen my husband so vulnerable as he clung to me like never before. Then and there I decided that I would never be unfaithful to him again, no matter what. Besides the notion that his mother would be looking down on us, I realized that it was the moral thing to do regardless of Henry's actions toward me. Tit-for-tat games would never make things right between us; and even though I did what I felt I had to do in order to keep peace of mind, I knew I would be held accountable for my own actions in the end.

Henry got a special reassignment to Saginaw, so that he could stay home with his family. He and a friend of the family drove me back to Fort Bragg, and I was so happy that Henry was acting like a husband again. I sat in the back seat from time to time, and I would grab him from the back and wrap my arms around him and just hold him. I loved him so much, and I was so attracted him. When he dropped me off, he promised to call and let me know when he would return to Jacksonville, but we both knew it would be a while before that happened.

Calvin had gone on a six-month float while I was gone. I had left so abruptly that I didn't get a chance to talk to him. I tried to call him once during the week I was in Saginaw, and that's when I found out about the float. We never saw each other after that.

Henry and I conversed over the phone quite a bit until one day I called and his sister told me that he had returned to Jacksonville. I called his job, but he no longer worked there. I then called the barracks, and they only had his old job's number. I was upset that he didn't let me know that he was coming back, but more so than that I was concerned about his well-being. After I kept getting the runaround and nobody seemed to know how to locate Henry, I called his commanding officer. The CO tried to find out if there were any problems between us, and I said, "No, I just want to know where he is." He asked for my number and assured me he would personally locate Henry and have him to call me. I thanked the kind man and said good-bye. Ten minutes later my phone rang, and the CO was on the other end saying, "Specialist Moore, I have your husband here and I'm going to put him on the line." Henry got on the phone stuttering like the cat had his tongue.

"G...wen, w...hat's wrong?"

"I just want to know where the hell you are!" I yelled because I was mad at this point.

"I've moved to a different barracks and job," he said and supplied the new numbers. I could tell that the CO was still there next to him by how polite he was being. He called later that night and demanded that I never call his CO ever again, because he could have gotten in trouble. I replied through clenched lips, "As long as you keep me informed about where the hell you are, there will be no need to call the CO."

I kept my promise and remained faithful to Henry from that day forward. That was April and he came to live with me in November of the same year. After that, Henry and I had a lot of good times. There were many more times that he came and spent weekends with me and I with him.

Chapter 8

1992: Henry woke up this morning with a really bad stomach ache. He didn't want anything to eat, and when I finally got him to at least drink some orange juice, he threw it all back up. I drove him to the emergency room tonight, because I believed that his stomach wound may have flared up. When Henry was stabbed during the cookout, the hospital had performed what was called a gastroscopy on him to examine his interior stomach, and fortunately they didn't find anything out of order. He has two cuts on his stomach, which are parallel to one another; one from the stabbing incident, and the other from the exploratory procedure. I could tell by the way he squirmed in his chair that he was in some serious pain. They stuck this long tube down his nose to reach his stomach, which caused him to gag so bad that I had to turn my head. I finally left after they admitted him, and I felt sorry that he had to endure so much suffering.

Today after work I picked Li'l Henry up from daycare, and we went to visit Henry in the hospital. I had tried to call earlier on my break to check on him, but the nurse said he was sleeping. The nurse permitted me to bring Li'l Henry into the room after I told her I didn't have anyone to leave him with. However, I was warned that he was too young, and it was against hospital policy to have him in the room. She told me not to bring him again. When we walked into the room and saw all those tubes hooked up to Henry's body, it was scary for me. He was so weak that he could barely talk, and his lips were extremely chapped from dehydration. Henry turned toward me, looked straight into my eyes, and said, "Gwen I don't think I'm going to make it."

I looked at him and nervously replied, "Please don't say that!"

When I left the hospital, I called my sister Jennifer, who lived in Fayetteville, and asked if she could keep Li'l Henry for a week or so. Jennifer was two years younger than me, happily married, and had two boys; the youngest was a year older than Li'l Henry. She was a seamstress and worked from home. She agreed to keep him, so I drove home and packed a bag for him. Since I had to work the next morning,

I made the two-hour drive that night, tried not to visit too long, and turned around and drove right back.

1990: On my way back those, words that Henry said in the hospital room danced around in my head. "Gwen, I don't think I'm going to make it." I prayed to God to keep him in His ever-loving care. All sorts of thoughts were floating through my mind that night as I drove back. It was selfish of me, but what crept into my mind was the time when I'd gotten out of the military and Li'l Henry and I had moved here with Henry in Jacksonville. I had developed a large cyst on my hind side, close to my rectum, and I had gone a couple of days in serious pain hoping it would burst. After the second day, I couldn't endure the pain any longer, so I drove myself to the military hospital. The doctor examined me and decided to lance it right then and there in the emergency room.

"Mrs. Moore, you have a very infected cyst that is about two centimeters away from your rectum," said the middle-aged, heavyset, deep-voiced doctor who had a Southern drawl. "It will eventually form a head and, with some applied pressure, it will burst to give some release. If that happens, you will have to squeeze the cyst until you see a white spongy-like cork pop out. Then you would need to keep it covered with gauze until the remaining fluid drains. However, I can't tell you when that will happen. It could be tonight, tomorrow, or next week. I could prescribe some pain pills or I can go ahead and lance it for you today."

"Please lance it right now, because I cannot deal with this pain any longer," I replied.

He instructed me to return to the knee-chest position while he gave the nurse instructions. My face, forearms, knees, and the front of my feet were against the examining table, and my rear end was hoisted with my legs spread apart. What an awkward position! After about three minutes, the nurse came around front of me where I could see her and said, "Mrs. Moore, the doctor is now ready to lance the cyst."

"Okay!"

I felt a hand grab my cheeks and spread them apart and then a very sharp pinch. Liquid began running down my leg, and this indescribable stench enveloped the entire room. "This may be painful, Mrs. Moore, but I have to squeeze out the excess fluid and the core from the wound.

Afterward, I'm going to pack it with medicated gauze." I didn't say anything because I was already biting my lips from the pain.

After he bandaged my wound, I got dressed. The throbbing pain was almost unbearable. The doctor reentered the room and instructed, "Your gauze has to be changed daily, so I need for you to return tomorrow. I see that you are married, so bring your husband with you so he can watch. If he feels comfortable enough to change your gauze, then you won't have to come back every day for the next two weeks."

That must be a very deep wound to take two weeks to heal, I thought, then said, "Okay," as I tried to contain the tears that were forming in my eyes. He handed me a prescription for Vicodin for the pain. "Take one daily with food, as needed," were his last instruction as he left the room.

I slowly walked down the stairs, dropped off the prescription, and waited for what seemed like forever. As soon as I got my Vicodin, I went straight to the water fountain.

I laugh in remembrance of this because I had my rear-end lifted up in so many people's faces. After that, I felt that I was placed in a predicament where I had to rely on Henry and be nice to him. We had been going through some disagreements, and I kept it at a "down-low" because of what he had to do for me. Even though I thought there was a chance he could be spiteful, in the back of my mind I really didn't want to believe that my husband would actually permit a small matter like us getting angry at one another or arguing about something to stop him from packing my wound.

Sure enough, there came a day when I just couldn't hold my silence any longer and I told him a piece of my mind. Just as I had anticipated, when it came time to pack my wound, he said, "Stuff it your damn self." I found a way to do just that. I can still remember getting the wall mirror, propping it against the bathroom sink, and bending over to try and pack a wound on my backside. I left Henry shortly after that.

It's funny how the tables turn, but of course I have no intentions of not being there for Henry. As a matter of fact, I plan to visit him every day after I get out of work, because I want to be there for him and I know that he needs me. The doctor diagnosed him has having a volvulus, which is the twisting of the intestine upon itself and is common in infants. It caused obstruction to the bowel flow, and that was why his stomach was hurting so bad. Henry stayed in the hospital for an entire week, and oh man was he skinny when he came home. Just the way I liked him!

I drove to get Li'l Henry from my sister's house, and Henry rode along. She and her husband invited us to dinner, and we stayed a while. It was incredible how my sister had gotten Li'l Henry in the habit of eating everything on his plate. I used to try and force him to finish all of his food, but I heard that it could cause obesity later in life. Now he wasn't being forced, and as a matter of fact he was enjoying it. My sister is a better cook than I am; she got that from our mother, who is the best cook in the world. Henry and Mark, my brother-in-law, went into the living room after dinner while I helped Jennifer with the dishes. We couldn't stay too long because I had to work the next day. Henry wasn't going back to work yet, because he was placed on a 30-day convalescent leave. That's time that you get off when you're sick and it is not deducted from your annual leave. In other words, it's free time off.

Well, I thought I had it made in the shade. I've always wanted my husband to spend all of his free time with me and stay out of those streets, but the last two weeks have been pure hell. I've even suggested that he go hang out with his friends so he could get the heck out of my way. Since he wasn't budging, I decided I would go and play Bingo. Not far from where we live there is a bingo hall where I like to play, and the cost is only a quarter per game. The payout is anywhere between $10 and $20. It's fun and relaxing, and I don't have to spend as much money as I normally do at those regular bingo places where I go sometimes.

I ended up staying at the bingo hall all day, because I was winning more than I was losing for a change. When I finally ran out of quarters, I went to the car to confiscate the change from the ashtray, because I wasn't ready to leave just yet. I had to take the gear out of Park in order to reach it. I was in such a big hurry to get back inside to play bingo that I forgot to return the gear to Park. Needless to say, when I got ready to leave, I couldn't start the car. Try as I might I just couldn't get it to start, so I called a cab and went home.

When I got to the townhouse, I asked the cab driver to wait while I ran upstairs to get money to pay him. Henry was already looking out of the window because of the late hour.

"Gwen, where the hell is my car?" he yelled as I was going back out the door. After I paid the driver and walked back inside, I told him the car wouldn't start. Henry walked all the way to the bingo hall, about two miles away, to get his precious Volvo. When he got home he told me that I'd forgotten to put the gear in Park and that was why it wouldn't start. I thought that he was going to be angry with me, but surprisingly we laughed about it together. While we were laughing he asked, "Why do women sit and play bingo all day long, and when it's time to go, we haul butt home?"

Just to think of him being aware of that reality made me laugh even more, because it was so true.

Henry hasn't been drinking since his operation, and it was nice to be able to laugh and joke with him on a regular basis. He said he was afraid to drink, because he thought it would cause stomach pain. That must have been some excruciating pain to make Henry not want to drink anymore!

Next week, Mama is coming to get Li'l Henry to spend two weeks with her in Florida. As a matter of fact, she's asking for all of her grandchildren, which is something she has never done before. She's up there in Saginaw right now picking up Diane's and Debra's kids. They are my two oldest sisters. She'll be coming to Fayetteville to get Li'l Henry and Jennifer's two boys, so I have to drive him there on Saturday. This is going to be a treat to be able to enjoy myself and take it easy. I haven't been apart from Li'l Henry since I went overseas. I hope I don't overreact when he leaves me. I'm sure I won't, since he'll only be gone for two weeks and he will be in the best of care.

Sandra, a girl from work, asked me to go out to the club with her. Li'l Henry had already gone, so I said yes. Sandra was married, too, and had a little girl the same age as my son. When I first met her at the hotel, she talked to me like she already knew me. She was friendly, had a great personality, and talked a lot of junk.

When I got home around 2:00 AM, Henry was mad and waiting up for me. I had no idea what he was mad about, because I had told him I was going. The clubs here close at 3:00 in the morning, so I didn't stay till the end.

"Gwen, what the hell do you think you're doing, coming home at 2:00 in morning?" Henry asked.

"Why, is that not a decent time to come home, Henry? I wasn't doing anything," was my condescending reply. Needless to say, we got into this big argument, and he started throwing my clothes down the stairs and telling me to get out. You're my wife and you don't come home at 2:00 in the morning!" he yelled.

I wasn't about to leave, and I didn't pick those clothes up, either. Both of us walked across those clothes at the bottom of the stairs for about two weeks before he decided to pick them up and put them away. He only did it because his friends were coming over. That incident made me realize something different about Henry. Since I've been here in Jacksonville, I've noticed that it didn't matter how angry he got; he did not lay a hand on me. He once threw something at me and missed, but we haven't fought. As a matter of fact, when I was here before, he never touched me, either.

Chapter 9

1990: I can remember a time when we got into it about who was going to keep Li'l Henry. "I'm sick and tired of sitting at home while you run the streets like you're a single man," I told Henry one day. This was right before I left him, because he had just bought the Volvo. His buying that Volvo was the reason why I left him. It was actually the straw that broke the camel's back.

One day I decided I would pretend that I was going out. I wasn't going anywhere, because at that time I didn't know a single soul here in Jacksonville. I used to do that sometimes when we were in Fayetteville. I would get dressed and park somewhere. I would sit there until I thought he was good and mad, and then I would come home. I never wanted to go to the clubs without him, and I definitely didn't want to go alone. I would put on my sexiest dress and make up my face. I waited until he would get home so he could see how good I looked. He would ask where I was going. "I'm going out to the club," I would say. When he announced that he wasn't keeping Li'l Henry, I would get mad and started talking smack to him and then leave anyway.

We got into this big argument and, as I recall, he didn't hit me. He started punching the walls and he tore down the bathroom door, acting like a lunatic. I warned him that if he puts his hands on me, I would call his CO to report it. I learned to threaten to call his CO from when I called that time while I was in the Army and couldn't find him after his mother died. He kept saying, "Call the police and call my CO. I don't give a damn!" All the while he was saying that, he was punching the walls and his voice was becoming hoarser and hoarser. That really scared the hell out of me, because I thought he was going crazy. He finally calmed down and left, so I got my baby and got out of there, too. I got a hotel room and Li'l Henry and I spent the night there. I imagine he always had it in the back of his mind that I might just call his CO again. I don't think I would have ever done something like that, because I wouldn't want to cause him any trouble. After all his troubles were my troubles.

1989: We used to get into some crazy brawls when we lived together in Fayetteville. The worse one was when he gave me a black eye and chipped my tooth. I never told a soul, because I can't believe I stayed with him afterward. It happened one day when he was gone and some girl called. I can't remember her name. When I questioned why was she calling she asked, "Who the hell is this?"

"I'm Henry's wife!" I almost yelled.

"Oh, well, Henry told me he lived alone with his son," she said with attitude. Apparently she'd met my son. She also said, "He told me that Li'l Henry's mom lived in Michigan and that he wasn't even married to her."

She claimed that Henry had just left her house and was supposed to return later to take her and her girlfriend to rent a car. As she explained this to me, Henry walked through the door with my son in his arms. "Wait a goddamn minute," I cut her off and immediately asked him, "Oh, so you and I are not married? You and I are not together? This girl on the phone said that you are not married!" I yelled.

Henry grabbed the phone as I stood right there awaiting an answer, and he said to her, "Hell no, I'm not married. Let me call you back."

He hung up the phone, and at that point I was speechless. I felt my eyes begin to burn and sobs were approaching my throat. I then yelled at the top of my lungs, "Give me my keys and get the hell out of my house!"

He told me that he wasn't going anywhere. We argued for the longest time, and it reached a point when I was saying, "Please leave."

"Where am I going to go, Gwen? I don't have nowhere else to go."

I reminded him that he could go and live with his cousin, who was staying right there in Fayetteville at the time, but he refused to budge.

The phone began to ring again, and I believed that girl was calling back maybe to verify if he was still going to take them or to find out what was going on. We both made a mad dash to the phone but he got to it first. He unplugged it and wouldn't give it to me. "Give me my damn phone, Henry!" I yelled as I grabbed for it.

"You're not getting this phone!" he yelled back while holding it in one hand above his head. My adrenaline was flowing at a level beyond normal at this point. However, I found a way to turn around, walk out of the house, get into my car, and drive away.

As I drove around, I wondered how Henry could do this to me, his wife. What had I done so badly to him, to anyone, to make him treat me like this or even think it was okay? "God!" I screamed out with a shaky voice as the tears began to flow. "What have I done wrong that deserves such humiliating treatment from someone who says he loves me? He doesn't love me, he can't love me. Why doesn't my husband love me, Lord? Why, God, can't I have a normal, caring husband who puts family before anything except you?"

"Drive the car into a tree and kill yourself," I heard a voice say. I drove into a parking lot and stopped the car. "Kill yourself, Gwen, because Henry doesn't love you, he doesn't want you. You'll show him and he'll be sorry for all he's done to you. Do it! Do it! Do it!"

I turned the ignition and started the car back up. As I drove slowly I was totally incognizant of my surroundings. I started speeding, driving faster and faster, and the tears were streaming down my face. "I can't live like this!" I shouted. "I won't live like this anymore!"

The thundering of my heart was all I could hear. Pain was all I could feel in my hands as I gripped the steering tighter and aimed the Hyundai toward the only tree I could see. "I'm going to do this, damn it!" I sobbed. I floored the accelerator and closed my eyes. I could feel my body being pushed against the leather seat as the acceleration increased. I opened my eyes for just a second to adjust my tracking so I would hit the center of the tree. That's when I saw him. Li'l Henry standing in front of the tree holding his tattered teddy bear, crying out to me, "Mommy, Mommy, I love you!"

I jerked the steering wheel but it was too late. The front passenger side rammed into the tree and sent me into what seemed like a never-ending spin. I screamed, "Help me! help me!"

When I opened my eyes I realized that the car was not on, and I was still in the parking lot. I finally went home after realizing I needed to live for my son if for nothing else.

Henry was sitting in the living room watching TV. "Where is my son?" I asked.

"He's in the bed asleep."

I looked around the room and didn't see the telephone. "Where is the telephone?"

"You are not getting that phone, Gwen," he said without even looking away from the TV. I didn't say anything else, but I searched for a while and couldn't find it. I finally gave up and slept on the couch that night, because I did not want him anywhere near me.

The next day, I called home from work to see if he had reconnected the telephone, and he picked up. I slammed the phone down hard enough to crack the receiver. Henry was unemployed at this time and he would babysit Li'l Henry while I worked. The bills were beginning to pile up, and we had several discussions about what he needed to do about it. He was in the process of enlisting in the Army

When I came home from work that day, he walked out as if he had something to be mad about. I wasn't falling for that "I'll be mad so she can get over it" bit this time. He got into the car and left. I looked around again for the phone, but still I could not find it. When Henry walked through the door, I said, "Henry let's get one thing straight about my car. I pay that car note and you better not get in my car no more."

"Watch me," he replied.

Henry's car had gotten repossessed, and I had bought a brand new Hyundai right before it happened. He had his own set of keys to my car, so I knew I couldn't physically stop him from driving it. This madness went on for about two weeks. It had gotten to the point where he wouldn't even permit me to drive my own car once I came home from work. He kept removing some part from underneath the hood. When he removed this part, the car wouldn't start, so I wasn't able to go anywhere. I grew so frustrated with him dominating me that I picked up a knife while we were arguing one day. When he got too close, I cut him on the hand. It was a deep cut, and I really didn't mean to do it, but I was mad. He picked up a chair and hurled it at me. I ducked behind the refrigerator, and the chair hit the wall. He ran upstairs, and I ran out the back door.

He always claimed there was a gun in one of his duffel bags, but I never saw it. I immediately thought of that gun, which was why I ran. I walked over to my girlfriend Deidra's house and stayed there for a while to let him cool off. Deidra was in the Army and a good friend of mine. She let my family live with her for about two months while we waited for on-post housing. When I returned, Henry had a bandage wrapped around his hand and claimed he had gone to the hospital. I was sorry for cutting him, but I didn't tell him. I thought he would try to get even, but, surprisingly, he didn't.

When I went to work, I pulled up the hood of the car and stared at the engine. I tried to figure out what it was that Henry was removing. I know now that it was a spark plug, but try as I might I couldn't figure it out then.

One day after I got off work, I thought, I'll be devious and park the car somewhere else in the housing area. We were living in on-post housing and it was pretty big, so I felt I had parked the car a good distance away. As I walked home, I thought to myself, Bet he won't get my car this day. As soon as I got home and Henry didn't see the car, he asked where it was. "Where is the phone?" I asked. He sarcastically asked did I want to know where the phone was? Then he unscrewed the large air vent that was alongside the wall, reached inside, pulled the phone out, and plugged it in. He called his cousin to come and pick him up, then unplugged the phone after they hung up.

"I'm going to find the car, and you still ain't getting this phone," he stated. I was so angry that I even thought about getting it disconnected, but I figured it would only hurt me in the long run because I would have to pay a reconnection fee. He was getting the best of me, and it was eating me up inside, because there wasn't a thing I could do about it. It took Henry a while, but he found the car and drove it back home. His cousin may have talked to him and convinced him to do the right thing, because he plugged the phone back in when he got back.

I could not believe that we were behaving that way. It was as if we were playing a game and the loser would suffer dire consequences. Adults shouldn't behave like this, but I didn't care because I felt he had no right to disrespect me with other women and think he could do whatever he wanted with my stuff after I confronted him about it. He was living in my world, and he didn't even have a pot to piss in, yet he wanted to tell me what to do. Naturally, I tried to outsmart him in every possible way. I endured all of this on my own, and I told no one, because I didn't want to put my personal business out in the streets.

I finally decided to settle down for a few days, and I didn't say anything to Henry. He came and went as he pleased. Continuously looking out the window one night, I waited for him to come home. As soon as I saw him get out of the car, I ran out of the back door, jumped into the car and drove away. He had stopped taking the spark plug out of the car when I gave him the impression that I didn't care. I thought it was a smart move and I stayed away for about an hour, just savoring the idea that I'd out-slicked him.

When I arrived back at the street that we live on, I noticed Military Police cars with lights flashing everywhere. I drove up and realized they were at my house. I didn't really know what to think, so I got out of the car to see what was going on. As soon as I neared the front door, and it was wide open might I add, two MPs stopped me and one escorted me over to the patrol car. "Ma'am, your husband has called us regarding a domestic dispute, and I need you to sit inside this car until we figure out what is going on," the officer advised.

As I sat in the back of the MP car, I became embarrassed, because all the neighbors were looking out of their windows and doors at me. Some people were standing on the curbside trying to find out what was going on. The MP finally approached the car and explained the situation to me in detail. He said that Henry had alleged that I pulled a knife on him. "No, I didn't," I interrupted while knowing that I had two days ago.

"Well, he said that you did, Ma'am, so according to protocol we called your First Sergeant and he is on his way over as we speak."

After informing me of what to expect, the MP walked back into the house and left me in the squad car for about 20 more minutes.

I saw the First Sergeant drive up, talk to the MP, and head toward me. He opened my car door and told me he was going to drive me to the barracks. "The MPs are going to escort you inside the house to get some overnight items," he said. I didn't say anything, and I did as he instructed. I didn't even look at Henry when I walked inside; I just went upstairs and packed an overnight bag. I got into the First Sergeant's car, and we drove away.

The First Sergeant and I were pretty cool, so he began talking to me. "I knew something was bothering you, Specialist Moore, because you haven't been acting like yourself." The First Sergeant was the main reason why I received my E-4 Specialist stripes. He always asked, "Private Moore, why haven't you made Specialist yet? I'm going to promote you to Specialist," he would then add. He did just that, too, and he also recommended me for the E-5 Board. That's when you stand before a group of high-ranking officials and they ask you a series of questions about military procedures, political and governmental issues, or just what was happening in the news. A person didn't automatically become a sergeant after passing this board, but he or she would then be considered E-4 promotable. Once a person obtains that status, it's a matter of a cut-off score lowering to meet their accumulated points. If that score decreases to the accumulated points, he or she automatically gets promoted to Sergeant and obtains an E-5 status.

Anyway, I started crying right in front of the First Sergeant. I told him everything that had been going on. He had met Henry before on several occasions when he used to pick me up from work. The First Sergeant said that he had no other choice other than to take me to the barracks, because Henry was my dependent. He explained that whenever there is any type of domestic dispute, the one in the military had to leave. They couldn't very well take the dependent to the barracks.

When I got to the barracks, I was issued linen, a blanket, and a pillow. They gave me a key, and I went to my room. I sat there on the bed quietly for a while, just thinking. Nobody gave a damn about my son. How did anyone know if Henry was capable of taking care of him? I just could not believe he had gotten me put out of my own house. I got up, went to the pay phone down the hall, and called him. I told him that he was dead wrong for what he had just done. "That is my apartment, my furniture, my world, and you need to be the one to go," I whispered through clenched teeth.

"Do you want to spend the night at the barracks?" he then asked me. I suspect at that point he was feeling guilty about the whole ordeal and wanted to make amends.

"Hell no, I don't want to stay here," I answered. He picked me up that night and I spent the night at home.

The next morning I got up and drove to PT, but I just could not get out of the car. Everybody was looking at me, because PT was mandatory, not an option. Sergeant James finally came over to my car after PT was finished. She was my NCOIC, but she was also a friend. She saw that I was crying, so she got into the car and asked what was wrong. I explained everything to her, and she persuaded me to go and get Li'l Henry and spend the weekend over at her house.

After PT, Sergeant James usually took a shower and got dressed for work at the barracks. I waited for her, and she trailed me home. She came in and sat down on the couch in the living room while I packed a bag for Li'l Henry and me. Henry and I started arguing right in front of her. I yelled at him, "I can't stand you with your black ass, and I'm getting that phone disconnected." "There isn't any food in this house, and I hope you starve to death!"

I didn't tell him where I was going or how long I would be gone. I grabbed my baby and drove away in my car. When we got to Sergeant James's house, she told me that she knew I was mad because she'd never heard me talk like that before. She told me that I didn't have to come into work that day. "Stay here, make yourself comfortable, and calm down," she said before she left for work.

We had a four-day weekend off from work because it was some holiday; I can't remember which. Li'l Henry and I stayed there the entire four days alone, because Sergeant James and her family went out of town. I called to disconnect the phone, and the telephone company assured me it would be cut off by Monday morning. I thought maybe Henry would try to run up my telephone bill since he thought I'd left him.

I called Deidra to tell her what had happened, and she advised me to call the Inspecting General. The IG is who to call when you feel you've been done an injustice and after first using the Chain of Command. In other words, if my NCOIC couldn't resolve my problem, then I would go to the First Sergeant and so on up the ladder. I did take her advice and called the IG, because I felt it wasn't right to make me leave my own apartment no matter what the circumstances were.

Unfortunately, my First Sergeant heard about it and had me standing at attention in his office when I returned to work. He reiterated to me the procedure concerning domestic disputes that he had informed me of the day he drove me to the barracks. He wanted to clarify the fact that I didn't have to remain in the barracks, and that I could go home once things cooled down. I could tell he was somewhat disturbed about it, so I apologized for calling the IG, because I wasn't trying to get him in trouble. I also thanked him for making me understand that I could in fact return home even though, little did he know, I already had.

When I came home that Monday afternoon, the phone was still on. I called the telephone company, and they explained that Henry had called after I did and requested they keep it on. I argued with the lady because I felt it was wrong, considering the phone was listed under my name only. I decided to just keep it on since I had returned home. Henry tried to look sorry and then he asked why I had stayed gone so long. I just looked at him and continued unpacking our bags. As far as I was concerned, I didn't have anything to say to him anymore. We spent the next two days in total silence. I didn't cook for him nor did I sleep with him.

Wednesday of that same week I had just laid Li'l Henry down to take a nap, another girl called. Maybe she could have been the same girl trying to mess with me; I don't know. She said that Henry had just left her house and that he was her man. I hung up in her face and she kept calling back. I picked the phone up and slammed it back down.

Finally, Henry walked in with a beer can in his hand. I glared at him and said, "Your woman just called." After he asked who she was, I demanded to know who the hell he thought I was, his personal secretary? I was so mad that before I knew it I slapped him as hard as I could. I'm sure he saw stars. He didn't even see it coming, and I know it shocked him, because it was totally out of my character. I had never hit him first before in my life, only defended myself from him. This time I wanted to fight. I felt that by fighting I could alleviate some of the hostility that I had bottled up deep inside of me. He pushed me back so hard that I stumbled and fell down on my butt. I jumped up and rammed straight into him, head first. We started fighting, and as always I ended up on the floor trying to kick him in the groin. If I had my way, I would have jammed his testicles straight up into his stomach.

I can't remember whether he kicked me or stomped me in the face, but one of the two happened while I was trapped on the floor. I couldn't feel anything when we were fighting, but once we finished the pain set in. Henry took off in the car as usual. I went into the bathroom and looked in the mirror. I discovered one tooth in the back of my mouth was chipped and hanging loose. I pulled on the chipped part until it came out. After rinsing the blood out of my mouth, I took some pain killers to ease the toothache. Li'l Henry woke up after I had taken a shower and I prepared him something to eat. I couldn't eat anything and all I could think about was what a mess my life was. I couldn't help but wonder how could a man who once loved me, treat me in such a way? I was angry and I didn't want anything else to do with him. When I went to bed I let Li'l Henry sleep with me. I heard Henry come in the wee hours of the night. He never came upstairs and he slept on couch. I didn't realize that I had a black eye until the next morning when I got up for PT. So instead of going to PT, I went to Sick Call complaining of a toothache.

Sick Call is when you go to a military medical clinic, and they determine the severity of your illness. It is also the place to go to obtain quarters, which is a note instructing you to stay in the house, barracks, or wherever you live for a certain amount of hours, usually 24, 36, or 48. They referred me to the dentist and gave me 24-hour quarters. I was happy because I didn't want to go to work so everybody could see my shiner. I then went to the dentist, and he put a very large filling in my tooth. He asked about the black eye, and I lied and said I got hit in the face with a baseball at the game the night before. I believe he took pity upon me, because he extended my quarters to 48 hours, so I wouldn't have to go to work that Friday either. By Monday morning I was able to conceal my black eye with makeup.

Henry kept saying how sorry he was and tried to show me the scratches I'd made on his face. I didn't give a darn about some petty scratches when he had bruised my face and chipped my tooth. The dentist had to reconstruct the chipped part because it was so large and it broke very close to the root. I also had to get a cap over that entire tooth. This was a permanent injury, and I felt those petty scratches would go away far faster than my black eye. He tried to give me a steak to put on my eye, but I didn't want to take anything from him. I realized I was the one who started the fight, but how did he expect me to react to women calling my house and he not acknowledging to them that I am his wife. I was angry and that's why I slapped him and I didn't care what he would do to me.

I finally came around after maybe a couple of weeks of him apologizing and telling me it would never happen again and him catering to me as if I were a sick puppy. When I used to watch those movies on TV about battered women, I swore I would never allow that to happen to me. Even on TV the husband always apologized and the wife forgave. Henry basically begged for my forgiveness, and after a while I believed that he was truly sorry for what he had done and I still loved him. I guess you don't really know what you'll endure from a man until you actually live it.

Chapter 10

October 20, 1992

Dear Willie:

Three weeks from now I am going to live with Mama in sunny Florida. Henry has to go on another six-month float. I didn't want to stay here in Jacksonville until he returned, so we're going to give up the townhouse. We won't have a problem breaking the lease, because all Henry has to do is show the landlord his orders. Since Li'l Henry is already there, I asked my mother to keep him in Florida until I come.

In case you're wondered how I was able to write to you so often, I wrote at my job. I kept paper, envelop, and stamps in my locker at work. I took paper with me on my cart whenever I went to clean the rooms. The supervision at Hampton Inn was very relaxed. Sometimes I would sit down for about ten minutes or so and write you. We had twenty-eight minutes to clean a room and I usually finished in about fifteen to twenty. I wrote on my lunch hour sometimes and my fifteen minute breaks at other times. Just think, you'll be able to write again. I'm sure you have plenty to say to me. It seems I can't stay in one place for any extended amount of time. I love the military life, but as long as I'm a part of it, there's always going to be living changes. I hope that when

Li'l Henry starts school I'll at least be somewhere stable, because I know moving here and there is not good for him at all.

Well, anyhow, I wanted to let you know that even though I haven't said it, I still love you. I just didn't think it was appropriate for me to continue expressing it to you while I'm here living with Henry. My feelings have not changed at all for you. I still remember everything we've been through together when I was home. That has remained in my mind as well as my heart all of this time, and I will never let it go. You have made me feel more special and more loved than any man I've ever known.

I'm not going to write anymore until I arrive in Tampa. As soon as I get there, I'll write you, and maybe we could get a chance to talk on the phone. Take care, Babe, and I'll talk to you soon.

Love,

Gwen

PART II
SAGINAW, MICHIGAN

Chapter 1

May 5, 1991

Dear Willie:

How are you doing? Fine and very much healthy, I hope. I imagine you're shocked to your knees to hear from me. Then again, you probably knew I would find a way to communicate with you after my sisters informed you of my return.

My sister Diane told me what happened over the phone right before I came back home. I was sort of following your case in the newspapers after that, but it wasn't very informative. I planned to write before now, but I'm sorry to say that the thought emerged, faded, and then drifted to the back of my mind. I've also been preoccupied with working two jobs. I've just recently quit one of them, with the intent to rectify my improper eating habits, which caused excessive weight loss. When I was working the two jobs, I would forget to eat, but since then my food consumption has increased and my weight is now stable. I want my butt back if nothing else. I feel insecure walking around here with a flat booty looking like a white girl.

There really isn't anything going on in my life right now. I've been in Saginaw since last year. I requested to get out of the Army after reenlisting for Germany and discovering the tour was unaccompanied. After arriving there, I was informed I could in fact bring my family, but getting on-post housing would take up to a year. I decided the Army wasn't for me. I love the Army and will miss it very much, but I grew sick of all of that running without a destination. It's not a suitable place for a female with children, because separation will occur from one time to another and I can't deal with being away from my son. Yes, I do have a son now. He is three years old and is the most important person in my life.

Well, Willie, so much about my life. What's going on in yours besides this little mishap? How do you feel? Are you still married? How many children do you have? I was there at your sentencing yesterday. I caught only the rear view of you, and it sure looked good. I wish to know if I may come to see the front view, too. I want to know if my name can be added to your visitation list. Write back in response, because I won't come unless I'm certain you have indeed added my name.

Take care, Hon.

Your friend,

Gwen

* * *

May 13, 1991

Dear Gwen:

What's up! You're right; it was definitely an eye-opener to receive a letter from you. Of course immediately afterward I indeed added your name to my visitation list. I took it upon myself to schedule your visit for Saturday at 4:00 PM. I hope you can make it. If not, perhaps you can tell me what's convenient for you. Visiting days are Tuesday, Thursday, and Saturday between 4:00 and 8:30 PM.

My goodness, you are a blast from the past! I am a fortunate man to have you in my corner. Had I only known you were at the sentencing, I would have turned around so I could get a good look at you. Don't doubt for a moment that I've forgotten how sexy you were.

I suppose your sisters enlightened you about my gory incident. I was evidently in the wrong place and not at the right time. In time maybe I'll share with you my interpretation of what happened. In response to your question, I'm still married, but my wife and I were separated long before this happened. I have three girls; two from my marriage. You do remember Tracie, my oldest daughter from back when you and I were together? She's presently living in Germany with her mother. It's difficult to believe you have a son considering your unchangeable stubbornness to be childless. I'm happy that feelings do change, because I believe every woman should experience bearing a child at least once in a lifetime. So where are you working and what do you do? I hope you're happy to be home, because I know that I am.

Well, it was really nice hearing from you and hopefully I'll see you on Saturday.

Take care,

Willie

* * *

May 18, 1991

Dear Willie:

I received your letter, and Saturday will be fine since I'm not working that day. I ordinarily work every weekend, so I suspect Providence is working in our favor. You probably won't get this letter earlier, but I'm sending it nevertheless so you can have another one to open. I remember us being fairly close at one point in time, yet I find myself developing anxiety as the day nears for me to visit. It has been a long time.

I'm currently working at the Hampton Inn Hotel in the housekeeping department. After my discharge from the military, I got into housekeeping because jobs were very scarce in Jacksonville, North Carolina. As it turns out, I enjoy it because it's laid back with no supervision, and above all I get to watch the soap operas daily. It's nice to be back in Saginaw, because I've gotten an opportunity to talk with some of my old classmates. Do you remember Vicky? Well, she and I have been spending a lot of time together, just like we used to before.

When I was there at the sentencing, I saw your mother and sister but I don't think they noticed me and, besides, they wouldn't remember me anyway. They were crying their poor hearts out. I really didn't understand the sentence that the judge ruled. I remember him repeating six years over and over. Does that mean you have to serve three six-year terms, or are they concurrent?

Until next time,

Gwen

* * *

May 25, 1991

Dear Gwen:

My goodness, Babe, you are as sexy as ever! You're right about that butt, though. I do remember it being much bigger. You may have lost weight from lack of eating, but do you think maybe separation from your husband is also a contributing factor? What happened with your marriage, anyway? Are you divorced? Were there any "oops upside your head" going on? In other words, did your husband ever put his hands on you? I thought you guys were a match made in heaven that would last forever, considering my inability to capture your heart. You were in love with that Negro because although he was in Japan when we met, you made sure I knew he was "The Man." I remember that was a quality I liked about you. You were always straightforward as far as your relationship with him. I figured I could snatch you away, considering he would be away in Japan for a year and I was there alone with you. I suppose fate deals the deck in ways we don't even understand.

I wouldn't say that I was in love with my wife when we married. There were many complications in our relationship, but she had my children. If for no other reason, I wanted to do the right thing for my daughters. My first daughter was without a father figure in the house, but I played my part in her life as best as I could. I just became discontent with busting my back by working two and three jobs in order for my wife to stay at home. She graduated from college yet didn't want to work. She wanted to remain home with the kids, which was okay initially; then after a while that got old. It wasn't just that, either. She was a jealous and self-centered woman, and I grew disgusted with it all. That's basically what happened with my marriage. I suppose you know she's staying in my house next door to your daddy.

By the way, I received your letter the day after your visit. Vicky, of course I remember her. I'll never forget her because she's the reason why I had an opportunity to meet you. Then again she's the reason for your abundance of negativity concerning me, too.

I really enjoyed seeing you again and would love if we could keep in touch in the future. When am I going to see you again, Gwen? Can I call sometimes? I'm asking because it will have to be collect.

I'm looking forward to hearing from you again soon.

Be sweet,

Willie

P.S. The six years are concurrent.

* * *

June 1, 1991

Dear Willie:

In case you didn't know, that was my first time ever visiting anyone in jail. It was strange because I thought they were going to pat me down like they do in the movies. They just took my ID card and told me to empty my pockets. I supposed they were making sure I wasn't sneaking anything in to you. When I walked in and saw a room filled with small round tables surrounded by chairs, I was amazed. I thought you and I would be separated by a glass window. I'm sorry if I seemed disconnected, but the hug you gave me when I walked in really surprised me. I was unaware that we would be able to embrace, and then I was concerned about the amount of time we could do it. Visiting a jail wasn't at all like I'd expected it to be. Those 30 minutes did go by pretty fast, and before I knew it the guard was calling your name to go back. It was too short, but it was really nice seeing you again.

I had a letter prepared for you sealed with a stamp that I had written the night after leaving there. Upon receipt of your letter, I decided to discard it because it was only casual talk. I'm thinking you would prefer that I am straight up with you and share exactly what I'm feeling, especially after our visit. I will include some of the strong points of that letter, though.

A month after I left Henry, we began conversing over the phone. He came home last July determined to get Li'l Henry and me, but I asked him to wait until Labor Day weekend, at which time I said I would go back to Jacksonville. The reason why I decided to reconcile was because I felt I couldn't make it without him. I've got so many bills, and then there was medical coverage to think about. I basically wanted to make amends because I was afraid of failure in attempting to make it on my own.

I later called him with this great idea about stopping at Cedar Point, which is an amusement park in Ohio, and maybe spending the night in a hotel on the way back to Jacksonville. He flat out said no. That was my incentive to try again to make it alone. All I wanted was to initiate something we could do as a family, and as always he shot down my idea and replaced it with nothing. I said then and there, "Forget it and forget you; I'm not going back." That gave me the determination to make it on my own.

You know what Willie? I don't miss him, and I don't know if I still love him. Seriously, I doubt if we will ever resolve our differences. I want a loving husband who enjoys doing things as a family. He just wants a wife to be at home awaiting his arrival whenever he decides to take a break from the streets. In response to your question, no, we are not divorced yet. Until I reestablish myself, remaining his wife would be a sensible plus for me. Until we're divorced, I'm 100% medically covered through the military.

I've been through an abundance of changes with my marriage. Although I feel he is solely responsible for the destruction of our marriage, he holds the opposite point of view. He always felt that I was to blame, basically because I wouldn't accept everything that he dished out without an argument. From the time he was discharged from the Marines and came to live with me, we've had problems. I believe in woman's liberation, and the fact that I was the main supporter of the family really didn't bother me at all. He worked part-time jobs here and there, and for a six-month stretch, he wasn't employed at all. What I wanted was an equal relationship, but I suppose he needed the upper hand because he was the man and he felt he had to uphold his dominance. After viewing his disposition, I felt it was my responsibility to continuously remind him who was basically bringing in the money.

We lived in a furnished one-bedroom apartment until we were called for on-post housing. Babe, I singularly purchased the bedroom set, and the living room and dining room furniture. I cared for both my husband and my son as I should have, and I had no beef about it. After a while, it became extremely difficult for me to satisfy our creditors, because I was the only one employed at the time. It was also taking too long for him to enlist in the Army, so he decided to reenlist in the Marines. It worked out pretty much okay for a while, because he came home on the weekends. Prior to his reenlistment, I reenlisted for Germany with the notion that we would all be there together. When my order came as an unaccompanied tour, we found an apartment in Jacksonville, I discharged from the Army, and this man began playing the "This is my house" game. I guess he wanted to flip the script, since he was now in the Marines and I was working the minimum-wage job. Willie, I prepared his lunch and cooked dinner every day, plus I worked a full-time job. I maintained our apartment as far as cleanliness and made sure all of our bills were paid. I considered myself to be the perfect wife, and I wanted to do these things for him. The three topics we argued about were his female friends, my infrequent slackening of daily rituals, and sex, sex, sex, because my drive wasn't as strong as his. How could he expect me to even want to make love to him all the time when he treated me so bad? Nevertheless, I continued holding on to the marriage.

We battled many times, and I fought back because I'm not the type of person who allows a man to bash, slap, or punch me without returning the courtesy. There's one particular fight that comes to mind that was quite funny. It happened in 1987 before Li'l Henry was born, and we were living in our first apartment in Fayetteville. I came home from work ready to spend a nice, quiet evening with my husband. When I walked in, he headed toward the door, and I wasn't able to share my plans with him. In a desperate attempt to detain him, I stated that I had somewhere else to go.

I remember us both entering the car while tussling to prevent the other from going anywhere. He was in the driver's seat and I was in the passenger's. We started fighting right there inside the car in the apartment complex parking lot where we lived. I remember there not being enough room to hoist a fisted hand far enough upward to render a blow with sufficient force. I think we might have tussled in the car for a good five minutes before we called truce. We somehow hit and jammed the horn, causing it to honk the entire time, and I'm convinced that everybody was looking out their windows trying to see what the hell was going on. The horn continued to blow even after we got out the car, and that's when I noticed it. When I think about that now, I laugh, because it was very funny.

To sum it all up, I have had knots upside my head, a black eye, and a cut in the back of my head once. You better believe he has scars to remember me by, as well. He's had scratches on his face and arms and a cut that required stitches.

There have been this girl and that girl and telephone numbers galore. I've never caught him with another woman, but I've always found telephone numbers. I endured all of this hoping one day he would change. I never liked to go to clubs without him, and when I played bingo, which was the only place I ever went for enjoyment, we argued when I returned home most of the times. He, on the other hand, went out when he felt the urge.

I'm not trying to paint a dog's picture on his face, because there were good times too. He took me out to dinner quite often, he informed me where he would go prior to leaving, and he cared for Li'l Henry while I went to bingo. But Willie, he wanted to live from paycheck to paycheck. After discussing our financial situation, we agreed to deposit $25 into our savings every month. I'll be darned if that man didn't withdraw that money every single month. I wanted to buy a house one day, but he didn't want to save anything. I had established my credit fairly well; I had Visa, MasterCard, and MasterCard Gold, so I knew the credit portion wouldn't be a problem. That was all I wanted besides a washer and dryer—and that, too, I never got. I wanted us both to work two jobs and just save, but then he would comment on how we would never get to see one another, which was a bit of sarcasm. I said that the lack of seeing each other is a small sacrifice for a fulfillment of a dream. "We could enjoy each other later when we are benefiting from our dreams. We don't have to buy a house, let's just rent one," I said.

Willie, I can go on and on about this 20/80 relationship, but

I think you've gotten the picture. Anyhow, he bought a Volvo without discussing it with me beforehand. The note on my Hyundai was due, bills were unpaid, and there wasn't any food in the refrigerator. I suppose he thought he had his priorities straight. That was the last straw! I sold all the furniture and I "got out of Dodge" before he came home from work one day. I sold it for far less than it was worth, but I needed the money. I called and asked Diane to come down and lead the way back to Saginaw. All of my sisters came: Debra, Diane, Charlene, and Pam in order from oldest to youngest. Jennifer, who was already living in Fayetteville at the time, ranked after me and we were between Diane and Charlene. We all met at Jennifer's house and spent the night before making the trip back to Saginaw.

Now, I feel good because I don't have to worry about placing someone's feelings above mine. I can go anywhere I want without fear of someone developing an attitude about it. And get this, Willie; I was totally faithful to Henry the entire time we were together in Jacksonville. I'll get myself on track in a little while. I'm getting ready to return to school next term. I'm waiting on my DD Form 214 which is my military discharge papers to apply for a civil service job. I will definitely be ready to take the post office test that will come available next year. I will secure a good job one day, hopefully, and I will get everything I lost plus more, just like Job did in the Bible. All I have to do trust in God, and He can make it happen.

You and I married some knuckleheads. Maybe we should have gotten married; but Willie, you really terrified me back then. I felt I needed to safeguard my heart from you, because of the fear that you might shatter it. I felt you were dating other women besides me. Hell, you never mentioned that you loved me, so I assumed you didn't. I cared a great deal about you, because I remember sometimes awaiting your arrival and feeling disappointed when you never came. Then there were times I'd sparkle when I saw you coming. There wasn't a doubt in my mind about how I felt for you, but I just didn't want to get hurt. Willie, I believed you cared about me, but I suppose I needed you to find a way to show how much. If you could have given me some type of indication that there could have been a future for us, I would have certainly given Henry the boot. Your tenacity to play the cool dude made me second-guess your intentions. Now that I've learned about your marriage and your perseverance to make a life for your family, I think I may have misjudged you. I supposed I can say I may have missed out.

I'll end on that note. I'll keep in touch through letters, and maybe whenever you reach your destination and it's not very far I could visit again. Before I close, I would like to say that you looked real good, and I'm pleased to see you're not allowing this misfortune to take away your morale. I needed to see for myself, or else you would have acquired my everlasting sympathy, and I know you don't want that. After attending the sentencing, I could not release you from my mind, and it's such a release to know you are okay. And another thing: I sure would love to grab that nice butt you got back there (ha, ha!).

Take care "Hun,"

Gwen

* * *

Chapter 2

June 7, 1991

Dear Gwen:

I enjoyed our telephone conversation yesterday. It seems as though things haven't changed very much for me as far as my feelings for you. I find myself thinking about you quite a bit lately, and it's very odd considering that many years have passed since we were an item. We've lived separate lives with two people we had no business being with whatsoever. All I can say is, "If I could turn back the hands of time..."

I don't understand how you could be afraid of me back then, because I felt I portrayed my feelings for you explicitly. I realized

I'd never proved my feelings for you, but I really did love you. I just couldn't allow myself to voice it, because you belonged to someone else. In a way I suppose I was trying to shield my heart as well. Then, after you left for basic training, I thought that I would never see you again. I remember writing once or was it twice, I forget. I really didn't see the point in pursuing you any longer, because my only advantage over Henry was being near to you and that was all that I had to hold on to. Once we were apart as well, I felt I didn't have a chance in the world.

I read your last letter over and over, and I can't believe that man didn't take care of his business as a husband should have. You were right to leave his ass. You were the only one giving, and a marriage is all about give and take. There's no such thing as one partner continuously receiving while the other is always giving. It should be a 50/50 affair. That's exactly what happened in my marriage, and nothing good can ever come of it. I made the right decision and got out, because at one point prior to leaving, "oops upside her head" was beginning to penetrate my mind. I've never hit my wife the entire time we were together. I felt that if an argument got out of hand, the best option for me was to leave until things cooled off.

I have faith in myself, and I believe that when I get out of here, life has rewards waiting for me. I always think positive no matter what situation I'm in, and it has worked to my advantage. Maybe you should adopt those concepts and see how they can work for you. You'll be just fine, because there are plenty of single mothers out there who are doing damned good and you can, too. You've conceived it and perceived it. Now believe it and achieve it, so you can receive it.

With love,

Willie

P.S. Remember to tell your son you love him three times a day.

* * *

June 13, 1991

Dear Willie:

Such a beautiful letter coming from a man who I thought was not sentimental at all! I should have supplied you with a piece of paper and pen back then, so I could have really known how you felt. I recall the one time you wrote while I was in basic training, and never in a million years would I have thought you could express yourself on paper so well. I remember that letter being trivial and containing no emotions whatsoever. I felt it was just something you quickly transcribed because of your promise to write. It compels me to wonder if your feelings are different now than they were before. This letter was warm, sincere, and very intimate. This is the type of letter that can make me say, "Willie cares about me," and truly believe it. Thank you, Baby, for sharing a part of you that I never knew existed.

Although some things change, I see one that has stayed the same. I enjoyed our telephone conversation, but let me ask you something. Why do you sometimes call me "man"? Do I look like a man to you? That was another expression you used a lot when we dated that caused me to question your sincerity. I didn't particularly like it much, but I supposed I should have asked you to stop, right? What would you have said?

I would like to enlighten you about my position concerning Henry's integrity before I went to basic training. He didn't reassure me that our relationship was worth a "one-year separation" prior to leaving for Japan. I anticipated being surprised with an engagement right before he left, but that didn't happen. I was so upset that I told him I wasn't going to be faithful while he was away, and I meant that. Believe me, I'm not the type of person who fools around for the sheer joy of it. If he had done right by me, I would have never given you a chance. I thought it would just be a fling between you and me, because although Henry and I were on bad terms when he left for Japan, my feelings for him were nevertheless the same. It all backfired in my face when I fell head over heels in love with you and couldn't let you know. How could I, after throwing the fact that Henry was my man in your face every chance I had? Besides, I thought you were involved with other women, too, and that made it extremely difficult for me to expose my true feelings.

Just maybe this is our second chance. Maybe fate has brought us back together for a reason. Only time can tell this story.

Love,

Gwen

* * *

June 20, 1991

Hi, Gwen:

Here's the black-and-white version of the picture we took together last week. I bought two copies for the price of one. I hope you're doing fine with your nice, round butt. Can you see how well it fits in the pocket (between my legs)? (smile) I think our feelings for each other are mutual. When you said you wanted to take me home with you, I could see the sincerity in the words that you spoke through your eyes. When we took that picture together, the way you were holding my hands, I got a feeling that you have wanted to hold me tight for some time now. I love standing behind you and wrapping my arms around your waist. I look at that picture 50 or more times a day and feel that very way. I ordered a 5×7 color version, and I'll send it when it's developed.

I don't know what it is about you in white, but it just drives me crazy. I've only seen you in white twice, and it does something to me. You said you were going to wear some pink shoes. No, no, the white ones were best. I wasn't even paying attention to your feet, but they are quite sexy without socks. So if you want to entice me, just wear white. I remember when we first met. You had on those white jeans with the stripes, and I wanted you for my own so bad. I didn't think you would give me the time of day. When I got your number, I thought, "Yeah!"

Well, I'll end this letter, so be sweet.

I love you,

Willie

P.S. You are something else

* * *

June 27, 1991

Dear Willie:

What's up, Babe? Of course it's you. Now I understand my take on why we didn't kiss much when we were an item. I always played the "I don't really want to kiss" game, knowing all the while I wanted every kiss you were willing to give. However, I didn't want you to be aware of that. I suppose my playacting was convincing, because I can't believe you actually thought I didn't like to kiss you. That was so stupid, wasn't it? The only sense I can make of it is that I used that strategy with every guy I met, and they played along by turning my head and taking the kiss regardless. So in actuality, I preferred the kiss to be taken as opposed to my giving it willingly. I felt that by pretending, men wouldn't detect my real feelings. I theorized that as long as they were unaware of my feelings, they would continue to strive at winning me over. You were the only one who didn't follow suit, and you believed I didn't want to kiss you.

Well, anyway, I really enjoyed your touches on my arms, legs, and my face when we kissed. I like the feel of your hands on me everywhere, because it allows me to tap into your passion. That reminds me of the time when I took off my clothes and lay in your bed only wearing my pantries and bra. I was lying sideways with my back toward you, and you were lying behind me facing my back. Both of our heads were propped up by our idle hands. I remember how you gently touched me from the top of my neck all the way down to my thighs. I placed my free hand upon yours and allowed it to glide along as you encircled my nipples and then my belly button. I remember you removing my bra and then proceeding to touch me softly up and down, driving me wild; so crazy that I had to surrender to you that night. I wanted to be close to you very badly that night. I bet you probably don't even remember, huh? I remember that night very clearly.

Baby, I really liked that prison. I felt uncomfortable at first because we were the only ones in the visiting room. The guard didn't have anyone else to watch except us. Once the room began to fill, I became more relaxed. It's nice that you can have contact visits. It's exceptionally nice to know that I can hug and kiss you at any given minute. If it wasn't for visiting hours being over, I would have never left your side.

It took exactly two hours, and I made it home at 10:00 PM straight up. I passed Diane's house and saw Debra's car. Since she was babysitting Li'l Henry, I turned around with the intentions of picking him up and going home. Everybody was over there drinking, partying, and playing cards. I didn't leave until midnight, so I didn't get a chance to begin a letter to you last night like I normally do. My feelings for you are at their strongest point right after visiting you.

The reason why I like to write a letter when I get home is because that's the best time to express them to you. It's as if you make me so weak when I visit, and when I write the letter I let down my guard. I don't care that I'm revealing everything to you. I don't care that you may perceive that I really do love you, and it's no joke by the words I write. It's not words that I'm saying just because you've said them to me. It's not expressions I'm releasing only to make you happy. And it's definitely not emotions I'm sharing because I just think it's the right thing to do. I want to be with you all the time. Since you asked me to come back Monday, I'm sitting here contemplating how to make it happen. And you know what, Babe? If it is a short day at work on Monday, I will definitely come, not only because you asked me, but because I want to see you, too. So, Babe, I must state that you've managed to get into my heart once again when I thought I was protecting it so well. I'm happy that we are connecting, because I've always cared about you.

I'm going to end on that good note.

Take care, Babe.

Love,

Gwen

* * *

June 30, 1991

Dear Willie:

Happy Birthday! Listen, I asked Vicky to mail your birthday card for me. She implied that I was cheap because I didn't want to send the card and the letter in separate envelopes. Would you call that being cheap, or simply wanting to save a stamp whenever there is an opportunity? I took some pictures of me to the store to get developed the other day. I thought about sending one picture at a time in future letters to you, starting with clothes on and ending with them off. I want to tease you, because I feel you're purposely making me wait for the color version that you have of us. However, I realize I shouldn't play tit-for-tat games, especially after I got the pictures back. I'm sorry to tell you that every last one of them did not turn out clear. I'll send them anyway so you can see I don't know a thing about taking pictures. I will try taking some more pictures soon.

I was reading a letter I wrote to you, and I inquired about a couple of issues that you didn't address. I asked if you would have tried to quit calling me "man" if I'd asked before when we were "an item." I also asked, "Are your feelings for me today the same as they were before?" It appears sort of odd that you neglected to answer both questions. You ignored me, Babe, and I want to know what's up with that?

I received the black-and-white version of us, and my head seems twice as big as my body, but you look good. You have the brightest smile and perfectly straight teeth. As I look at this picture, I can see how handsome you are with your smooth caramel-colored skin. Our heights are so in proportion; your 5'10" to my 5'4". I love your slim physique, and your body molds right into mine. You're behind me with your arms wrapped around my waist. Your head is cuddled on my right shoulder and mine is snuggled up against it. I'm holding on to your hands and I didn't want to let go. I enjoyed that closeness with you very much that day

Bye, Baby.

Gwen

P.S. I'll send the rest in intervals, because I don't want to overstuff the envelope. Not a single picture came out clear!

* * *

July 5, 1991

Dear Sweetheart:

I'm very sorry that I didn't answer your questions, Baby. As far as my feelings for you, I would say they are basically the same when comparing now to then. I can still remember when you and Vicky walked into my store that very first time. When I first saw you, I had to do a double-take, sort of like I did when you first walked into the jail to see me. I checked you out and said to myself, I'm not letting this girl step a foot out of this store before I get her telephone number. When I first saw you in the jail, I felt exactly the same way. You look the same with your light skinned, flawless complexion, shoulder length dark brown hair, and petite body. You are everything I like in a woman. I would say definitely, yes, my feelings are the same.

If you had asked me to stop calling you "man," I would have tried to do as you asked. I don't think I would have succeeded, because it is a habit that's hard for me to break. About mailing the card and letter in the same envelope, I don't feel you are cheap because that's something I would have done myself. So tell Vicky she better lay off my Baby.

Babe, why do you think I'm keeping the 5×7 colored version of the picture from you? Girl, I will never torment you in such a way. I know how bad you want to see it in color. As soon as I get it, you'll get it. I'm glad you sent the pictures—and you were right, they are messed up. At least your face is clear in every picture. That's the most important part and the most beautiful. I just want to be surrounded by you, and your pictures are the next best thing to you being here. Please hurry and send the rest, because I can't wait to see more of you.

What do you mean you were reading one of your letters to me? Try as I might I couldn't figure that one out. Please explain.

Love,

Willie

* * *

July 11, 1991

Dear Babe:

I remember when we first met very well. I walked into your convenience store with Vicky, and I remember you trying to talk to me. Believe it or not I, was attracted to you almost immediately, too, but I had to play a role because, again, I didn't believe you were a single man. You were so outspoken and didn't give a hoot about the impact of your words. You were nosy as hell, too. After that day, I would visit Vicky all the time because, since she lived next door to your store, I figured I would get a chance to see you. I tried to pretend that your actions didn't impress me. All that hugging and kissing on me and those nice words you always had to say to and about me really allured me in the worst kind of way. You were the first guy to take me to Red Lobster and introduce me to the lobster tail. We spent a lot of time together, and I can't believe I let you slip through my fingers.

Babe, I write a second copy of all the letters I send to you. I like to reminisce about the letters I write from time to time. Another reason is so I won't repeat what I've already said to you. It's just a woman thing, I suppose.

I love you,

Gwen

P.S. Looking forward to seeing you soon.

* * *

Chapter 3

July 19, 1991

Hello, Love:

I'm just lying in my bunk looking at the picture we took together when you came to visit. I agree, we look very good together. Next week is not advancing soon enough for me. I can't wait to hold you in my arms again. It's such a wonderful feeling that I want to refresh myself with.

I have fond memories of the first time we met, too. Normally I would have surrendered the pursuit of a woman who seemed to be uninterested, but there was something about you that made the chase worth the effort. I thought about you incessantly after you left the store that first time. I just had to have you in my life. All those first times for you were events that I didn't do to impress you (which was my usual motive). I arranged them because I really wanted to spend some quality time with you to get to know you better. I always wanted you to be by my side whenever I went places. I was grateful to Vicky for introducing us and speaking to you on my behalf; but, after we finally got together, she began bad-mouthing my loyalty. It was as if she wanted us to bond but also needed to regulate how close we became. I was so angry at her for telling you those lies about me being with other women. She really didn't know what the hell she was talking about. I felt you slipping away from me after that.

Remember when we would get mad at each other, and I wouldn't come around for days? Well, it took all I had to refrain from coming over there. Let me confess that you meant a great deal to me right from the start, and you still do.

I'll close on that note.

All my love,

Willie

* * *

July 24, 1991

Dear Willie:

How are you doing? I'm fine and in the best of health, heart, and spirit. I enjoyed our visit today. I always leave there feeling warm and tingly all over. All the way home, I reminisce with a smile on my face. After I arrive home, spend some time with my son, and put him to bed, I write a letter to you. Like I said before, I like to write when the memories of you are still fresh in my mind. Your cologne lingers on my shirt, and every now and then I raise my collar to my nose to inhale that Polo fragrance. The sweet, soft, sensual kisses that you branded me with are rewinding and playing in my head. My mind spins like a never-ending whirlpool. Remembrance of entwining our fingers, and the sensation of our sweaty palms, inspires an irregular beat within my heart. The embrace of your entire body close to mine just generates chills up and down my spine. I'm visualizing those baby cheeks of yours, and its increasing my desire to cover this envelope with soft yet wet kisses. The feel of your lips ignites sparks that give my body an electrifying sensation. What a man! I am definitely in love, and it feels so good.

Babe, guess what happened when I arrived home tonight? I hit the lottery for $360! My three-digit number came out straight in the Michigan Lottery. When I walked through the door, Mama asked did I play my numbers today. I routinely play the same numbers every day, and she knew what they were. I began jumping up and down, screaming, and asking, "Did I hit the lottery?" Someone would have thought I won a million dollars by the way I was behaving. I didn't care; I was happy with whatever God decided to bless me with. I'm going to send a $40 money order in this letter to put on your books.

I've registered for school and everything's all set to go. I'll start next week, and I'm so excited. Of course you know I may not be able to write as much, because I need to study. Actually, the only difficult class I'm taking is accounting. Hopefully, it won't be as difficult as I anticipate.

I'll talk to you soon.

Love,

Gwen

* * *

July 29, 1991

Dear Sweetheart:

Gee, that was the most inspiring, uplifting, motivating, and exciting letter I have received from you yet! Damn Baby, where did you learn to talk like that? I suppose there's more to you than meets the eye. You have been holding back on me. I think you have come a long way since those bashful days, and believe me, it's a good thing. If you can compose a letter like that, there shouldn't be one course in college that you can't master. I will always understand about study time, homework, and all that knowledge-seeking stuff, and writing me should come second. Allow me to reiterate that: *second*, next to your son, of course (ha, ha!). I love you, Girl, and you just make my day every time I hear from you.

I finally got the 5×7 picture and, as promised, I'm immediately sending your copy. I think it is a great picture of us together. I also wanted to thank you for putting that money in my account. That was very nice of you. Sometimes I need a little help, because we have to buy our own personal hygiene supplies. My mom and sister usually take turns sending a little something every week. I wouldn't dare ask you to, and it was very considerate of you to take the initiative. They have jobs in here that pay 50 cents an hour, but I haven't been able to obtain one as of yet. I'm working on it, and I'm pretty sure it will come soon. I've got this gig (arrangement) selling snacks to the inmates. I worked out an under-the-table deal with the man who replenishes the snack machines. I always find a way to make a little extra money.

So Babe, why don't you share some more of that diary with me? I was shocked when you read it to me over the phone. It's nice to hear how you thought about me then. It's funny how you candidly let me know now what I needed a top-secret clearance to hear then.

I love you, Babe,

Willie

* * *

August 4, 1991

Dear Willie:

I suppose I look somewhat improved in color as opposed to that black-and-white version you sent before. Thank you for sending it to me in a timely manner. I'm glad I didn't hold my breath while I waited (ha, ha!).

This is dated March 5, 1984 in my diary, and it appears we hadn't known each other very long.

> Dear Diary: When I got home from work, I drove my cousin to the store. When I returned, Willie was here. He took me over to his house, and we stayed until 2:30 AM. We just watched television and kissed while lying on his water bed. He really excited me tonight and I wanted to go further, but I don't think I would have if I wasn't on my monthly. He's nice when he wants to be, and I really think he likes me a lot, but he's not my type. I like aggressive, but he's a bit much. Still, I do like him.

Next day:

> Dear Diary: Willie didn't come over today. Maybe because I told him that I was on my period and he has no use for me. If he doesn't come over tomorrow, I'll know what he wants, and he doesn't ever have to come over again.

The next day I didn't even mention your name, so I assume you didn't come over and my presumption was correct. The following day you came, so I imagine I just forgot all about my intent to dump you.

On March 9, 1984, I wrote:

> Dear Diary: Willie and I went riding to Midland, Bay City, and Flint, and we talked about a lot of things. He said he wanted to get to know me better. I don't know, it seems like I'm unable to speak on important issues concerning "us" in his presence, because he's so intelligent and talks over my head. Whenever I open my mouth, I stutter on my words, which is very unlike me. I suppose he makes me feel dense.

Come to think of it, I always felt at a loss for words when you were around. You had a far broader vocabulary than I did, and I was very much aware of that. You also made me nervous because I felt I was inexperienced.

Well, Babe, I'll continue to share the diary with you from time to time.

I love you, too.

Gwen

* * *

August 10, 1991

Dear Willie:

I enjoyed our telephone conversation the other day, but I think we've been spending entirely too much time on the phone lately. Although I enjoy it, I don't want to dig too deep into your pockets. I'm sure there are other important things that you could do with your hard-earned money. Hopefully, your friend is being lenient with charging for the use of his telephone card since I've introduced him to my cousin. Speaking of the phone, I felt bad when you commented on the other line ringing. I felt maybe you thought the other line was for me. I want to state for the record, when I placed you on hold, the other line was never for me. I don't know why I feel the need to explain this, but I suppose old habits are hard to break when it involves defending myself.

Henry always placed me in a predicament where I felt I was guilty but knew I wasn't. Even though I know you are more understanding and mature than he ever was, it's hard to change. You are so much more than I ever thought you could be. After getting to know you better and developing closeness to you, I catch myself comparing you to Henry all the time. I have no idea why I chose him, because you should have been my choice all along. I feel so stupid now.

I'm planning to come to visit next week, and I've already asked for the weekend off from work. I've also been thinking about driving there on my days off regularly. I really do enjoy my visits with you. Before I close this letter, I will share a word from my diary.

On March 11, 1984, I wrote:

> Dear Diary: Willie came over while my sisters and I were playing Monopoly. Boy, I really like him. I went over to his house and stayed until almost 5:00 AM. I helped him count

the money in his store. He only allowed me to count the food stamps. Maybe he doesn't trust me with the money. Afterward, we drove to Chuckey's Take-Out, where he owns half the business. He prepared food for us in the diner while I watched, and it was so romantic. We ate and went back to his house and just held each other tight. It was very arousing, but, yet again, I didn't do anything. I could tell he wanted me bad, but I still didn't do anything.

Next day:

Dear Diary: I know I still love Henry, but I can't stop thinking about the closeness that Willie and I are now sharing. I finally had sex with him. I wanted him more than ever, and I kept hearing in my mind, "Henry had sex with Annett," and that was enough to alleviate my guilt and release Henry's hold on me. Willie was much gentler than Henry, and he takes his time with me. I'm beginning to really care for Willie and question my love for Henry.

I didn't get a chance to answer your question when we were on the phone. I haven't been with anyone sexually since I've been here. I don't just have sex for the fun of it; I have to care about someone first. Don't you remember how long you waited? (smile)

Going to end now.

Love,

Gwen

* * *

Chapter 4

August 13, 1991

Hi, Babe:

I would like to begin by saying I like your morals. It's nice to hear you won't allow anybody to make you compromise on your sex ethics. Now I know why we didn't have sex when we were at Mackinaw Island. I think that anybody who has sex just to have fun might as well get a gun and play Russian roulette with life.

Hey, Babe, I'm sorry for making you feel guilty about the phone situation, but I don't understand how I could have done that. I was just joking around about the other line ringing so much. Darn, you can't see the punch line of a joke? In all actuality, I never thought the other line was for you.

I think your feelings for me are very special, considering I'm constantly put in a class with Henry, the one love of your life except me. (smile) That class is exclusive. I plan to keep it that way if I have anything to do with it, because, Babe, I want you as much as the earth needs the sun. With you, I can blossom to any height.

I like the thought of you coming down here to see me more often on your days off. I think you're beginning to unveil your heart by the thoughts you're expressing to me, and I love that. Without a heart, everything dies; and Babe, you just keep my blood at a boil. I hope you can keep this raging fire inside of me forever.

I was telling my sister about you one night on the phone. She was surprised to hear I was talking to someone who I really care about. She and my mother wanted to know more about you after I told them about the pictures we took. They wanted to know who was seeing their baby. I told them a little about you but just enough to tame their eagerness to know more. You are a mystery woman to them. I think my sister might remember you from back in the day, or, as you call them, "growing-up times."

I was also thinking about limiting my calling you so much. Hey, have you noticed that we think alike most times? Gwen, my phone bill isn't as high as it used to be, so please don't feel bad. My friend Tony and I are pretty cool, since he's talking to your cousin Stacy. He's not charging as much as he normally would. The last call didn't cost anything at all. Some days I just want to talk to you so bad, but I will try to control myself. I don't want to risk getting upset with each other by talking on the phone too much. There's a guy in here who said he and his girl ran out of topics to discuss and just began to argue about trivial things. I don't want that to ever happen to us.

Speaking of the phone, I almost got into a fight the night I talked to you while you were on hold. I hope you didn't hear the nonsense that took place before I returned to the phone. This man tried to disrespect me by grabbing the phone I was talking on, and for a quick second I contemplated knocking him out right in front of the guards. I thought it over and changed my mind. I hoped he would swing first, but he didn't. I'm trying to get home to you, and that's the only reason I didn't throw the first punch. The person who swings first will receive the greater punishment.

Gwen, if I had hit him there would have been a riot in here. I'm talking about blacks against whites, and I would have gotten the blame for the whole thing. These brothers wanted to go at it, too. They said, "Man, you are a better person than me. I would have blasted him." I know I did the right thing, though. The next day this white guy who I'm pretty cool with said, "Man, you did the right thing. It wasn't worth it over a telephone. It would have added more time onto your sentence."

I'm going to end this letter now because it's 1:00 AM and I have to get up at 4:15. I'll write again this weekend, because I have much more to say.

Love,

Willie

P.S. I go to bed thinking about you every night.

P.P.S. Give your son a kiss.

* * *

August 21, 1991

Dear Willie:

I'm sorry it took so long for me to write again. I'm also sorry that I have to convey some bad news. I can't come to visit the weekend I promised. My boss forgot and scheduled me to work on that Saturday. She said she couldn't change the schedule, because they didn't have anyone else to do laundry. Being the nice person I am, I agreed to work. The understanding was I would be off the weekend following Labor Day. However, that weekend won't work for me either, because it doesn't fall on a payday. We'll have to wait to see what the next schedule looks like and decide then.

So Willie, I was reminiscing about us and wondering what really happened between us. Why didn't we continue seeing each other? I turned to my diary for answers, and now I think I understand. When I got back home from basic training, things had changed between us drastically. I heard you were dating someone in college who was also staying with you at your house for the summer. I remember being crazy about you before I left for the Army, and I still had feelings for you when I returned. Listen to this:

On July 25, 1984, I wrote:

> Dear Diary: Willie came to visit today, and he looks sexy with that Jheri curl in his hair. He has someone else, and she's living with him, too. I wanted to kiss him so bad...

And August 10, 1984:

> Dear Diary: Willie has only come to visit twice since I've been back home from basic training. I suppose he really likes this girl that I'm hearing about, but I can't help it—I still care. I still think about him all the time. He complimented me on how my body has changed and how good it looks. He said I filled out in all the right places. I blushed but felt he was saying it only to spark up a conversation between us since the tension was so high. If I looked as good as he claimed, he would put forth a stronger effort to spend more time with me. He's full of it, and who does he thinks he is, anyway—he's staying with a girl and visiting me! Boy, I still adore him anyway, stupid me. If only I could gain his attention as I had before I left and get him away from her. That's a chance in a million, I think.

That's two days of writings from my diary after I returned from basic training. Can you now understand how I felt? I cared about you, but I kept it to myself because I didn't want you to hurt me. It's funny that you spoke about Mackinaw Island. I still don't fully understand what went wrong between us when we were there. I remember getting the job in Michigan, at the Grand Hotel on Mackinaw Island, after I returned home from basic training. I also remember you drove three-and-a-half hours there to see me. Come to think of it, you also drove to Lansing several times to visit when I relocated there. Looking back, I can now see that you must have cared a lot for me to travel so far to see me so many times.

I also don't understand why I would have sex with you before leaving for the Army but wouldn't after I came back, especially after you drove to Mackinaw Island just to see me. I remember we stayed in a hotel in the city, because the ones on the island were so expensive, but I can't recall much about that time. Do you remember anything else? After we drove back from Mackinaw Island, I didn't write in my diary anymore. I remember you being very angry with me, but I don't recall why.

Willie, I'm going to end now. I'm sorry for the bad news, but you know the longer we are apart, the more we'll want to see each other. The more we want to see each other, the better our visits together will be.

Take care, Babe.

Gwen

P.S. I can't wait until I see you again!

* * *

August 25, 1991

Dear Gwen:

Hey, Baby, I'm sorry to hear that you won't be able to visit the Saturday we planned, but I do understand how mix-ups can happen. However, they had better not let it happen again or I'm going to break out and give someone a piece of my mind! Just kidding. I'll just have to wait out this undying desire to hold you in my arms that I thought I was getting close to fulfilling. I try to be a patient and understanding man, but sometimes it's very difficult.

So, you've become curious about Mackinaw Island? I remember making that drive and being excited about spending some time with you and also visiting the island. As I remember, it seems like a dream getting on that ferryboat to ride across to the island. It was only a 30-minute ride, and I remember it being so peaceful and calm. When I arrived at the island, I remember the first thing I saw was that Grand Hotel. It was the biggest building on the island, and it looked like a castle situated at the center. I wish I'd taken the time to see the inside. As I walked to the hotel that you worked at, I felt as though I was in a movie. Do you remember the scenery on *Little House on the Prairie* when they went to the big town that had those pubs and hotel rooms? That is exactly how Mackinaw Island looked to me. They had all the fudge shops and B&B's on both sides of a dirt road in those old-fashioned buildings. There was also a big bicycle rental place that was a main attraction, because, remember, there were no cars there, only horses and bikes. I waited until you finished work, and we rode the ferry to the hotel. We slept together but we did not make love.

If you can remember the day we were to leave, I got sick. I'd asked you to drive and you said no. I had to drive three-and-a-half hours back to Saginaw, sick as hell, and I was highly pissed off because you acted like you could care less. We didn't utter a single word to each other the entire way home. I dropped you off and left without seeing you to your door. I can't remember when or if I ever came back over there after that. I really felt that you didn't give a damn about me.

That girl who you spoke of in your diary is who I married. She was only visiting me from college for the summer. If you paid close attention to your diary, you would realize the reason we didn't make love while we were at Mackinaw Island was because you thought I had a girlfriend at the time. Believe me when I say there would have never been an opportunity for her had I known your true feelings. I dated her, and we broke up before I met you. Sometime after you left for basic training, we got together again. I knew it was not right to continue to visit you after you returned home, but I knew that I still cared about you, and I wanted to see if we still had something together. What I discovered was you were still hung up on Henry, or that's how it appeared to me.

What can I say? We should have been more open with one another.

I'm glad that we're getting this out in the open now, so there won't be any misunderstandings about our past. We can learn from it and move forward. I see you in my future as clear as I'm writing this letter to you today. Remember that I love you always.

Willie

* * *

August 30, 1991

Dear Willie:

How are you doing since I last wrote? I suppose you know I have you on my brain every minute of the day. Whatever you're doing to me needs to cease, because I have to get back into my schoolwork. I slacked off a bit, but I have regrouped and hopefully I've gotten priorities back in line. My next task is to get out of Mama's house. Getting a second job is the only way I'll be able to save the money I need to move out. I checked out this apartment that's owned by Rodarte Realty, and they completed a financial worksheet on me. They didn't think I earned enough money to handle a $290 a month rent. Most times at my job I'll be lucky to get 30 hours a week. Maybe they're right, because I don't want to get in over my head.

Speaking of work, I got into an argument today with Annie, the assistant supervisor. A couple of Sundays ago, she took it upon herself to punch out our time cards while we were still working. She came into the room and informed me afterward. I finished cleaning my room and didn't say anything when she explained it was because we were going over the time allotted. I don't know everyone else's excuse, but the reason why I fell behind was, number one, I originally had the day off. I was called in to wash, dry, and fold because they thought Maria, the laundry person, wasn't going to show up. I walked in at 8:00 AM in an anticipation of working in the laundry but saw Maria standing there. When she saw the confused look on my face, Annie laughed and said she tried to catch me before I'd left home. So, the reality was they didn't actually know who really had called off work.

I didn't develop an attitude until she wouldn't allow me to punch in. The room attendants were scheduled for 10:00 AM on Sundays, and she wanted me to wait around, off the clock, until she figured out who wasn't coming in. I waited and finally she allowed me to punch in to work four hours in the laundry room, since her many calls to ascertain who wasn't coming in remained unresolved. I supposed she perceived I was growing very impatient.

I punched in at 8:30 AM and around 10:15 one person still hadn't shown up. Annie instructed me to stock the cart so I could begin cleaning the extra rooms. There wasn't any laundry available on the shelf. I had to start 30 minutes late with only six big towels and ten double sheets. I didn't even have any king sheets, wash or hand towels, bathmats, or pillowcases. Because of my limited supply, my routine became to complete whatever I could in a room and continue to the next. Annie became infuriated because all of my rooms weren't finished. She would stop me in the middle of what I was doing to send me down to the laundry for towels, only to acquire a mere handful. There weren't enough towels on the shelves to even make the trip worth the while. There were no pillowcases at all, so I still couldn't fully complete the rooms. I was beginning to get upset because I felt she was wasting my time.

To sum it all up, I started 30 minutes late, there wasn't enough linen on the shelves whenever I came to replenish my stock, plus she called me in on my day off. So, you know I wasn't trying to bust my butt to get done; I was taking my sweet time.

Initially, I wasn't going to say anything about her punching us out early, because I know how Annie is. She would get upset with me, and I didn't want to cause any conflict in the workplace. As time progressed, I could not refrain from thinking how unfair it really was. I began to feel like she'd gotten over on us big time, and nobody was going to say anything about it.

After sneaking a look at her time card and discovering she hadn't punched her own self out, I decided to report it. I had to tell because even though I tried, I couldn't think of anything else. The attitude that was forming within me was about to explode. I told Linda, Annie's supervisor, and as I suspected she had no idea. She reinstated our stolen time and apologized for the misunderstanding. Annie was recently promoted to assistant supervisor, so she had the audacity to use the notion that she's still learning as an excuse.

Babe, I held my tongue two days before I decided to report it to Linda, during which time Annie and I conversed like we were best friends. I think she talked to me more than she ever had, because perhaps she figured if anyone would tell, it would definitely be me. I'm well known for disputing my hours, and I know she only befriended me to pacify my urge to spill the beans. After speaking with her supervisor, she didn't mumble another word to me for the remainder of the day. I assumed she was aware that I was the informant, so I didn't say anything else to her, either.

About a week later, we had a monthly meeting with the big boss to review the rule book. I thought it was a good opportunity to clarify some issues that I personally had problems with. So I asked about being forced to come in 20 minutes earlier to stock carts prior to punching in. The big boss totally agreed it was against policy and promised to talk to our supervisor about it. Now Annie is steaming hot with me. I really wasn't trying to piss her off, but she and I had words when she initially instructed us to do this. I retaliated by stating it was unfair for me to pay a babysitter for an extra 20 minutes that I wasn't getting paid for. I basically wanted to get this rule straight once and for all. Following that, Annie just balled up with anger, only talking to me when she had to. I got a kick out of the whole ordeal, because although I wouldn't say anything to her unless she spoke first, I greeted her when I came in the morning and said good-bye when I left. She would never reciprocate, but I continued to speak—I guess out of respect.

I worked in the laundry yesterday and sat down to take my second 15-minute break. Although Annie didn't tell me how long I would be working, I assumed it would be eight hours. As fast as I loaded the shelves with laundry, the girls came and swiped it off. So that made me feel they needed me for the full eight hours. When Annie saw that I was sitting down, she asked me to get the remainder of the wet towels dried before I went home. I wasn't finished with my break, but I went ahead and complied. I worked eight hours that day just as I had anticipated.

Today she was nice enough to inform me I would only be working four-and-a-half hours. I worked from 8:00 AM to 12:00 noon and then sat down to take my 15-minute break. I didn't have a chance to take it sooner, because I was barely keeping enough laundry on the shelves. Do you know what she had the audacity to tell me? She said I didn't get a break today, and to make up the time I just took I could work until 12:45, but I had to punch out at 12:30 PM. Who the hell did she think she was? You know I wasn't having that, and I don't know how many times and ways I could communicate to her that I didn't work for free. Needless to say, our discussion led into an argument, because I was sick of her. I tried to be mindful of the fact that she was much older than me, so I did not utter one curse word. In an attempt to end the disagreement, I simply said, "I disagree with you because by law I am entitled to one 15-minute break for every four hours that I work." Once again, I said I was going to speak to Linda tomorrow, because she wasn't taking a single minute away from my time. "If I work until 12:45, I want to get paid until 12:45," I demanded.

"You ain't nothing but a backstabber, and whatever you have to say about me, say it to my face," she spat out. I didn't know where the hell that statement came from, but I stood up and stated that I had something to say. She turned to walk out of the break room, so I asked, "Why are you leaving? I said I have something to say." She nonchalantly turned around to listen. I told her I never talked about her behind her back. "I don't work for free, and I'm getting sick and tired of your trying to accumulate brownie points at my expense. By the way that you are behaving right now, it was best that I addressed it with your supervisor because you and I would never resolve anything. You think you're right, I know I'm right, so there. I heard rumors that you were calling me a tattletale. Is that true?"

And Babe, we went back and forth about he say/she say until finally I said again, "I will talk to Linda tomorrow to get this straight." I told her that I wasn't going to argue with her about it anymore, and besides, she was screaming at the top of her lungs. Everyone in the break room was listening to us and getting a big kick out of the whole ordeal. Afterward, I know she felt pleasure in being able to release all of that hostility she had bottled up inside. I'm going to feel pleasure in knowing I proved her wrong yet again.

I think they are going to fire me, because I could tell the big boss wasn't eager to comply with my request about punching in early, but she had no other choice. I'm planning to take a one-week vacation next month to look for another job. If I'm unable to find one, of course; I'm not going to just quit. I'm at that job every scheduled day on time, and I clean my rooms spotless just so Annie won't have any reason to send me back. They can't fire me, so I'm not worried about that.

I know you're probably tripping out over this letter, and that's why I shared it with you. I wanted to give you a good laugh.

Love,

Gwen

* * *

Chapter 5

September 3, 1991

Dear Gwen:

It's such a nice feeling to know I am constantly on your mind. I definitely don't want to be the reason for your failing in school, so I'm pleased to know you've gotten your priorities in line. For me, I don't have anything better to do than think of you all day and dream about you all night.

Babe, moving out on your own just takes time. I understand that you want your own space, but you must be prepared financially before you make that move. It may be beneficial for you to deal with living with your mother as opposed to moving out without being ready. Think about it before you make a decision is all I ask.

I think you made the right decision on that job situation. By keeping your mouth closed in accordance with everyone else would have condoned that sort of treatment forever, believe me. She would feel she had the authority to do anything to you whether she was right or wrong. That's how people develop their level of preeminence. They determine how much you'll take and then dish that quantity of bulls--t every time. You did good, Babe, and I am very proud of you. I'm sure everyone else thinks so, too, because you said what they wanted to but were too afraid to say. Let her know you're not taking any mess. Let me know what happens after you speak to Linda about Annie.

I would like to do something nice for you, but I want to surprise you. The plans are already in the making, but I need one small favor from you to complete the task. Do you think that you could be home next Thursday between 12:00 noon and 3:00 PM? I'm hoping it's a day off or maybe there's enough time to request it. If you can, I would appreciate it very much. Let me know what to expect in your next letter.

I love you,

Willie

* * *

September 7, 1991

Dear Sweetheart:

I cannot believe you accomplished that. That was very sweet of you. I was leaving to go over to Diane's house when the man pulled up with a rose. How did you manage to arrange something so special like that? I suppose you're an all-around Romeo. What makes it even more special is the fact that it's not a holiday or my birthday. As always, you put a smile on my face today, Babe. I love you.

When I come to visit this weekend, I'm bringing my son along. Since you've asked several times to meet him, I figured it's about time to introduce you two. When was the last time you've seen your kids? You never talk about them coming to visit, and I was just wondering had they ever been there? There is something else I've wanted to ask you but felt the time was never quite right.

I've heard so many stories about what took place from so many people, and I really would like to hear your interpretation of what happened. I heard you were set up by your wife and you and this guy fought right before it happened. I never questioned you before, because I felt it might have been a touchy issue since you never volunteered to talk about it. Now, I feel the closeness that we share has developed strong enough where I can ask of you anything that I maybe curious about. Babe, please don't blow this off, because I really would like to finally know your story.

Thanks again for sending the rose. I guess you do love me, and I love you back.

Gwen

P.S. I decided not to say anything to Linda after all, because Annie never deducted the 15 minutes from my time.

* * *

September 10, 1991

Dear Babe:

How are you? Well, me, I'm still floating on cloud nine from our last visit. I enjoyed myself as always. I love you so much. I'm glad I got an opportunity to meet Li'l Henry. He should have been my son. Well, I'll tell you what, as far as I'm concerned he is my son; the son I never had.

Now let's address the question at hand. So you're curious about what really happened? Well, as I told you before, my wife and I were not together at the time. She was living with her mother. One day I went over there and she was in the company of a guy whom I was very familiar with. Before we split up, they were talking and laughing together at a store that I happened to walk into, and she said they were only friends. I was pretty pissed off to discover she had lied, and I'm sure they saw it on my face. Her boyfriend tried to check me for coming over there without calling, and we began to argue, which turned into a fight. I kicked his ass pretty good.

About a week later, I had my youngest daughter, Cynthia. She was over at my mom's house, which is where I lived at the time. She wanted to spend the night with me but didn't have a change of clothes. I called my wife to inform her that Cynthia was spending the night, and she volunteered to bring a change of clothes. Well, needless to say, she never brought the clothes. The following day, I telephoned my mom from work, only to discover that my wife still hadn't brought over the clothes. I told my mom to ask her to send the clothes in a taxi, and we would pay the driver upon arrival. They were never sent.

After I got off work, I called her and she claimed she didn't have transportation at that time. "Why the hell didn't you put them in the cab like my mom asked you to?" I screamed in her ear. She didn't say anything. I finally said I would come to get the clothes myself, and you know I was mad.

I stored my gun underneath the seat in my car following the fight with my wife's boyfriend, just in case. When I arrived there, I saw about three cars parked in the driveway. I vigilantly walked to the door, knocked, and heard my wife's brother yell he'd be right out. I waited and waited. About three minutes elapsed and I started to get cold, so I got back in the car to warm up. I sat there for what seemed like another three minutes, and finally the front door opened. I saw her brother step onto the porch with the clothes in his hand, but he froze in his tracks as if anticipating something. I saw another guy come out, walk to the driver's side of my car, and stand there. Last, out the door came my wife's boyfriend, who positioned himself in front of my car. "Get your ass out of the car," the boy who stood next to my car demanded. "I have something to talk to you about."

"Man you don't know me, so you and I have nothing to talk about," I replied.

I reexamined her boyfriend's position through my peripheral vision. He held a drink in one hand while his other was stuffed inside of his jacket pocket. After being asked a third time to get out of my car, I disgustedly got out with my gun in my hand. This guy punched me in my face and I shot the gun but missed. After tussling for about 10 seconds, I shot the gun again. It hit him, and he finally fell after a short delay with a surprised look on his face. I immediately turned to her boyfriend, who had stayed put during the brawl. He hurled his drink and it hit me upside my head. He then began walking toward me while continuing to hold his other hand in his pocket. He was well aware that I had a gun but proceeded nevertheless. I shot him right in the chest, because at that particular moment I really felt I had no other choice. My brother-in-law never stepped off of the porch, and my wife never came out of the house. I felt like I was set up, and if my wife had stepped one foot out of that house that day, I truly believe I would have shot her dead and I would be serving a life term right now.

I drove over to a friend's house and explained to him what had just happened. He called his police friend who explained some technicalities to me. I got something to eat and then I turned myself in.

I later learned that the first guy who I shot was my wife's boyfriend's uncle, and he didn't die. I truly believe God blinked an eye that day, because I asked around about her boyfriend and learned he wasn't a bad person at all. It just happened so fast. He didn't have a gun and still to this day I don't understand why he kept coming at me knowing that I did have one. I have to live with the fact that I killed a person for the rest of my life, and it is hard sometimes.

I wanted to discuss this over the telephone, but it doesn't seem like I'll be able to call you tonight. Everybody's holding on to the phones like their lives are depending on it.

I love you,

Willie

P.S. I've only seen my kids once since I've been here. My sister brought them to visit.

* * *

September 13, 1991

Dear Babe:

I thought you would have called by now. I suppose you took my advice to refrain from calling so much, but this was definitely not the time to begin. After leaving from visiting you last week, I got into a car accident. I was driving about 60 mph when this person ran the stop sign. He pulled right out in front of me and I swerved to avoid him. I went into a ditch, came back up, and collided into a telephone pole. Li'l Henry was thrown to the floor of the passenger's side. The other car drove away without stopping. Luckily there was someone at the opposite stop sign who saw the entire incident. He ran over to the car and asked if I was okay as I lifted myself out. I didn't feel anything out of the ordinary, so I told him I was alright. Other than a nosebleed, Li'l Henry was okay, too. The man instructed me to write down the license tag number because he had memorized it.

Instantly, a group of people surrounded us. There was an old lady among them who offered the use of her phone to call the police and my mother. She offered Li'l Henry some cookies and was just as nice as pie to us as we waited for the police. She volunteered to drive us half the distance to meet my mother in order to save her from driving so far. I tried to offer her some money for gas, but she refused to accept it. She drove approximately 45 minutes to meet Mama. Now, you know Mama talked junk all the way home about me coming to see you. My neck was sore the next day but it wasn't too bad. I lost my glasses, too. Now I'm waiting to hear whether the car can be fixed. I hope it's not totaled.

Well, Babe, I love you. I just wanted to inform you of what happened.

Love,

Gwen

* * *

September 18, 1991

Dear Babe:

I'm so sorry about what happened. I called and Diane informed me on the phone before I received your letter. How's Li'l Henry doing? I'm so pleased that you both are all right. I feel so bad about this. I thought about your decision to leave earlier that day and how I insisted that you stay a little while longer. Something just went through me when Diane told me. I felt as though I was solely responsible for this tragedy, and I feel the need to make it up to you somehow. I hope the car isn't totaled, but the details make me think otherwise. I hope my thoughts are wrong, because

I know you need your transportation. I tried to call before now, but I could never get a phone. When I finally got one, you weren't home. I'll try to call tonight if at all possible.

I love you, Babe. I just felt the urge to say that. I really do appreciate your taking the time to drive up here to visit me. I also appreciate your writing and making me feel like I am special someone in your life. You are someone very special and dear to me, too. One day we will be together forever, and no one will ever be able to take you away. I'm going to commit my life to making you the happiest woman in the world, because that's what you deserve.

Love,

Willie

* * *

September 21, 1991

Dear Willie:

It's not your fault, Baby! That accident was going to happen whether I visited for one hour or ten. The car was totaled, and the insurance didn't pay off the entire balance. They paid the blue book value and left a $1,700 balance. I refuse to pay a car note for a vehicle I don't have. Since I'm not going to get a new car out of the deal, I imagine visiting you won't be happening anytime soon. Mama drives me to work, but I catch the bus home. Things are pretty much working out. I really don't enjoy being without a car, but I suppose my only choice is to deal with this for now.

Babe, I talked to Henry, and he'll be here next week. He picked the perfect time to come home, considering I'm down on my luck. He'll certainly think I need him, since I don't have a car. I told him about the car accident but excluded the part about visiting you. I fabricated a story about trailing Vicky to return her boyfriend's car. I don't know why I lied; I just did without realizing it. Even though this doesn't change anything, I thought I should at least let you know, because I don't want to keep secrets from you. I want us to have an open and honest relationship forever.

So, that's what happened, huh? I'm happy that you solved the mystery in my mind. I was curious about it for such a long time.

Thank you for sharing your story with me. Now, a word from my diary:

On March 13, 1984, I wrote:

> Dear Diary: I had sex with Willie again. I'm petrified now because he assured me he wore protection, but I don't think he did. There was a lot of white stuff in my panties, and I don't think it came from me. Man, I hope I'm not pregnant! Afterward, I became rather quiet just thinking about the consequences, and he asked was I all right. He wanted to know had he done anything wrong. He made me feel very much cared about tonight and really displayed true concern for my feelings. Small expressions like that will make me always remember him. I stayed over there until 6:30 AM. I was afraid to come home, because Mama would surely be mad. She didn't hear me come in, thank God.

And on March 19, 1984:

> Dear Diary: Today I got up and finished packing. I went over to Vicky's house and treated her to a banana split at Toney's. Afterward, I went to visit Willie, but he wasn't in the store and I didn't want to go over to his house. When I got home I called, and he told me he'd be right over after I informed him I would be leaving in 45 minutes. Willie knocked at my door 10 minutes later. We kissed and said our good-byes.

Then March 20, 1984:

> Dear Diary: Today is the big day for me. I am presently in Detroit, Michigan. I woke up at 4:00 AM and ate breakfast at 4:30. We went to the Military Enlistment Processing Station at 5:00. I was all prepared to leave when the nurse pulled me from the line and informed me that my pregnancy test was positive after being checked twice. I was spooked in my mind, which felt like déjà vu. I knew Willie didn't wear protection that night we had sex, I thought. She asked did I want to go to the Medical Center to get a third opinion? Of course, I said yes.

I arrived at the hospital at 8:30 AM but didn't get the results until

1:30 PM. I was so nervous that my arm was trembling when they drew the blood. All types of thoughts were progressing through my mind as I waited for the results. I called Willie all kinds of bad names. I then decided that if I was pregnant, Willie would never know. I would get an abortion without telling a soul. Nothing or nobody was going to interfere in my plans to enlist in the Army Reserves.

The people from the MEPS called the hospital several times asking for the results, because it was only supposed to take two hours. Finally, the results came in and they were negative. I was so happy that I couldn't refrain from smiling from ear to ear.

It was too late to submit my paperwork in order to leave today, so I have to wait until next week. I rode that bus back home when I should have been on that plane to South Carolina.

Take care, Babe,

Gwen

* * *

Chapter 6

September 27, 1991

Dear Willie:

What's troubling you? Why haven't you called or written a letter to me? I think I have an idea of why. You think Henry is here, don't you? Well, you're right, but is that a reason to cease communication?

Willie, I wish I could reassure you regarding Henry, but I can't. I realize that I still care about him, and he wants to reconcile. As I said when we talked on the phone, I have considered it this time because it's the best solution to my problem right now. I would get away from Mama's house, which is what I unsuccessfully tried to do. I wouldn't have to worry myself with paying bills, because Henry would pay them and I wouldn't have to struggle, attempting to make it on my own. I have my doubts about Henry, because after talking to him, I can sense his childishness; but I also sense a need for his family. Maybe that necessity will overshadow his immaturity.

I love my freedom, not having to care about another person's feelings when I want to do something, but I feel that's a small sacrifice. I enjoy my life now. I like being apart of your life and that's why, when comparing, I try to avoid focusing on the feelings I have for you. I do this so I can concentrate on what's best for my son and me. If you were here with me and your feelings were legitimate, then my choice would be made. There wouldn't be any reluctance on my part, because I know together we can make a decent life for us and our children. We are both strong willed and independent, and I like the way you think. I know you're a "make it happen" type of guy. However, that's not the situation here, and hard as I try to scramble through this maze, I find myself always sitting and thinking, standing and thinking, working and thinking, and going to bed and thinking about what to do.

Then employment possibilities materialize like that GM job offer, and I think maybe someone wants me to stay and try to make it on my own. Just yesterday, St. Mary's Hospital called about an interview for a temporary full-time housekeeping position. I think maybe God is placing these opportunities in my way so I won't go back to a failed marriage. Who's to say that if I get the position at the hospital, and after the temporary period has elapsed, they won't hire me on full-time?

Yet, I get into a car accident on the way home from seeing you, and I think maybe God is trying to tell me something with that, also. After all, I am a married woman and I shouldn't be coming up there to see you as more than friends. Friends don't kiss and touch one another like we do. It's against God's laws of matrimony.

Maybe God thinks I belong with my husband, because, when thinking back to the accident, I recall Li'l Henry getting sleepy and I took his seatbelt off. He laid down in the front seat no more than three minutes before it happened. I know upon impact he would have flown out of the window, but he was spared. So, I feel that was a blessing of some sort, and in return I need to do the moral thing. Then I think about the fact that I'm getting too involved with you, that I'm neglecting other things that are important as well. Just like I called in sick that day so I could come to see you, and they wrote me up.

Then there are other issues you're unaware of, such as the time I put money in your account while knowing my baby needed tennis shoes. I held off on getting his shoes until my next paycheck. I'm not saying that it's your fault, because it's not. I want to be there for you. I want to come see you and talk to you on the phone and do little things for you, but I have to regroup and get my priorities straight. Li'l Henry is the number one priority in my life, and that will never change. Babe, I sit down and I compare these positive and negative feelings toward this situation, and I can't figure out a perfect solution.

As you can see, I have a lot on my mind. I don't have a car to come visit you today, which is Saturday, and I'm disgusted because I can't see you. On the other hand, I'm sort of scared that something might happen if I try. Just give me a little time so I can get myself together, okay, Babe? I haven't made a decision and the interview isn't until Monday. Please write back, call, or do something.

All my love,

Gwen

P.S. I suppose you're saying, "Two letters in one week!" I say you're worth it, and I want you to know you are a special person who I love very much.

* * *

September 30, 1991

Dear Babe:

I'm sorry I didn't respond to your previous letter. I was just at a loss for words. Even though you informed me in the beginning you didn't love Henry anymore, I still had my doubts. It's not that I didn't trust you, Baby, I just felt you were releasing a lot of hostility that may have been built up from Henry's wrongdoings.

It's hard to hate the one you have loved for so long. He might have done you wrong, but still it's difficult to hate. I also understand the situation you are in right now.

If you feel your best option is to go back to him, I can only accept your decision. I know that we'll always have a special bond between us no matter where you are. If situations were different and I wasn't locked up, there would definitely be a different story to tell. All I ask is that if you decide to go back, stand your ground. Don't let him walk all over you, and demand your respect.

If you were to go, I understand that there will be ups and downs in our communication because of your relationship with Henry, so I'm telling you now to never feel guilty. Whatever you get into, I know I'm in your heart and on your mind. I know I have whatever you need to make you feel good in a time of need. I don't want to make your decision hard for you by trying to convince you to do something because of me. I want you to know that I will always be your friend first, and I want you to be happy. I want you to do what's best for you and Li'l Henry.

Well, now that I've cleared the air, I would like to comment on that previous letter. I recall that time before you left for basic training, and I really had sorrow in my heart, although I didn't let it surface. I also remember you coming back, but you never told me the reason why. So you thought you were pregnant and with my child? Let me get one thing straight right here and now. I don't even want to think about the possibility of the test coming up positive, because an abortion is something I could never deal with. I think I better leave that subject in the past where it belongs.

I'm going to end here and, Babe, please try to settle your mind, because I don't want you to worry about this. Whatever choice you make, I will stand by your side.

I love you forever,

Willie

* * *

October 4, 1991

Dear Babe:

Well, I had the interview and they said they'll call me. I know what that means. Babe, I'm going to go back with Henry. I just think this is the best thing for me to do. You and I will always have a bond that no one else will ever be able to penetrate. I won't stop writing you and that is something I promise. Believe it or not, I still believe when you get out, we will be together.

Babe, we just won't see each other as often, but that holds true if I stay because I don't have a car anymore. Maybe this Gulf War has changed him as far as the importance of family. Maybe he'll put Li'l Henry and me first before himself. Maybe he is now ready to do the right thing as far as providing for his family. I've got to try it once more, because if I don't I'll always wonder. We'll be leaving tomorrow, and right now I'm taking a break from packing. I didn't want to leave without saying goodbye and assuring you that once I get settled, I will begin writing again. I won't lose contact.

Stay sweet, my love. My thoughts are forever with you.

All my love,

Gwen

P.S. Enjoy the poem, because that's how I really feel.

Sunshine
All my life I've wished for sunshine
Try as I might I could not find
A kind of brightness that makes hearts glow
Combined with warmness that makes love flow
One yellow circle of brightness
Mixed with warmth and gentleness
Blended with touches of softness
Releasing rays of happiness
To bring out the glow of love inside
The love I've always been known to hide
Deep down securely tucked away
In hope to be released one day
The day has come since I've met you
I was confused at first on what to do
Unaware I was that my sunshine had come

I didn't open up to you at once
At first I ignored the warmth of your smile
Intentionally I guess because I knew all the while
That you were my sunshine as bright as can be
And the glow in your love, it surrounded me
I love you my sunshine
Finally, I can say this
I thank the Lord for being kind
I've truly gotten my wish

* * *

Chapter 7

October 25, 1991

Dear Willie:

I'm back! We just arrived yesterday, and I'm now living with my grandmother. Henry and I couldn't find an apartment, and the money he'd saved ran out, so Li'l Henry and I caught the bus home. I really hate riding that bus, especially with Li'l Henry being so young.

Babe, you're not going to believe this, but Henry and I argued all the way to North Carolina about the past. He dropped us off at my sister Jennifer's house in Fayetteville, and boy was he mad! He didn't bother to tell me his plans as far as how long we would stay there or even if he was still committed to making the marriage work. After a couple of days of not hearing from him, I tried to call, but I couldn't reach him. So at that point I said to hell with him.

Li'l Henry and I moved in with Cheryl, my girlfriend who lives off base with her two kids. Her husband is in the Army but is now stationed in Panama City for a year or so. She had plenty of room and was glad to have us there. Cheryl said I could get Henry for abandonment, which was something I never would have thought of. She started making calls and finally located where he was working. She gave the receiver to me when he got on the phone. Henry immediately started explaining about how hard he had been trying to find an apartment but to no avail. He said he called Jennifer's house several times and I was never there. I told Jennifer not to tell him where I was, but she also did not tell me he had called.

Henry finally came to collect us from Cheryl's house, and I was ready to go because I felt she was beginning to get tired of us. Li'l Henry kept making her son cry. When we arrived at Jacksonville, we stayed in a hotel room for two weeks. Every day we looked for an apartment, but no one would take a chance on us. They discovered the truth about that apartment we had before I left. I found out Henry didn't even live there for the full term of the lease. He abandoned the apartment shortly after I left him. They were sure as hell bad-mouthing us, which made it difficult to get into another place. Finally the money ran out, and we had no alternative but to come back to Michigan. Henry promised to continue looking and said we wouldn't have to stay here for very long.

So now I'm back, and I'm sorry I didn't write, but I wasn't away for very long. You probably haven't missed me at all. Well, I've definitely missed you, and I'm so happy to be back. My present task is to figure out how in the world I am going to get to my Baby.

Hurry and write back.

Love,

Gwen

* * *

October 28, 1991

Hello Babe:

The first thing I noticed on the envelope when I held it in my hand and after seeing your name was the postmark. I saw Michigan and I thought, My Baby is back! It was such a treat to hear from you. I tried to condition my mind, because I'd thought I'd never hear from you again. I know you promised to write before you left, but still, I always think of you as doing the moral thing. Writing me would not have been the moral thing to do. Yet, I still hoped that you would.

I'm sorry you guys couldn't locate an apartment. I know how bad you wanted to get out on your own. Now you have to come back just to live with someone again. The good thing about it is you've gotten another opportunity to see me, the love of your life. I think that's worth a little praising of the Lord.

Well, I've finally got a job working as a librarian in the bookstore. I'm responsible for the checking in and out and replacement of books. It pays a whopping 55 cents an hour. I'm happy to be working again, and I'm reading many books, enhancing my mind somewhat.

Take care.

With love,

Willie

* * *

November 2, 1991

Dear Babe:

How are you? I've got some good news. My sister Charlene is going to let me drive her car to see you. It's not in the best of shape, but she feels it will make it there, considering all the running around she's done in town. I'm going to chance it, because I am definitely in dire need of my "fix."

I think I'll be here for a while so; I'd better start looking for a job. Henry started an allotment for us before I left, so that will be the only funds I'll have. I don't exactly like to depend on someone for income, especially when I'm capable of making my own way. I definitely don't want him to feel like he can tell me what the hell to do. I'm planning to go back, but I don't know exactly when as of yet.

I'm happy to hear that you found a job and are making big bucks, too. I'll be there Saturday, and I can't wait to see you again. Ooh, I'm going to get my "fix"!

Love,

Gwen

* * *

November 5, 1991

Hello, Sweetheart:

Well, you must have read my mind, because I was already trying to work on a ride for you to get here, but to no avail as of yet. You know me, if there is a way I will definitely find it and make it happen.

Girl, I thought about you constantly. I wondered if you and Li'l Henry were all right. Sometimes at night I wondered what you were doing at that particular moment. There wasn't a minute that went by that I didn't think about you. I kept hoping for a letter, but I understood why you didn't write. I respect you for always trying to do the right thing.

I'm doing fine now. I must add that any time I'm thinking about you, I know I'm doing well, because you deliver warmth that keeps my heart ever so loving. I was feeling so good the other day, I went out of my room and talked to people and even played ping-pong. I was feeling so good about you that I was talking a lot of stuff and "beating a lot of butt." A lot of guys didn't think I could play very well, because they've never seen me in action. I must say it's because my Baby is back in town.

So what's up with that diary? Do you have it with you, and, if so, can I hear some more of your true feelings, please?

Your love,

Willie

* * *

November 9, 1991

Dear Willie:

Well, I made it home in one piece. If you had seen Charlene's car, you never would have thought it could have made it all the way there, but it did. I must reemphasize that I was long overdue for my "fix." Every time we kissed, I felt this tingling inside of my body that was so unreal. My heart thumped extremely hard, but it all felt so good.

So you want to learn more of the diary, eh? By the way, I took that diary with me when I went back with Henry. I have nothing to hide because he read the entire diary. He came to visit me one day when I had Charge of Quarters in the Army one weekend. I smuggled him into my room, because I wasn't getting relieved until the following morning. I thought he wanted to go to sleep, but I discovered later that he read my diary all night long. After that, he kept throwing in my face the time I thought I was pregnant by you. For some mysterious reason he always found out everything that I tried to hide from him.

Anyhow, do you remember this day?

On March 22, 1984:

Dear Diary: Today I forgot that Willie was going to take me to the game in Ann Arbor, and I told Mama I would pick up Debra from the doctor's office. When I walked toward the door, sure enough, Mama asked who was going to pick up Debra. I just turned around and went back into the room. I called Willie in there to tell him I wasn't going. When he left, I started packing my clothes. My aunt Grace asked why was I packing, and I told her I was spending the remainder of my days with Vicky before I had to return to the MEPS. Aunt Grace asked why, and I told her Mama didn't like Willie and I didn't want to put up with it any more. I said she's always trying to find something for me to do when he's around. She could have very well picked up Debra so I could go to the game with Willie, because she wasn't doing anything. My aunt told my Mama that I was upset. I was crying because I was so angry, and Mama told me she didn't dislike Willie and he could come over here anytime. I told her I didn't feel comfortable with Willie when she was around. She said she was sorry for making me feel uncomfortable. She didn't want me to leave, and I felt sort of good inside considering just that morning she said she'll be glad when I go.

Willie didn't go to the game after all. He came back to take me to the movies but we were too late, so we went bowling instead. I beat him two games to his one. After that we got doughnuts and then went over to his house. I fell asleep and came home at 5:00 AM.

On March 23, 1984:

Dear Diary: While I was over at my girlfriend Ann's house, Willie came by. He called twice while I was in the tub. When I went to sleep, he finally came and woke me up. He told me that he wanted to go to the movies. He also told me he was crazy about me. We talked a while and then he left.

Love,

Gwen

* * *

November 11, 1991

Dear Sweetheart:

Baby, do you know how much I've missed you? You are still looking so good with your sexy self. I could have kissed those soft lips all night long.

I'm glad you made it home in one piece. I'm kind of skeptical about that car, so I've worked out some transportation for you. I talked with a friend of mine who's going to talk to his girlfriend who comes up twice a week. I don't see it being a problem for you to ride with her.

Babe, I'm so sorry that I didn't call you back. I've never used the phone that early before. I didn't know it was "first come, first serve." Those inmates stayed on the phone for hours. If I knew what I know now, I would have called you right after head count at 11:30 AM and just held it. I was trying to cut it close to the time I said I would call. I went to eat in the chow hall and thought I'd be back in plenty of time. As you can see, it didn't work out that way. I was mad as all outdoors. I know one thing: I'll be calling next Sunday. You can bet on that.

I love you,

Willie

* * *

November 9, 1991

Dear Babe:

Well, I've moved in with my daddy, but you can continue writing over to Diane's house. Of course, you know that I'm living next door to your wife. I wonder if she knows that I've been visiting you. I'm very curious to know to what she looks like. Every time she goes outside, which is not very often as I can see, she never turns my way.

I'll tell you what, living here is just like being alone. My daddy is never here. I think I'm going to enjoy living here. Don't get me wrong, I like living with my grandmother, too, but I prefer being here. Mama is getting ready to move to Florida with her sister. She let Diane move into the house, and she's in the process of packing. She says she needs to find herself. I'll miss her, but I suppose she knows what's best for her.

There's something else I need to tell you that is not the best of news but it is important. Henry is coming next week to get us. He had an operation of some sort and is on leave, so that's why he's able to come. He doesn't have a place for us to stay yet, but he wants us to come back. I don't know what's going on, but I will find out and you'll be the first person I inform.

Love ya,

Gwen

* * *

November 24, 1991

Dear Sweetheart:

I hope this letter gets to you before Henry does. I really don't understand why he's coming to get you two if he doesn't have a place yet. Then again, I can understand him wanting you near him, because that's all I ever dream of. I suppose we won't be seeing each other again soon, but I just want to say that I'm happy

I got another chance to see you and kiss you and feel your soft skin. It's really fresh in my mind, and I imagine it'll keep until the next time. There will definitely be a next time, because I have faith in us.

Babe, I wanted to let you know about our nice Thanksgiving dinner. I didn't think they would go all out for us, but they did. I had a lot to be thankful for, because someone has brought you back to me and I truly believe it was fate. You know what, Babe? I think we have a good thing going on now. I hope you can have faith in us to keep this dream alive of us being together one day. I will have you for my very own. I am getting to know you so much better through your letters and your diary. What you never knew was that you were always able to calm the beast in me. I was always able to take matters slow with you. I have always wanted what I wanted and wanted it right now. I think that's what made me so crazy about you. I never dated a lady who made me want to consume my time, without sex being a major issue. I just enjoyed being with you, and I want that feeling to last forever.

I'm going to go now, so be sweet wherever you are.

I love you,

Willie

* * *

Chapter 8

December 3, 1991

Dear Willie:

Babe, I am still here. We were leaving to go back to Jacksonville last Saturday, and the car broke down. Thank God we had only been driving for about 15 minutes, so we hadn't gotten far. Henry finally got the car started and drove back. He took a plane home because he had to report to work that Monday. Since then, I've gotten the car repaired. It needed a new alternator. Baby, what

I'm trying to say is, I have transportation now. I'm coming to see you tomorrow and I don't give a doggone because I'm in dire need of my "fix."

He found out about my wrecking the car while I was coming to see you. I can't believe Pam's loose tongue slipped and said it right in front of him. Instantly the room grew very quiet, because everybody heard it. I immediately made small talk to break up the monotony. I didn't think he caught on at first, but he mentioned it to me later that night. I just said it was the only time I had ever been there to visit, and I did it out of curiosity. I wanted to know how jail life would be. He didn't buy that, but after a while he just let it rest. I believe that increased his desire to take me back with him even more.

Well, Babe, I'll be there tomorrow around 1:00 PM. I'm going to spend the entire day with you. I hope nothing happens to this man's car, but rain or shine, I'll be there.

I love you,

Gwen

* * *

December 10, 1991

Dear Gwen:

I enjoyed our visit today. Girl, you made me feel so good and special, too. Sometimes I have doubts about your feelings for me because of your situation with Henry. I know that it would be different if I wasn't locked up, but sometimes it's difficult to maintain those positive thoughts. I was thinking about some of the things you mentioned in your diary and the conversation we had when you were here. I have never thought of myself as a monster, because I only have warmth and compassion in my heart for you. I think what you meant to say was you always felt I was playing you for a fool. I think you were intimidated by me. I never knew it then, but you must have liked me very much to put up a wall so high that I couldn't climb over. To know you came back to me under the conditions that I'm in shows how much you care about me. The way you have unveiled to me, I know the wall has

113

lowered to my level. Believe me when I say I want to come in and be an "item," as you call it.

When you first mentioned driving Henry's car to see me, I felt strange because I could envision myself in his place. I wouldn't want you driving to see another man and especially not in my car. Then I began thinking if this man had played his cards right and treated you with dignity and respect, this wouldn't be happening. It's his doggone fault. I don't give a darn about him because I want to see my Baby.

Love,

Willie

P.S. Thanks for the pictures. They came out perfect. You look so sexy in all those different outfits. You look good, Girl.

* * *

December 16, 1991

Hello, Willie:

Well, well, well, so you want me to take chances coming to see you, huh? You want me to risk it, huh? Well, it's about time, Babe. You're talking words I like to hear, because no one needs to show consideration for Henry except me. You are right: I would be a better wife if he had been a better husband. So keep talking like you're talking, because it warms me up to hear you want to see me just as bad as I want to see you.

Unfortunately, I am without car again. Henry came and took the car a couple of days ago. He stayed two days, asked me to return with him, and of course live with Jennifer until he finds a place. He claimed it was extremely hard for him to search because of lack of reliable friends to chauffeur him around. I couldn't exactly get mad about it because, after all, it is his car. I was contemplating returning at first, but at the last minute I changed my mind. I told him I was sick and tired of living in other people's houses and didn't see the significance in leaving here to go live with somebody else. Then he started talking about my family's concerns about him leaving us without a car, as if he cared about what they thought. I just stated that it was sort of unethical. His comeback was, "Well, you would have transportation if you hadn't tried to see the punk in jail." Well, that finally closed my mouth. I should be going back to Jacksonville by the first of January. We agreed that if push came to shove, he would rent a trailer home. We both dread living in one, but as a last resort, it's better than nothing.

So, ever since he left, you know what's been on my mind: How in the world am I going to get to my Willie? We know me; I'll make a way out of no way sooner or later. I should have followed my first mind and visited you on Thanksgiving, but, then again, if I had you probably would have missed that nice turkey dinner. I definitely wouldn't want to be the cause of you missing that nice treat.

Anyhow, I wanted to share something with you that I thought was funny. The last letter you sent sat over at Diane's house three days before I could enjoy it. After Diane told me a letter had come from you, you know I was eager to read it as always. Henry clung to me like static those two day. I am not lying. My sister Diane needed my daddy's car one day, and I drove it to her while Henry trailed me. Babe, when we approached Janes Street, I deliberately turned out in front of a car, which prevented Henry from turning behind me. After that I became "speed lightening." Every light I approached was changing to red as I drove through, and I didn't have to stop for any. Then I started speeding and made it over to Diane's house about a good five minutes before Henry. I dashed into the house, opened the letter, and read the first page. You know what, Babe? It wasn't even worth it because I read so fast that I didn't get a good understanding, and I knew I wouldn't be able to finish.

So, after Henry went back to North Carolina, I went over to Diane's house to retrieve the letter that I had stored underneath the sofa cushion—and it wasn't there. My baby sister, Pam, said she saw Diane's son Jerry with it and told him to put it back. Jerry wasn't there and I thought, "Got Dog, I've waited all of this time and still I can't read the letter!" Come to find out, my oldest sister, Debra, had moved it while cleaning, and she gave it to me. So I just sat back, curled up, and read my letter like a hungry baby sucking her bottle.

I'm glad you enjoyed the pictures, and thank you for your many compliments. They made me feel special. I would also like to thank you for answering my questions. By the way, you're getting quite good at that. You're even answering questions that I haven't asked.

Babe, I'm sorry I didn't finish my fantasy on the phone. I just felt you would be able to feel the rest. Listen, Babe, I like to kiss before and during from time to time. I like to be caressed and touched all over, especially where you can feel the wetness. My neck is my second most-sensitive spot, wet kisses not dry. If you play with my ears just right, you can really arouse me. I like my fingers fondled with your mouth and to be passionately kissed down my back and chest. I like my lips to be encircled with your pointer finger; and every previous thing mentioned, I prefer you to use the same. And of course I wouldn't expect all of this good treatment in one session of lovemaking, but it sure would be nice. Last but by no means least, I like long, slow strokes up until it's almost time to climax. Then, just at that instant, I like short, slow strokes where you're barely lifting up, but a little bit harder and never, never fast. Why you would want to know now is beyond me. You take the fun out of exploring, but I suppose there's always more to know. Then again, there could be some details I left out—unintentionally, of course. You never asked questions like that before when we were together. You just plunged right in. (ha, ha!)

Listen, Babe, Henry will never find your letters. I store them all on the top shelf in Diane's garage, and every time I finish one, I place it right up there. I'm so careful now, Babe, that careful could be my middle name. I've noticed you haven't made a comment about the picture getting wet. I'm really feeling bad about wasting water on it and smearing part of your face. Say something, Baby. Don't make me wonder.

I'm going to end, and I won't give up hope.

Love,

Gwen

* * *

December 20, 1991

Dear Gwen:

I was happy to receive a letter from you today. I'm glad to hear that you will be here for a little while. Hope is still alive. By the way, I'm working on something to get you up here with me for a day, so keep your fingers crossed and I'll let you know when I talk to you on the phone

I must tell you, this letter is one for my classic collection. Out of all the letters I've received from you, there are only two that are classics that you have masterfully put together. As I read this letter, I put each individual page behind one other, and upon reaching the end, I wanted more because I still had paper in my hand. I had to read it again to make sure I hadn't missed a page. This letter is the one I really craved for like a baby that has an empty bottle and is still hungry. Gwen, I love that letter! I liked the baby bottle scenario, so I had to send it right back to you. (smile)

I think I'll title this letter "The dog that couldn't stay on a trail." Girl, you had me rolling in my bed talking about that car chase. My jaws were in pain for hours from laughing so hard. You better be careful driving Troy's car. I don't understand why Henry had to follow you over there, anyway, unless you two were going someplace else from there. Your sister could have driven you back, and he could have waited for you at the house. What is that man trying to catch you doing?

I don't understand why the trailer home option wasn't implemented right after plans A and B failed. I know I wouldn't let you go back while knowing there was something I could do to keep you with me. I do think it is senseless to keep moving from house to house. By the way, he knows you didn't particularly like living with them. I don't know why he would ask you to live there again. Stupid prick. He was probably trying to avoid making another trip up here to get you two.

I feel so bad every time I think about what happened to your car. I think about it all the time. I don't know how I will make that up to you, but I will try for the rest of my life. Now to hear that he hurls that in your face to make you feel bad makes me feel even worse, but I will heal that wound one day.

I ask questions about a lot of things because I do want to know what makes my kitten purr. I didn't inquire back then because you would have never revealed anything like that to me, considering how shy you were. Now that I know where to start, I certainly know how to finish. I reversed those things in my mind. I pictured you doing them to me and, Girl, I got warm inside. You really know how to make a man's hair stand erect.

I'm glad to know we are thinking about the same things. To hear you answering questions that you haven't read yet lets me know that we are thinking alike and have some kind of ESP when it comes to each other. We are in sync, as one.

I'm sorry for having you wonder about how I felt concerning the drawing getting wet. I thought that when you told me while you were visiting, you understood my feelings. I gave that drawing to you. Not for you to safeguard until I'm able to get it back one day. I wanted it to be a 16×20 substitute for the real thing until I can be there in person. We'll take a bigger and better one of the two of us when I get out, okay? I was only telling you to take it over to my mother's house so it wouldn't get lost, that's all. No big deal. As a matter of fact, when I get out of here, you can wet me up as often as you like if you get my meaning. (ha, ha!)

Love ya,

Willie

P.S. I've got one of your pictures hanging in my locker. I just can never seem to close the door because I can never get enough of looking at you. By the way, that lipstick looks ravishing. So the next time you come to visit, have some on, okay? The last time you wore some, I love it so much I was scared to kiss you, because I didn't want to smear it. Then you started eating it off yourself. So this time I would love to eat it off your soft lips for you.

Love,

Willie

* * *

December 21, 1991

Hello, Love:

How are you? Fine, I hope. Well, I imagine I didn't receive a letter from you today because you probably think I'm gone, since I haven't written in a week. I sure was looking for one today, but I can understand that.

I got some bad news and I've got some bad news, but I still have some good news. The bad news is I can't think of a single way that I'm going to get up there before I leave. Diane was going to get Charlene's car fixed, until she was informed it would cost $600 for the parts alone. She said forget that. The bad news is I'm leaving for sure some time after Christmas. Henry is supposed to come back to get us, and I hope nothing happens to the car this time. I'm so sick and tired of going back and forth, and this time had better be it or else. The good news is I love you and always will. (smile)

Do you recall when Henry came back that first time to get us? Well, he was back only one day when his stomach started hurting real bad. He was admitted into the hospital in North Carolina prior to coming, and he told me some story about it happening at a cookout, I don't want to get into the details. He had an operation before he came, and he was on convalescent leave. Anyway, I thought maybe that happened to him because of his wrongdoings of leaving us in Fayetteville with Jennifer, or whatever else he was doing. I don't care what you say, Babe, I believe that was some type of punishment. So I say to myself, "Self, you were doing wrong by going to visit Willie." I think my punishment was to be left here without a car so I wouldn't have a way to see you again. Let's face it; the bottom line is, if I still had a car, I would continue to come. I don't ask Troy for the use of his car anymore, because I'm a jinx with cars in everyone's eyes since the accident.

Guess what, Babe? I took your advice about talking to my sister Debra again. Yesterday she asked Troy to let me take her to cash her check. When I picked her up, I told her that we're talking again and it's fine and dandy, but I wanted to get one thing straight. I wasn't going to be called upon to do things for her, and I advised her not to expect me to because she did pawn my microwave and I didn't get anything in return. Do you know what she had the nerve to say? She said she didn't feel she owed me anything, and she asked Troy to take her to cash her check, not me. Since Troy didn't feel like doing it, he wanted her to ask me. She said that she's paying for the microwave in her own way, because she doesn't have anywhere to live. She's living with Diane, by the way, but Diane is not very happy about it. She called me a materialistic heifer because I refused to talk to her after she pawned the microwave that Mama gave me. We argued and she made me so mad that I said, "Forget this, I'm taking your butt home," and I turned the car around and did just that.

All she had to say was she wouldn't ask me to do anything for her and nothing else would have been said. Babe, she made me so mad that if I hadn't been driving that car, we would have fought. So now I don't care what anybody says, I'm not talking to her ever again. She may be right in saying that she is paying for what she did by her own problems, but the fact is she didn't pay me anything.

Well, so much for that. Guess what I did to my head? You know the fat braids that people are wearing now? Well, I'm wearing them too, and it looks nice. I'll take some pictures and send them to you. By the way, I like that little picture of you on the bottom of the letter. So you found a way to get a picture of you to me after all. That was very clever.

Since I won't be seeing you again anytime soon, I got to at least talk to you on the phone. Here's what we'll do. See, the problem is I don't want to hear Troy mouth about you calling here collect, so I was trying to figure out a way for you to call while he's at work. You should get this letter by Wednesday. Either Wednesday or Thursday, I want you to call me at 7:00 PM or 9:00 PM, whichever time is good for you. I'll make sure that I answer the phone. Troy goes to work at 5:00 PM and get back at 6:30, so if you can call between those hours, it would be perfect. I think those hours correlated with head count time, right? Let's hope he doesn't have a hold on the phone.

You know, Willie, I've seen your wife a few times. She's always turned, facing in the opposite direction, but this time she turned my way. I couldn't see her face, but she saw me. I wonder if she knows who I am. Then I feel funny, because if she does know who I am and also knows that I come up there to see you, boy, what she must think of me!

I'll talk to you soon.

Love,

Gwen

* * *

December 25, 1991

Dear Gwen:

How are you doing? I hope you are in the festive spirit of the holidays. As for myself, I'm doing as well as can be expected. One thing I have noticed is I was feeling bad about Christmas coming about a month or so ago, and it was all anticlimactic because now that it's here, I don't feel bad at all. I thought about not being able to be with the kids and all the big dinners my mother prepares. I'm going to be taking pictures out in the visiting room today, so I will get to see a lot of people enjoying being with their families.

Debra is a lost soul. When you told me she felt she didn't owe you anything, I thought to myself, she is lost. She's sounding just like my brother. Those kinds of people think everybody owes them something. When I went to Atlanta, my brother took a TV and my cash register and pawned them both for $75. The cash register alone cost $500. I was pissed, and he felt he didn't owe me anything, either. That's a crack head's way of thinking. They will go on and on taking from their family and thinking nothing of it. I just stayed away from him and didn't allow him into my house, because I knew he was up to no good. That was the best way for both of us so I wouldn't have to hurt him. That might be the best thing for you, too. She's got the nerve to take your stuff and then call you materialistic. Keep your hands off of my materials and you won't have to worry about me or my stuff.

I bet you look pretty with those braids in your hair. I hope you don't think that you don't look just as good without them. Gwen, you know that's one of the many qualities I liked about you. You always felt good about yourself and didn't feel the need to use artificial stuff. I didn't even know what my wife really looked like, because she was always wearing someone else's hair on top of her head. I can't wait to get the picture of you. You know me; I want to see you as many times as I can.

Babe, I hope you just used the wrong words when you said you were doing wrong by seeing me or wanting to, and because of it you're being punished by not being able to visit me at all. I know you love me and want to see me, so with that there could never be anything wrong about it at all. As you can see, I have made a way for you to get here. There can't be anything wrong about us.

Gwen, I know that you're getting ready to go back to North Carolina and you are glad to be getting back on your own again. I must say for the record it is not a happy time for me, and I am definitely going to miss you. Drop a postcard as soon as you get there, please.

I love you always,

Willie

PART III
TAMPA, FLORIDA

Chapter 1

November 10, 1992

Hello, Love:

Henry has finally left. We've been here in Tampa a week so far. He decided to spend his last week of leave down here. Babe, he was so nice to me and behaved like a real husband and father. I'm planning to work while I'm here, but he insisted on starting an allotment for Li'l Henry and me, nevertheless. I could see a change in him, and it really felt good to know that he wanted to make sure his family would be taken care of.

When Li'l Henry and I drove him to the bus station, he gave us both a big hug, and it was very sad for me. I didn't cry in front of him, but I did when my sister Pam kept asking questions about our parting. Something changed with me for him. I can't quite pinpoint it right now, but when I figure it out, you will be the first to know.

So here's my mother's address, and please write me as soon as you get this letter. I can't wait to hear from you. Do you know how it feels to write letter after letter after letter and not get a response at all? If it wasn't for the stories I shared with you while I was in Jacksonville, I definitely would have run out of subjects to talk about. At one point I almost got a post office box so that I could hear from my Baby. Well, I'm no longer in North Carolina, and we've got six months to communicate as much as we would like. Don't waste any time, Babe. I'll be waiting to hear from you.

Love,

Gwen

* * *

November 15, 1992

Hey, Babe:

What a relief, I can talk again. I feel like my mouth has been taped shut for many, many months, and someone has finally taken pity upon me and allowed me to speak again. It's pure delight to be able to talk to you. Do you have any idea how many questions I wanted to ask about your stories? I wrote them all down as they popped into my mind, and I'm enclosing that list along with this letter. Before you started writing about your and Henry's life, I started reading this book. I became so engrossed in what would happen next in your life that I couldn't concentrate on the book anymore. Needless to say, I never reopened it again.

Babe, you know it's really nice to hear that Henry wants to make sure you are taken care of. Hell that is his responsibility. I would really like to think it's within him to do the right thing, but after reading about you two and your lives, it's somewhat hard for me to believe. Maybe he doesn't want you to do anything wrong like cheat while he's away. He probably thinks that if he treats you decent or in a special way just before leaving, you'll be less inclined to mess around on him. I know what kind of person you are, so I know he does, too. I don't want to destroy any good feelings that you may have, and I really do hope his actions are legitimate. I'm just providing you with a male prospective on the situation.

Baby, Baby, Baby, you have no idea what has happened to me. A couple of months ago there was this fag who came here. I tried to stay clear of him because I didn't want any dealings. He must have had some kind of implant surgery done, because he had breasts like a woman. I assumed he must have gotten in trouble prior to altering the other part. We had to take showers with this freak, but like I said, I stayed clear of him.

Well, one day when walking out of the recreation room, I ran smack into him. I didn't have on a shirt, so when we bumped, his chest hit against mine. Babe, they felt real as hell. He's no longer here now, though. They moved him to another facility a month ago. I'm sure the men were visiting his cell frequently while he was here.

I am now working in the kitchen. It pays 65 cents an hour, which is more than what any of the other jobs here pay. It has its advantages, too. I'm able to eat a variety of food other than what we serve the inmates. By the way, I no longer eat pork. I'm not Muslim or anything like that; it's just that they've never served pork to us since I've been in prison. I've gotten accustomed to not eating it. I didn't know this until one day while I was working; I spotted some pork chops in the freezer. I swiped and cooked them and felt my mouth watering as I anticipated eating them. I was sick as hell afterwards. Now I don't want to even smell it, because I'll never forget how I felt that day.

Well, Babe, again I want to say I am very happy to be able to speak with you again. I am so looking forward to conversing with you extensively. Take care and hope to hear from you real soon.

With love,

Willie

P.S. Questions:
1. How did you find out Henry went to the movies with Valerie?
2. Referring to the section about the operator calling for Henry to charge a call to Valerie. Did you take the hold off the phone by that time?.
3. What happened after Henry said Charkeshia wasn't his child?
4. Did you and Valerie ever meet up at Henry's job with the kids?
5. When did he finally admit to Charkeshia being his child?
6. What was the outcome of Henry going to jail?
7. You mean to tell me Jody tried something with you while those other people were in the room?
8. How did you know that Larry wanted to get with you?
9. When you were in the Army, when did you get a car to take Calvin to eat and Douglas home?
10. Did you ever hear from Calvin again?
11. Why did Douglas kiss you on the lips? What type of relationship did you two have?

* * *

December 1, 1992

Dear Willie:

I was so happy to get your letter. I started smiling as soon as Charlene walked through the door asking me to guess what she had in her hands. Of course I'm going to answer all of your questions, because I don't want my Baby to wonder about anything. I shared this part of my life with you because I wanted you to understand how I lived. Maybe it will answer why I act certain ways or say strange things.

Valerie and I never met. As a matter of fact, we never even talked again after we made plans to confront Henry. Henry called her, trying to prove something to me again. He referred to Charkeshia as her baby once again, and I just didn't ponder it anymore. When he came home after the Gulf War had ended, he had a picture of Charkeshia in his wallet. He showed it to me, and that's when he actually admitted it; not in words, but in his actions.

When we moved to on-post housing, I didn't keep the hold on the phone anymore. I predicted that since he was unable to call her for so long, he was too embarrassed to do it then. Believe it or not, there weren't any calls to her on the bill after we moved. After finding out about the baby, my mind retreated to that night Henry went to the movies and I questioned him about it. He admitted that he was with Valerie that night.

I talked to Jody once since that night, and I never heard from him again. He promised to visit and I waited, but he never came. He had given me his sweater before we left; I suppose to reassure me that we would see each other again. I tossed it into the trash shortly after our telephone conversation. So, now I know the myth is true about giving it up on the first date. He didn't respect me after that. To answer your question, yes, he did try something with me while they were in the room, but we were underneath the blanket.

I knew Larry was attracted to me because when he drove me back that time after Christmas, he came up to my room for a while. We lay across the bed and talked about getting together. He wanted assurance that I would get a divorce, or so I imagined. That's what prevented us from going any further. I kissed him that night because I was sort of fond of him, too.

That November after I enlisted in the Army, Mama brought my car to me. She hitched it onto her car and drove it all the way to Fort Bragg from Michigan. I was thankful and glad to have it, because I didn't really learn my way around until I started driving myself.

Calvin is the one I'll never forget. After Henry returned, he somehow met up with Larry in Jacksonville. He confronted him about me. He thought Larry and I had something going on between us. Larry spilled his guts to Henry about Calvin and me. Larry probably relayed the story to Calvin, so maybe that's why he didn't call anymore. At some point in our relationship, Calvin had asked me about getting a divorce, and I contemplated doing it. So if Larry revealed to Calvin the fact that Henry and I were back together, I'm sure that's the reason he stopped calling. He did call once while he was on the float, and that was the last time I heard from him. I really cared about him, but, again, getting my marriage back together ended up being more important.

I don't know what happened after Henry went to jail. He was very hush-hush about it. All I know is he never went back to jail. When he was involved in doing something illegal, it was hush-hush and he did not want me to know. I remember a couple of his friends coming over, and we were all sitting in the living room. They brought up the subject about the tires. Henry was sort of standoffish at first and then asked could I leave because it was only fellows in the room. I left because I knew he was embarrassed about it, plus I didn't want to cause a scene in front of his friends about him asking me to leave my own living room.

Douglas was someone I was really attracted to in high school. We never got together as a couple, but we always flirted with each other. It was just that way between us.

So, Babe, did that fag ever try anything with you? I bet that was weird. I bet he made everybody feel uncomfortable. What I really can't believe is you don't eat pork anymore. No ham, ham hocks, pork chops, bacon, pork ribs, pork steak, or pork chitterlings? Shoot, all of that meat comes from a pig. I just can't imagine not eating ham.

I'm glad to hear you're still working. I've started a data entry job through a temporary service. I've been working for a couple of days now. It's only a two-week assignment. I've put applications in every hotel I've seen. I've registered Li'l Henry in a daycare and hopefully one of those hotels will call or the temporary service will find something else before the job ends. I would hate to take him back out in two weeks.

I've learned this pattern in crocheting, and I've made a couple of blankets since I've been here. One of Mama's friends wants me to make a yellow-and-white one for her. Charlene is encouraging me to sell them at the flea market. Maybe I'll do that, because they are nice and they just might sell.

Well, Babe, I'm going to end now. Listen, here's Mama's telephone number. Call me, because I sure would love to hear your voice.

Love,

Gwen

* * *

December 19, 1992

Dear Gwen:

Today I was just sitting here thinking about our telephone conversation. It was nice listening to your lovely voice again. Gwen, I would like to take the time to tell you that you are someone very dear to me. Regardless of what's going on in your life, you will always hold a special part of my heart. You're unbelievably strong to have endured the things you've been through and are still able to play the loving wife. Yet, on the other hand, I sense your vulnerability in trying to contain the feelings that you have for me. Babe, I want you to understand that it doesn't matter what is going on in your life. I only focus on what we share together. Nothing you could ever tell me will change the relationship that we now have. If you and your husband split up today and you meet someone new, I want to know about it. I want to know about whatever goes on in your life. Like I've said so many times before, we are friends first, and I don't ever want to hear about you being lonely or unhappy, especially because of me. You don't ever have to feel as though you can't discuss something with me because you want to spare my feelings. When you tell me that you love me, I take it for just that. I believe it, and I don't relate it to anything that's going on in your life.

Let me tell you what I wish. I wish that I had been there for you after you left for basic training. If I had the mind that I have now, I would have felt your feelings for me. I would have waited for you and married you when you returned. I was so blind and very childish then. You were so shy and you didn't open up to me like you're doing now. I wish I had known you in this capacity back then. Well, it's too late to go back to yesterday, so I'm going to concentrate on right now. I want you to promise that you'll never stop writing before talking it over with me first. If there ever comes a time when you're unable to write, drop a postcard every now and then. Make me that promise, Baby, today. I feel so alive through your letters. When I read your words, I feel a part of you that I truly believe no one else can feel. I love you, Girl.

Remember those pictures you sent that were messed up? Well, I cut your face out of them and made a scrapbook entitled, "My One and Only Love." This guy was looking through the book one day, and he recognized you. He claims he's the first guy who ever had sex with. He and I hang out together all the time. I wonder can you guess who he is.

Well, I'll end on that note.

Love,

Willie

P.S. Merry Christmas!

* * *

January 6, 1993

Dear Sweetheart:

Now, why do you want to play the guessing game with me? The first guy I had sex with was George Harris, and there's no way

131

I'm going to believe he's in jail with you. Saginaw is a small town, but that would be a hell of a coincidence. So if George is not his name, then this guy has lied to you.

You know, Babe, that was such a sweet letter. First of all, I want to assure you that I do want to make you that promise. I promise that I will never stop writing without talking it over with you beforehand. I enjoy sharing the things that are going on in my life with you. I feel comfortable talking to you, because you listen to me and always give feedback at times when I really need it. I will always want to be a part of your life and have you part of mine.

I especially enjoyed our phone conversation. It's just that when you start asking questions about Henry and me, I think one day you're going to say, "To hell with you." You're going to feel as though there's no sense in loving someone who loves somebody else, yet tells you she loves you, too. I do love you, Willie, more than you will ever know. It's a feeling that's easy to recognize but hard to define and even harder to write on paper. I truly believe within my heart that if you were out here, I would leave Henry and live that fairy-tale life with you. Just imagine waking up happy every day—and, better yet, going to bed the same way every night. That's how I think my life would be with you: pure joy.

However, I can't concentrate on that right now, because the fact is you're not out here. The best thing for me to do is remain in this teeter-totter marriage and try to make the best of it. Ever since I was a child, I dreamed of getting married and living a happy life with my husband. Henry was my choice, and I'm not going to say that I don't sometimes wish that it could be that way with us; a fairy-tale relationship, that is. I have longed for it, but I know it will never happen. The reason why I hardly ever discuss the good times between Henry and me is because the bad times outweigh them. Then again, I only discuss the bad times because I need you to cling to our promise to one day be together.

I love you,

Gwen

* * *

January 18, 1993

Dear Babe:

How are you doing? Fine and in the best of health I hope. Well, that's more than I can say for myself. Last week, I got into this fight in the chow hall with another inmate. We were all laughing and having a good time. I suspect that I cracked on him one time too many, and he couldn't take it. He threw some peas at me and pissed me off. We started fighting, and I broke my baby finger on my right hand trying to take out his jawbone, but that is nothing compared to his injuries. I requested to see the doctor when I couldn't bend it, and he informed me that it was broken and put a cast on it. If my writing is sloppy, please forgive me because it's difficult to write when your baby finger is sticking straight out.

We didn't get into trouble, thank God, because the guys stopped the fight before any of the guards got there. I imagine that was a blessing in disguise, because it probably would have added time onto my sentence. Babe, I am trying hard to keep the peace during my stay here, but these men won't respect me if I just bow down every time someone jumps at me. If I use my better mind and just walk away, they are going to think I am a sissy.

I want to ask you to do a favor for me. Can you see if you can get a post office box there? I've got this connection with a guy who comes in weekly to refill the vending machines. He gives me a deal on supplies, such as batteries, lighters, pens, and things of that nature. I in turn sell them to the inmates for a higher price. It's unbelievable how much they will pay for a pack of batteries. They can't give the money to me directly, so I figured I'd ask you to get the post office box. Then they could mail it there, and you can send it to me in a money order. I had someone else do it for me before, but I think I should change up. Please write back and give me an answer in your next letter.

I'll talk to you soon. Stay sweet, my love.

All my love,

Willie

* * *

February 1, 1993

Dear Willie:

So, you can't walk away from a fight? What do you think you have to prove to anyone in there? I think that you've only got two things to prove. One is that you can spend the remainder of your time in there wisely and get out on the date that you're scheduled to. Two is that you can be man enough to walk away and not give a darn about what people think. So, the question is now, can you prove that to me? Babe, just please try and do the right thing.

I am doing fine. I've got 10 orders for blankets, so I've got my work cut out for me. I'm working at the Ramada Inn now, and it's a permanent job. They called me two days before I concluded my temporary assignment. This may be an ordinary housekeeping position, but the benefits are outstanding. They have the regular one-week vacation after one year, two weeks after the following year, and sick time that starts accumulating from day one. They pay "time" plus eight extra hours if I work on a holiday, and if I don't work, I'm still paid for eight hours. Get this: Your birthday is considered a holiday! After 90 days, I qualify for medical coverage, and the company pays 80% of the cost for the employees and 50% for their families. They'll reimburse for college if I major in something hotel-related, and they promote from within. They provide free lunch every day, and we have monthly meeting where we're given opportunities to win money. They pay cash for suggestions if they use them. It's laid back with no supervision, just like the other hotels I've worked at. Hell, the inspectors barely check the rooms after I'm finish. I think I'm going to love it here.

I checked with the post office, and they said my name would have to appear on Mama's mail box in order to purchase one. It was the craziest thing I'd ever heard. Why do you need a post office box anyway? Just have them send the money to Mama's address. Don't worry about Mama, because she already tried to question me about you writing here. She said it wasn't right because I'm married. That's funny, considering all the "not right" things Henry has done. She's crazy about Henry, and he's got her fooled about the kind of person he really is. I never shared with her all the abuse

I had to endure with him. No one else is good enough for me in her eyes. I made her aware of the fact that this is my life and I'm going to live it the way that I choose to.

Take care, Babe.

I love you,

Gwen

* * *

February 10, 1993

Dear Gwen:

What's up? Well, as you know, that was my method of finding out who was the first guy you ever made love to. You're right, his name is not George. It's Jesse Carter, and I've caught him in more lies than a little bit. If he chooses to twist reality in order to keep his sanity in here, then what can I say. We all need something to keep us going, and I suppose he's just dreaming a little dream.

So your mom still doesn't like me, huh? I don't understand why, because I was always very nice and respectful to her when we used to date. I can't believe you told her you were going to do what you wanted to do with your life. I remember how negative she used to act toward me, and how you never said anything about it. It never bothered me, because I knew I hadn't done anything wrong.

Remember that day when you were packing your clothes to leave because you were fed up with her interfering in our plans? I came to pick you up for a basketball game, and as we were walking out the door, she asked who was going to pick your sister Debra up from the doctor's office. You never would say anything in your defense when it came to your mother, but, boy oh boy, that day you were mad! I'll always remember that day, because it made me understand the depths you would go to be with me.

Don't worry about the post office box, Babe, because I spoke with my sister and she said that she would do it for me.

So how are things going with the blanket business? Girl, you know you are very talented. One day you are going to be successful at something, Ms. Entrepreneur. Let me know when I can call you again.

I love you, Babe,

Willie

P.S. Tell your son you love him today.

* * *

Chapter 2

February 19, 1993

Dear Willie:

I haven't written in a while because I'm getting so many orders for the blankets. This lady at work wants to buy one blanket per month for the next six months. She wants to give one to all of her children. Thank you for the vote of confidence at the end of your last letter.

Babe, did I tell you about the roaches here in the South? You wouldn't believe how big they are. The other day I was sitting on the sofa crocheting, when I heard this noise. It wasn't very loud, but I noticed that it came from the vent on the wall that was about three feet away from where I was sitting. I heard it again, I immediately looked toward the vent, and still nothing happened. About five minutes later, I saw, through my peripheral vision, a big roach crawling out of the vent. I jumped up off the couch, ran into the dining room where Charlene and Mama were, and I hopped on top of one of the dining room chairs. Charlene watched as I jumped onto the chair and she climbed onto another chair without asking any questions. While we were both on the chairs, I told them about what had happened, and my Mama killed it. We laughed about it afterwards, but I was scared as heck.

That reminds me of a time when I was in Jacksonville and Henry had gone to the field for the weekend for his job. I had gotten home from the club and was in the bathroom preparing for bed. Out of the corner of my eye, I saw one of those roaches crawl up the wall. It scared the living daylights out of me. I envisioned squashing it with my shoe and the insides squirting everywhere. I was too scared to even try to kill it. I ran out of the bathroom and closed the door, thinking I'd locked something inside that could squeeze through a keyhole. Luckily, we had two bathrooms, because I was not going back in there under any circumstances! I remember sleeping with one eye open that night.

The next morning I waited until the next-door neighbors were up, went over there, and asked could he kill the roach. His 10-year-old daughter jumped up and said, "I'll do it." Try as she might, she couldn't find where it was hiding. She finally gave up and told me to come get her if I saw it again. Well, after that I went into the bathroom, and believe me I was cautious about anything I touched in there. When I reached for the tissue, I saw it. I didn't have a tissue holder and I usually sat it on the sink. The roach had positioned itself in the center part of the roll. I ran next door and got the girl again. She came and, after a while, finally killed it. I watched her the entire time, and when it tried to hide in a crack, she used her fingernail to pull it out. I squirm every time I think about that incident. I don't think I would be so afraid of them if I hadn't discovered that they could fly.

I know you didn't expect a letter on roaches from me, but I thought I'd enlighten you about the creatures from the South.

Well, I'm off on Saturday, so why don't you call then. I'll be looking forward to hearing from you.

Love,

Gwen

P.S. I did date Jesse Carter, but I never had sex with him. A lie from him doesn't surprise me a bit, because he was a liar back then, too.

* * *

February 20, 1993

Dear Willie:

Henry is here. I don't know what's going on, but he came back early. He arrived unannounced, probably trying to catch me doing something. I need you to stop writing until I get back in touch with you. I guess we'll be going back to North Carolina, so I'll try to write again before I leave.

Remember that I love you.

Gwen

* * *

February 28, 1993

Dear Willie:

Henry found one of your letters, and, man, was he mad! He took the car and is now gone back to North Carolina. I don't even know if he's coming back to get us. See, he's always snooping around. From my understanding, he was cleaning up and stumbled upon one of your letters. I don't even know which one, but I thought I had them all hidden together. When he came here unannounced, I asked Charlene to pack them all away in a box and store them in the back of the closet in Mama's bedroom. Can you imagine how I felt for the next two days that he was here, coming home from work thinking maybe he'd found another letter, anticipating his reaction? I couldn't look around because he stuck to me like glue.

I finally got a chance to get the remaining letters out of the house when he went to the store with Charlene. I threw the entire box in the dumpster—and Babe, I felt like I was throwing a part of my heart away. I really didn't want to do it, but I knew he would continue looking. He was hurt and I can imagine how he felt. That letter could have said anything from "I love you" to "leaving him for you." That night he discovered the letter, I thought he had driven back to North Carolina because he stayed out all night. I found out later that he slept in the car. He had nothing to say to me whatsoever. I hated to go to work, because he continued to clean the house in what I thought was an attempt to find another letter. I was afraid that he would.

He stayed here a week and treated me like a stepchild. He didn't touch me or say anything to me. I tried to apologize, and even begged for his forgiveness, but to no avail. I even tried to reason with the fact that they were only words and that we couldn't see one another. Even Charlene and my aunt tried to put a good word in for me. He didn't give a doggone because his pride was shattered. I suppose he knows now how I felt with all those other women he messed around with in North Carolina.

Now I'm catching the bus home from work. Mama drops me off in the morning on her way to work. I got stranded downtown for about two-and-a-half hours that first day I caught the bus. This is so embarrassing for me for him to leave me without a car. I have no idea what the future holds for Li'l Henry and me.

Love you much,

Gwen

* * *

March 2, 1993

Dear Willie:

I'm leaving tomorrow for North Carolina. Henry has finally forgiven me. He found an apartment and has everything all ready for us to come. I know this is short notice for you, and I'm hoping you haven't mailed a letter to me yet. If you did, I probably won't get a chance to read it. Maybe I could ask my friend Sandra to let me receive mail at her house, so we can keep in contact. Babe, I hope you understand that I feel this is the best thing for Li'l Henry and me.

Take care.

With love,

Gwen

* * *

$\mathcal{C}hapter$ 3

April 15, 1993

Dear Babe:

How are you? Well, I am once again in Florida living with my sister and mother. Henry and I split up, and I'll elaborate on the details in my next letter. It will definitely be a lengthy letter, because I have plenty to tell. I want to hurry and get this letter off to you; therefore I'll make it short but sweet.

Like I said, I'm here in Florida, and you can write to this address. I have missed you so much. I'm sorry that I didn't write during my stay there. I just didn't have an opportunity to. I truly needed to try and do this the ethical way. He'd already had the fact that he found one of your letters dangling over my head; I didn't want to do anything to jeopardize his faith in me that I was trying to reestablish. I know you are an understanding man, and I know you are a patient man; so there.

What's going on in your life? What are you doing to keep yourself occupied? It has only been about a month and a half, but it seems equal to a lifetime when I'm not conversing with you.

Love you,

Gwen

* * *

April 23, 1993

Hello, Love:

It's exceptionally nice to hear from you again. To be precise, it's been exactly a month and a half. Girl, I am going to bite you whenever I see you again for not at least dropping that postcard. All is forgiven.

Now what are you doing writing me about some lengthy letter, making me anticipate receiving it? You know it's not nice to toy with father Willie. (smile)

All I've been doing besides expecting a letter from you is lifting weights. I'm trying to build up my chest somewhat. I can recall a certain young lady informing me a long time ago that I had a bird chest. I really felt offended by that, but I didn't allow it to show. That has stuck in my mind all of these years, and finally I have access to a weight room. I said, "What better time than the present?" So, in other words, you won't be able to make that judgment of me ever again.

I'm going to end now. I can't wait to hear back from you.

Love ya, Babe,

Willie

* * *

April 26, 1993

Dear Babe:

I'm beginning from when I told you to stop writing because I was going back to North Carolina. Well, when I arrived there it was fine for the first couple of days. Henry was basically excited about me seeing what he'd accomplished as far as finding a decent area to live and arranging things without my assistance. After that wore off, I imagine he didn't particularly want us there anymore.

It began with Tameka, this young 17-year-old girl. He introduced her to me, and I could tell they had a "chummy-chum" relationship. She lived in the apartment complex adjacent to ours. She became pretty close to Li'l Henry and from then on came to spend time with only him. She picked him up, brought him things, and even sat and played Nintendo with him. Two other girls from Henry's job whom he wanted me to meet, Cathy and Julie, came over. Cathy was pregnant, and I noticed that Henry couldn't keep his eyes off Julie. Two additional girls came over another night, and he introduced them to me. I can't recall their names, but they sat there for about 20 minutes and all conversed as though I wasn't in the room.

I met Jeff, his friend from next door who seemed to be a down-to-earth kind of guy. He was married and had three kids. I asked his wife about their oldest daughter babysitting Li'l Henry when

I met her, and she said yes. I was secretly getting my ducks in a row in case Henry tried that "I'm not babysitting" mess if I ever tried to go somewhere.

At first, Henry would come home and stay with Li'l Henry and me, then he started getting in from work only to change clothes, eat, and go right back out. He wouldn't come back until it was time to go to bed. This went on for a while before I said something about it. When I did, we argued, and he attempted to twist it around to make it appear to be my fault. He also hurled in my face the fact that he found your letter.

Well, Cathy and Julie came over quite a bit. Cathy, the pregnant girl, lived in the same complex as us. I kept an eye on Henry and Julie, because I just knew something was going on between them, but I kept quiet.

Remember Sandra, the friend I went to the club with when I was there before? She and I went to the club again one night, and I left Tameka there with Li'l Henry and big Henry. I tried hard to trust him, and I didn't think he would mess with a minor. There was another time I was going out, and I guess he didn't want me to, because he said that he wasn't going to care for Li'l Henry while I was out. I went right next door and asked could their oldest daughter babysit, and they said it was okay. Jeff knew what was going on between Henry and me, because he pulled me to aside and told me he didn't want to get in between anything by allowing his daughter to babysit.

I saw Jeff at the club and discovered he liked my friend Tonya, who was a girl I'd worked with at the hotel when I lived in Jacksonville before. She was a beautician, and she styled my hair sometimes. Tonya was married and had a daughter the same age as Li'l Henry. Her husband was in the Marines and was gone TDY, which is temporary duty. She did mess around on him, but she wasn't attracted to Jeff. Jeff and I became closer friends, because he was trying to get to know Tonya through me. Well anyhow, I got home about 2:00 that morning, paid the babysitter, and she left. Henry didn't get home until the next morning. From then on I started sleeping on the sofa.

One day when Jeff and I were over at Tonya's house, he said he thought I was a mischievous person. He said Henry had told him I did something outrageously detrimental to him, and that's why he treats me the way he does. Jeff said now that he's gained some insight, it appears to him that Henry was the cruel one. I told him about Henry finding your letter and you were incarcerated thousands of miles away. He told me Henry was insensitive, and he didn't particularly like the manner in which Henry handled me by allowing all of those women to come into our apartment and disrespect me in that way. "I may cheat on my wife, but I will never bring another woman to my house and disrespect her," he said. And he said if I opened my eyes I could see what was going on. At that point it really didn't matter, because I had informed Henry only a couple of days ago that I was leaving. When I told Jeff, he advised me not to go. He said, "Make that nigger go."

So I went home and told Henry I wasn't going anywhere, and do you know what he said? "Oh yes the hell you are." I was astounded. I couldn't believe he actually wanted me to go. When I first mentioned leaving and started packing my clothes, he pretended he didn't want me to go. I said, "And another thing, I don't want anymore women coming into this house disrespecting me anymore." He said I couldn't stop anybody from coming there. I could tell he was surprised I was addressing him in that manner, because you know me, forever disassociating myself with reality by tolerating his screw-ups because I'd rather not appear to be the jealous woman. I always tried to deal with situations so our marriage could work. Hell, I felt if he introduced me as his wife, what could possibly go on between him and all of those women.

So I firmly said, "Let's get one thing straight. I am the queen of this castle, and there won't be anymore women coming back in here unless I say so. If you don't believe that I mean what I say, try me."

Do you know what this fool did? He went and got Tameka and brought her back to the apartment. Just as they got inside the door I stood up, and I was nervous as hell because this character wasn't me at all, but I had to develop an attitude to show him I meant

143

business. I said, "Look, missy, you've got to go home, because I'm not permitting women in here anymore."

This girl gazed at me like "Who the hell are you to speak to me in this manner?" While staring her straight in the eye, I started walking toward her as I asked, "Did you hear what the hell I said?"

Henry jumped in between us and she said she wasn't going anywhere. I then said, "Bitch, oh yes the hell you are!"

Henry said, "She doesn't have to go anywhere."

So Henry and I began arguing, during which time she left. Henry ran after her and I ran out the door after them, yelling, "And don't bring your ass back!"

A few minutes later, Henry came in and told me that I had better apologize to her because she was crying. "I ain't apologizing to anybody, and I don't give a damn that she's crying. Who the hell does she think she is? When I say leave, I mean leave!"

Henry commanded me to get the hell out of his house, went upstairs, and seized my suitcases and threw them outside. Then, Babe, he announced to my four year old son, who had come downstairs, "You and your Mama are getting ready to go." I brought my suitcases back into the apartment and didn't utter another word, because I figured I had pushed him to his limit and I didn't want to fight and make it any uglier.

The following couple of days we dwelled in complete silence. I had decided to get an extra key for the apartment and the car, just in case he tried some moronic nonsense again. From then on I answered the door every time the bell rung. Julie came over alone one day. She stood there wearing a Michigan jogging suit that was identical to my husband's. I expressed to her very nicely, "Females are prohibited from this apartment indefinitely." She said, "Okay," like it wasn't a concern of hers, and then she left. She surprised me, because I thought I would have to tangle with her, too.

See, Henry was very "short" in the Marines. Short is a label that's given to military personnel who have little to no time left to serve. All I knew was that it was nearing his termination of service date;

and the more leave days he had accrued, the sooner he could get out. Well, he told me that he was able to get out that succeeding week. He said the movers were coming to collect the furniture to put it in storage that Saturday, and it was Friday. He also said he would purchase Li'l Henry's and my bus tickets home, put some money in my pocket for food on the way, and once I got here, he would have the furniture delivered to me, which I could have.

I fell for it. He was very convincing and seemed to be sincere. I imagine in the back of my mind I didn't desire to linger somewhere I wasn't wanted any longer. I couldn't transport everything so, I packed a sizable box of pictures and kitchen items and took it over to Tonya's house, where she said she would keep until I could send for it. Henry assured me that he would ship the remainder of my belongings, which I had packed in boxes. At the bus station he embraced my son, and we only said good-bye. I was hurt, but I didn't cry, basically because I believed he would do the right thing by me.

Love ya, Babe,

Gwen

* * *

May 7, 1993

Oh, Babe:

Wow, I can't believe he put you through all of that. My heart saturated with tears as I read that letter. To think you had high hopes of making your marriage work. I feel very much at fault, because it was my letter that he discovered in the first place that started all of this mess. I am so sorry, Baby. I feel like killing that man for hurting and disrespecting you in such a way. He can't possibly see the real you. If he could only perceive you like I do, really know and appreciate the real you, he wouldn't desire to do anything but love and make you happy. Better yet, admire and cherish your existence because you are an extraordinary woman. Does he know that you would never cheat on him? Does he know you would take care of him in every meaning of the word if he simply treated you halfway decent? Can this dude recognize what kind of treasure he is messing over? Any man would be honored to have a woman like you standing by his side. He's a fool!

You'll be all right, though, Babe because I know you are a strong woman with a lot of determination, and you can build your own destiny. You can! Just believe in yourself, and you can achieve happiness beyond your wildest dreams.

I would like to question you about some of the things that he promised, if you don't mind? Did he send the furniture? Is he going to be a man and play his role in the care of his son? Shoot, I can't think of a doggone thing else to say, but I love you.

Love,

Willie

* * *

May 11, 1993

Dear Willie:

To answer your questions, he did not come through with anything he'd promised. I left so unexpectedly that I didn't get a chance to inform Sandra. Since I've been here, I've called her to let her know what happened and to give her my telephone number. She told me she went over there one day looking for me, and he was sitting there in a house full of furniture, completely intact. She said it appeared to her he wasn't going anywhere, anytime soon. As far as child support is concerned, he assured me he would help out, but I seriously doubt it.

So much for that. Guess what? I've found a job! I had only been here a little over a week when I found it. I'm good, aren't I? I work for a pharmaceutical establishment through this temporary agency. It pays $5 an hour, and that's rather good, considering that the most I've earned an hour, excluding the military, was $4.60. When I started, they were working 10-hour days, Monday through Friday, and eight hours on Saturday. Overtime galore! This week, we are working 12 hours a day. I've always been a workaholic, anyway. I'm going to save some money to buy a car, and then I'll be on my way to a brand-new start. I knew I could make it on my own, and I'm glad Henry made it possible for me to find out.

I've registered my son in a daycare right across the street. It's pleasant and decent, and they'll prepare him for kindergarten. He'll start kindergarten next year, and this will give him an advantage. My sister Charlene or mother picks up Li'l Henry, because I work until 5:30 PM on 10-hour days and 7:30 PM on 12. I suspect they are trying to help me out as much as they can, because they have sympathy for me. They don't have to feel sorry for me, because, although I felt pretty gloomy at first, things are much better now. I just want to get on with my life.

So let's talk about you, okay? Have you received any visits lately? You've got to be doing something else beside lifting weights. You know what, Babe? I love you. It is, in fact, possible to love two men at the same time. I am living proof of that. I suppose I need to narrow that down a smidgen, huh? What do you think? (ha, ha!)

Love,

Gwen

* * *

May 16, 1993

Dear Sweetheart:

How are you doing, working girl? See, I told you all it takes is a little determination and you can progress. That's my Baby!

Me, I'm just hanging in there trying to generate a good thing out of a bad situation. Sometimes I honestly cannot believe I'm in here. It's like a bad dream that I will wake up from one day. I have never done anything felonious in my entire life. I've perpetually lived life honest and to the fullest. I've always had aspirations of getting ahead, and I was on my way until this happened. Had I not been in the position I was in financially, I don't know what I would have done as far as paying lawyer fees. I will get through this, though, especially with my Baby by my side. I visualize the day when I walk out of here. Perhaps I'm being self-centered, but I am hoping you'll be there to welcome me. Jointly we can demonstrate to society just how this relationship business is supposed to function. (smile)

Guess what happened to me the other day? I walked into the recreation room and overhead two inmates talking about selling phone time. I heard the word "telephone" and instantly became inquisitive. I stepped up to them and asked, "How can I get in on this telephone deal?"

This is the deal: We pay $5 per call up to one hour. No gimmicks. It's a three-way deal where someone calls the number for you. They sat their telephone down while you talk. I suppose they're not eavesdropping, and if they are, who cares, they don't know us. I didn't ask any questions, because I absolutely crave to hear my Baby's voice. Please send your telephone number so I can call you this week, okay?

In response to your question, I have not had a visit since I can remember.

All my love,

Willie

P.S. What's your job description?

* * *

June 2, 1993

Dear Love:

Listen, Babe, I haven't written in a couple of weeks, but as you know I've been putting in a lot of hours. They've placed me on this assembly line that's known as the Money-Line. When everyone leaves for the day, the Money-Line is continuously working. This company has developed a mouthwash, which is a product they have never packaged before. By the way, the nature of this business is to package pharmaceutical products. We fold the miniature containers and insert the directions and mouthwash as the box travels down the production line. A machine then affixes a product code and expiration date. The person at the end of the production line is responsible for packing the finished product into larger boxes for shipping. I really like this job. It's interesting, I stay busy and I get plenty of overtime. Anyhow, the line I work on runs as late as 8:00, 9:00, and even 10:00 PM. One night we worked until 1:30 AM and still had to come back the following day at 7:30 AM. We have deadlines that we must meet daily with the mouthwash. A number of things could and have gone wrong that consume time. Sometimes the machine malfunctions, and they have to send us to another line until it's repaired. Regardless of what happens that causes delays, a specified quantity of mouthwash has to be packaged daily.

I'm happy that you are hanging in there. You are right in saying that shortly this separation will be behind us, and my intention is to be there waiting for my Baby when he gets out. When I thought about leaving Henry this time, I considered moving back to Michigan. I contemplated long and hard, because I really would enjoy living near you again. I haven't seen you in such a long time, and I do need my "fix." Actually, being near you would be the only good thing about moving back to Michigan. There's no one I would want to live with, no jobs, and no cars available to look for employment. My mother is here, and I felt that I had more of a fighting chance at making it in Florida. She's leaving for Louisiana next month, but she's making sure my transportation is straight before she goes.

You and I will be united one day, because it feels good and it feels right this time—unlike before, when we would develop animosity, not speak to one another for prolonged intervals, and act immature by not surrendering to one another's feelings. We are so much more than that now. We are able to voice our feelings for each other much better. There is no shame in our game, and I know we were meant to be together—I just know it.

I'm going to end on that note, and I hope to talk to you soon.

I love you, Baby,

Gwen

* * *

June 10, 1993

Hey Babe:

I'm glad I wrote this letter following our telephone conversation.

Every time I try to write prior to speaking with you, I invariably tell you on the telephone what I've already mentioned in the letter. It was so nice to hear your voice again. You still sound very sexy over the phone. It forces me to envision the body from which the voice comes from. I long for your visits. When am I ever going to see you again is indeed the question that's up in the air for us. If you were here, it would only take 20 minutes to drive to this prison. They've transferred me to St. Louis, the location that you've passed several times while driving to visit in Ionia.

My sister came to visit, and guess who she brought along with her? My two babies! I was so happy to see my girls. I hadn't seen them in almost a year. Cynthia, my youngest, was so happy to see me, because she just laid on my lap and wouldn't get up for anything. Oh no, I'd better rephrase that. She got up to get candy and chips. When she first walked in, she commanded, "You come home with me right now!" Cathy, my middle child, asked some powerful questions. That girl is very smart, and she doesn't beat around the bush. We reminisced about this card I sent Cynthia that I, at the time, thought was cute. Cathy said she had to put it away, because Cynthia would always cry when she read it. The card read, "Me Miss You," with a picture of a clown and his dog on the cover. The inside read, "Darn, I Miss You A Lot," with the clown and his dog crying big crocodile tears. When she shared that with me, I almost started to cry. I thought to myself, I'd better not send anything like that to them again. They just love me so much.

Well, I can honestly sleep soundly tonight, because I've gotten an opportunity to hear my Baby's voice and see my kids all in the same week. It was a weekend full of people I love. I've been truly blessed.

Love ya,

Willie

* * *

June 19, 1993

Dear Sweetheart:

You know what, Babe? Whenever I hear your voice, my heart

commences to fluttering in this peculiar way. It's like I can hardly breathe, but it feels good. You always have the sweetest things to say to me. You really make me feel special. What would I ever do without you in my life? I felt so good about talking to you the other night that as soon as I hung up, I was in a daze, during which I felt isolated because I couldn't be there with you or you with me. I know you can relate to it, because I could feel it in your voice.

I am so pleased that you got a chance to see your kids. I know how much you've missed them. I'll call your sister and thank her personally for bringing you some happiness. I love you.

I have some good news, too. I purchased a car yesterday. It's a Honda Civic '85, white with blue interior. My car payment is only $110 biweekly. I purchased it at a "Buy Here, Pay Here" car dealership. I'm happy that someone took a chance with my bad credit. I drove to work for the first time today. It was nice getting to sleep an additional hour, because I didn't have to catch that darn bus. It seem as though it takes longer to drive home than it ordinarily takes when I'm traveling by bus.

Well, got to go.

Love you forever,

Gwen

P.S. Here's a photograph of me that I would like you to have.

* * *

July 1, 1993

Hi, My Love:

I trust you are doing fine and maintaining good health. Well, well, well, so you've obtained that car? You go ahead on with your bad self. I'm very happy to hear that. I have a question, though. If it takes longer to get home driving, why not continue taking the bus?

Hey, Babe, here is a picture of me as the King of the Throne. Yes, that's right, me! There were a number of guys who could lift more weight than I could, but pound for pound, I'm The Man.

The event in the picture took place on Memorial Day. It took a lot of chin-ups for me to prevail, because there were over 100 people enrolled. Initially, I completed 28 chin-ups. I thought I'd won after all those guys put forth their best efforts and couldn't match my score, but the man standing beside me in the picture did. Then we had to compete again. I completed 35 but only received credit for 28 again. I was furious, because I felt all my chin-ups were done correctly. He matched my score yet a second time. This went on until I became fed up. I asked a Recreation Director to oversee. He flipped a coin and I won, so my opponent had to go first. This time he could only complete 15. I completed 16 and proceeded on until the guy who ran the event declared me the winner. I thought he was a tough competitor, but I discovered later that the mediator was my competitor's bunkie. I'd wondered why my competitor received credit for all of his chin-ups when I didn't. They attempted to cheat, but they couldn't defeat The Man. I took second place in a few other events.

With love,

Willie

* * *

July 2, 1993

Dear Willie:

I have to ask you to stop calling until I get in touch with you again. I'll let you know why when I write again. I'm so sorry.

Gwen

* * *

Chapter 9

September 7, 1993

Dear Willie:

I haven't written in a while, as you well know. I suppose I concluded that when you read my last letter, you didn't particularly wish to have anything to do with me. I thought that I'd provided an adequate amount of time for you to sort out your thoughts. I needed time to get my thoughts together, as well.

Babe, I realize I hold the key to whether we communicate or not. It is so inconsiderate of me to place you on a rollercoaster ride whenever the course fluctuates in my life. I decided to take a different path other than what we've discussed. I felt so guilty about my decision, I chose to ignore my feelings for you and terminate our communication. In other words, instead of confessing to you about newly made decisions, I just stopped writing. I'm sorry for being a chicken.

I think my head is back on straight once again, and I want to inquire about your lack of writing as well. Was it because of the letter that I sent? I know you have called numerous times, and I'm awfully sorry that I missed you, but I couldn't talk to you.

Here's a photograph of me that I took when my aunt, sister, and I were going to the club. I hope you like it. Babe, please write back, so I'll know what to say to you. I am really at a loss for words, because I don't know how you are thinking or feeling these days.

I love you,

Gwen

* * *

October 12, 1993

What's up:

It is good to hear from you. I must say I really have missed the beautiful letters that you write. As you can see, I have relocated, and it was not for a good reason. I busted this guy's head open with a book. They gave me an assault and battery ticket, and raised me to a level two again. The higher your level determines the duration of your stay. For instance, the inmates who are at level five have at least three years left to serve. We are also separated by levels, and that's the reason I had to move to another facility. It's very simple to get here, just East on 13 and South to 57. It takes about 45 minutes.

As you can also see, my pen does not want to write, because it has not been used in so long. I enjoyed the picture you sent. It made me yearn to kiss those juicy lips, and my mouth started watering. I'd better shut my mouth concerning that before I commence dribbling on the paper.

Like I said, I got your letter, but you didn't go into detail about the reason why I couldn't call you anymore, and that's why I didn't write. It messed my head up the way your sister "checked me" (set me straight) about calling there when I knew you weren't at home. I was hoping she would accept the charges so I could give her my sister's address, because I gave you the wrong one. Please let her know the reason why I called so many times and also tell her not to "check me" in that manner again. (frown) I must admit, she had me speechless. Then she hung up the phone in my face, so then I was astounded. Shortly afterward, I called my sister, and she conveyed to me that you had called and asked her to tell me not to call you until you inform me otherwise. It is taking a lot out of me right now to refrain from calling to hear your lovely voice. I especially felt bad when I called there before and a man answered the phone. I thought it was Henry. Was it him? If it was, I hope I didn't incite any problems. The man said he was going to pick you up at 7:00.

So what was the reason I haven't heard from you in so long? It rips a tiny piece of my heart every time you do that to me. I need to understand the basis for this "don't call me, I'll call you" nonsense. I find myself wanting to get angry when I can't talk to you, but then I realize you stuck it out with me longer than I with you during your Army basic training days. I can say on my behalf that I was unaware of your feelings for me then. I felt you had a man and I was a convenience. What can you state in your defense now?

This place is all right, I suppose. They have two men rooms which are exceptionally nice. Unfortunately, I've acquired a bunkie who I can't get along with. I am trying to move to another room. I don't like being in this predicament, because it makes me feel like I'm running from him or something.

There's a guy here who said he went to school with you. His girlfriend drives up twice a week, so if you ever come to town she can give you a ride here to visit. Well, I am going to close this letter until the next time. I hope to hear from you soon and with an explanation of why you stopped writing. I deserve at least that.

Love you, Babe,

Willie

P.S. Make sure you tell your son three times a day that you love him.

P.P.S. Can I call? (frown) I miss you.

P.P.P.S. What letter are you talking about?

* * *

October 19, 1993

It's me again:

This letter is simply the way I really feel. I want you to know what I'm thinking. I can't believe the stuff that you tolerate and why you continue going back to it. It is beyond me. What does it take for you to comprehend that you are being abused? That punk is messing with your head. If you don't wake up and smell the coffee, you are going to expect every man in your life to treat you in this manner. That punk is a flat out whore. I don't get it; does he have a mojo (spell) on you that yanks you back to him whenever you've developed an attitude of self-reliance?

Now I understand your sister's concern about the probability of you just upping and deserting her. This stuff you keep pulling is messing up my head. That punk hasn't done anything for you except make you look like a fool: I can condone his actions, because if you go for it then he hasn't done anything wrong. I'm surprised he hasn't sexed one of his whores right in your face. Dig this here: You must defend yourself at all costs, at all times. Forget that mess! Endlessly allowing his actions to proceed can only cause you more pain. A person will snatch and seize until you put an end to it, so stop his shit from the beginning, right now!

Now, that bullshit about him mistreating you because you've done an injustice. If that wrongdoing was communicating with me, then he is a chauvinistic pig. He claims he forgives you and wants you back but then messes over you because of it. He's a punk. As if that m-----f----- has never spoken to a lady who you ordered him not to talk to. Hell, for that matter, he's probably taken quite a few to bed. I bet you shit to gold he isn't exercising other methods like me such, as masturbating. It's not as though I don't have a chance in here—I can do some of these boys if I wanted to, but I'm a man and that's beneath me. Just because you talked to me, he wants to treat you like shit. You ain't shit! You've only talked to me; that's all. We're not fucking!

If you go back to him and tolerate that drunken bullshit again, you are a goddamn fool. You can do badly all by yourself. In other words, if you're going to barely make ends meet, why not do it alone? Always remember, God blesses the child who's got it's own. So, get your own and stop trying to find someone to take care of you. Be a woman of the '90s and do what you got to do.

Shit! I have tried to tell you that nicely for the longest time. Fuck that punk. The reason he doesn't want to save any money is because he's a trick. By saying that I mean Henry is definitely paying for some booty. Those women out there are milking his ass dry like they are supposed to do. I suppose you sympathize with him and don't want to take advantage. Hello! If you don't get his money, someone else will. Remember that time when you were going to give me something and you said, "I have his money." Wake up, that's why you pay all the bills, because he is giving his to those ladies, buying drinks all fucking night. Your mother didn't raise any fool, so I hope you have finally come to your senses and are finished with that drunken punk. If you need a man in your life, please utilize your ability to choose your husband's opposite. He means you no good. You've witnessed how he will lie to you at the drop of a hat.

I think you should be friends, and that's for your son's benefit. Hey, if you want sex, then sex yourself as I do. I must confess that it feels good, too. If you want, I could coach you through it over the phone. You can do badly all by yourself. Don't be his sucker anymore. I'm only telling you this because I love you. Keep that punk out of your life. He means you no good.

You know what I thought to myself after my sister informed me not to call you anymore? That punk's got her full of hope again. I wonder what he lied about and promised her this time. I want to know why the hell I haven't heard from you in so long, too.

Signed: Fucked up in the head

* * *

July 13, 1993 – first time mailed
October 17, 1993 – second time mailed

Dear Willie:

How are you? I'm not starting this letter off by apologizing, because we both know I'm wrong for not writing in all this time. I'm just going to explain what has happened since the last time I talked to you on the telephone. When we last talked, I was to leave for Michigan that following morning for my 10-year class reunion. I didn't tell you because I'd decided to come and surprise you. As it turned out, I'm glad I didn't tell you after all, because you would have anticipated seeing me and I would have disappointed you.

Henry was supposed to pick up Li'l Henry and me to drive us to Saginaw. He didn't come to pick us up like he promised. My sister Pam informed me that he was already there in Saginaw, so I telephoned his house and had words with him about it. He finally said there was money in the bank that I could get to catch a flight home. I thought he was lying at first, but after calling I found it to be true. I had $500 wired to me, then called the airlines to make Henry and my reservations. They quoted a $470 round-trip apiece. So I decided to service my car and drive myself.

When I got the oil change and tune-up, I was informed that the cylinders on the back brakes were leaking and I needed four new tires. Remember when I told you that guy looked at my brakes when they were squeaking and couldn't find anything wrong? I knew something was wrong because brakes just don't squeak for no apparent reason. I got the brakes fixed, which cost $140, two new tires, and one used since they didn't have two in stock that fit my car. I also got the air conditioner serviced. After paying for all of the repairs, I had only $120 left to travel with. I was so determined to see you that I was going regardless of what I had in my pocket. I knew it wasn't sufficient enough to travel so far away, but I kept in mind that I would have help with gas once I picked up Shala, our class president, who had asked to ride with me.

Li'l Henry and I made it to Atlanta, and it took nearly seven-and-a-half hours. We picked up Shala and her daughter and made it to Knoxville when the car overheated. I hadn't a clue how long the needle had been in the red, but I noticed it when Shala was driving. We stopped at a gas station, and a nice man gave us directions to Western Auto, where we could purchase a thermostat, which was what he thought I needed. He poured water on the engine, attempting to cool it down quicker, but in turn drenched the spark plugs. We had to wait until they dried before the car would start.

The car finally started and we drove to Western Auto, only to discover they didn't fix thermostats. They directed us to the Texaco station next door. The man there said the thermostat wasn't the problem at all. He said it was the engine head, and he couldn't tell whether it was blown or cracked but definitely one of the two. We didn't believe him and asked him to put the thermostat on anyway, which he did at no charge. We got as far as around the block and the car overheated again. We decided to spend the night in Tennessee, so we got a hotel room down the street. Shala telephoned a couple of our classmates who she knew were leaving for Saginaw the next morning and asked them to swing by and pick us up on the way. The following morning they came and collected us, I dropped my car off at the Texaco station, and we left. They were driving two cars, so there was plenty of room.

When I arrived at Saginaw, I had only $20 left in my pocket. Nobody had any money to loan. Diane's boyfriend was the only one who owned a car. Loaning it to me was out the question, but she promised to drive me to my class reunion get-together that

Friday night. What I was really concerned about was how I was going to get to see you.

Henry took the buy-out that the military was offering soldiers to get out of the Marines early. He bought this Cadillac with his severance pay, and he thought he was The Man. He took me to all three events, but I only allowed him to drop me off and pick me up because I didn't want him escorting me as if we were a couple. It worked out as intended as far as the "get acquainted night" and the dinner went, but I mellowed out before the picnic that Sunday and invited him to come along. His benevolence clouded my better judgment.

He really took care of me during my stay in Saginaw, and that is no joke. For once I can honestly say I relied on him and he came through. Anyhow, I was to remain there until Wednesday, which was when the man could look at my car to ascertain his supposition. He said he would call my sister's house to forewarn me of the debt I was soon to be in.

In the meantime, I continued contemplating how I could get to you. I thought to myself, I should have informed you of my plans, and then maybe you could have made arrangements for me to come. My aunt Grace was the only other person who had a reliable vehicle. My cousins usually transported her to work in arrangement to keep her car. I asked their opinion to the chances of my aunt allowing me to use her car to visit you. They explained how fastidious she was about her car as far as unnecessary mileage went. They were well aware that it was merely a 20-minute drive to St. Louis, but I suppose that was quite remote to someone who was patrolling her odometer. So I concluded that attempting to go without her knowledge, which was my second option, was out of the question.

Babe, I was disappointed I didn't get a chance to see you, the most important reason I came. I'm sorry things didn't work out as planned. I spent most of my time with Henry after he promised to drive us back to Tampa. We left that Saturday, a whole week later, and the car still wasn't ready. I had to return to work that following Monday so I couldn't wait. Before we left, Henry had problems withdrawing money from the ATM machine.

This is the "tripped out" part, so listen to me closely. When I withdrew the money from Henry's account prior to leaving, he had $1,000 available, from which I took half. When we were in Saginaw, he withdrew $100 several times that totaled well over $500. When I questioned him, he claimed he had opened a new checking account right before he left. This conniver was forever trying to be mysterious when it concerned his money. In order to prove he was telling the truth, the last time he withdrew money, he gave me the receipt that displayed well over $600 remaining. So, at this point I began to believe him, because I remember leaving only $500 in there and after his many withdrawals, he still had over $600 in the bank. I thought to myself, Maybe he really did have a checking account that I didn't know about.

So, listen to this. The bank stopped allowing him to withdraw money for some reason. He called the bank and requested a wire of $300, but they only sent $200. He still had me on board at this point, especially after he told me the computers were down and they couldn't monitor the money. He had to borrow money from his father in order to drive us back and told me he would pay it back as soon as he had access to his account. Might I add, he deceitfully continued his efforts to withdraw money after that.

On the way home, we stopped and checked on my car. He was curious as to what kind of car I was capable of obtaining without his assistance. After seeing that it was fairly acceptable, he tried to belittle my self-assurance by asserting that the car was once in a wreck because the paint on the front end wasn't smooth, which I believed could have been true. I just looked at him and said, "So?" When he had big bucks, he promised to pay for the repairs, but I knew I had to throw that promise out the window. Besides, the car wasn't ready.

When we arrived here in Florida, he still couldn't withdraw any money out of the bank. I was growing suspicious at this time. "There's no way in hell a bank can deny your own money for this prolonged amount of time, I thought. What was funny was I couldn't even verify it with the bank, because I didn't have a red cent to call from work and I couldn't charge it to my number because Charlene had that hold on the phone. Because my work hours were the same as the bank's, I couldn't call after I got off, either.

Finally, I got my chance to call and just as I suspected, he didn't have any money in the bank. He cleverly traveled all the way down here knowing good and well he didn't have one red cent. He claimed a job awaited him in Jacksonville, which I knew was also a lie because he would have very well made provisions to get there and he did not.

So he cunningly entered into my life again; such a clever scheme for a man with little to no intellect to place me in. If I wanted him to leave, I had to provide the funds to do so. Of course, I wouldn't kick him out, especially after he went out of his way to drive us back. I was content in knowing I had transportation to and from work, which made the whole ordeal somewhat tolerable. There I was depending on his butt once again.

There were many times I'd asked him to leave. I made sure he understood that love was not an element in our relationship anymore, and I would never forgive him for what he did in Jacksonville when I was there last. He would act remorseful, and I would sympathize with him. The reality was he had nowhere else to go, and although revenge is bittersweet, I didn't think I could ever live with myself if I threw him out into the street. So I let him stay until I quit my job and needed him there. I'll write another time and elaborate on that.

Lately, we can't get along. When we arrived here in Tampa, your picture was on a stand in the living room. That was the first thing he noticed. I didn't care, and I didn't see a reason to remove it. It remained there for nearly a week before Charlene took the liberty of taking it down. She was fed up with us arguing about it. He discovered another letter of yours, and I told him he shouldn't have pried his nose where it didn't belong. Basically, he was only hurting himself by doing so. See, Babe, I had an "I don't give a damn" attitude. I would listen to your messages on the answering machine in his presence. Why did you continuously call like that? Didn't you get my letter? I also asked your sister to tell you not to call until I got in touch with you to let you know what was up. I just engrossed myself in trying to find employment. I didn't write you in his presence because I thought I should at least give him that respect in reciprocation for what I would expect from him.

Charlene, Henry, and I were all paying one-third of the bills, which made it financially affordable to live. I didn't want to create problems that would ruin our arrangement. Now I'm at the point where I don't care whether he leaves or stays. I want to be able to do what I want, when I want, and how I want. If you decide to write back, why shouldn't I accept a letter from you? That's what I would want. If he leaves because of it, then I shouldn't give a darn. Maybe it's not fitting because he is my husband, but we're not together and we just cannot get along. There's no logic in me living unhappy or trying to conceal my one and only true love because Henry is residing here as well. It's probably better for him to go ahead and leave, so I can continue building my self-reliance.

By the way, this is the second time I've sent this letter to you. I mailed it shortly after I returned from Michigan, and I'm assuming it was returned because you'd relocated and I didn't write your inmate number on the envelope. Upon getting it back, I've updated it to give you a broader insight of what went on.

No matter how much you inspire me, that man invariably rips my self-esteem to shreds. I feel like I'm unsuitable for him or beneath his standards. He makes me feel like every woman in the world is his choice and I'm second best or someone he just settles for. I know this seems like an attempt to rekindle what you and I shared because my reunion with Henry has failed. It's not like that, although it does appear to be such. I knew we were doomed after his ruthless treatment of me in Jacksonville, and if he didn't care then, he couldn't possibly care now.

After we got here, Henry would linger at the pool, and he met a number of friends, one being a girl name Roxanne. I was unaware of it until she came over here asking for him one day. Charlene was the one who answered the door and informed her that I was his wife. See, Charlene already knew what was going on, and she "checked" Henry about it. She didn't reveal it to me at that time, because she figured she successfully handled it without my knowledge. Roxanne announced that she was unaware that he was married, and she left. I was sitting there listening to all of this. Although we were not together as man and wife, I felt it was disrespectful and I had to say something. So that was the first time I asked him to get out. I never heard him beg before, but he pleaded that time and of course I gave in. What I'm trying to convey to you is I didn't write you after this letter that I'm sending for the second time. I didn't want to render evil for evil. I didn't want to disrespect him merely because he wasn't respecting me. In my mind it just wasn't right.

Willie, if you don't write back I won't blame you, because I broke my promise to never stop writing without an explanation. It certainly appears as though I'm toying with you, but Baby, please don't think that. Even though I've procrastinated about keeping in touch as I'd promised, I've consistently thought about you. Don't ever doubt that. You will always be someone special to me. Nobody can stimulate my emotions as you do, and no one can be my companion as well as you can. You listen to and understand me at times when nobody else does. We are so compatible that it's a shame we can't be together. I keep doing things to mess up our relationship that I know I wouldn't do if you were here with me. You've got to believe that. Henry even asked, "You love that man, don't you?" Even he can see it, but I didn't answer and just looked at him in a weird way. Every time he insinuates anything that concerns you, I agree. For instance, the other day, he said, "Oh, Willie makes me feel special," impersonating my letter to you. I responded, "He sure does." When it comes to you, I've begun voicing what I truly feel without remorse.

Now that you understand what has happened, you can determine the character you wish to play in this cast. I love you and that will never change, yet I also respect you to be the man you know how to be, regardless of whatever situation you may be placed in right now. Think about this please. Write back if you want, but I wish you would. I will write again soon.

I wish I could stick $5 or $10 in this letter but that's impossible. They charged $470 to repair the car, and I don't have that right now. When I had it I lost my job, so I lived off of it. I haven't even paid a car note since my return from Michigan. Presently I'm not doing very well, but it's only temporary. Henry is employed and is paying my portion of the bills, so it's working out. I'll find a job soon, and this time I'll make my promises my priorities.

I'll talk to you soon.

Love,

Gwen

* * *

Chapter 5

October 21, 1993

Dear Willie:

Hello, Hon, what's going on? Did I tell you lately how much I love you? Well, I do and with a passion at that.

Well, I promised I would write and tell you about the incident with my job. When I returned from Michigan, I discovered that some temporary workers were hired on as permanent full-time employees. They bypassed me and hired workers whose start dates were after mine. I was justifiably upset, yet I tried to pretend it didn't bother me. When the supervisor approached me with her personal feelings about the matter, I became disturbed. She felt it was unfair that they didn't hire me. She expressed how reliable I was, never missing days and working all of those late hours on the Money-Line. She was upset, and I could see it in her expression. At that moment, I felt the sobs form in my throat and my eyes began to water. Babe, I really enjoyed working there, and I felt they would hire me once an opening was available.

Well, I left the line to go the bathroom, because it was becoming difficult to hold back the tears. After a "composure adjustment," I decided to address the head supervisor. I walked in and explained everything to him. How I especially desired to work there permanently, how I'd never missed a day, and how I always worked as late as they needed me to. I proclaimed that I was the first temporary worker employed there, and I had worked there over three months. I also mentioned the test that everyone including the temps were required to take and reminded him of how I was the one who excelled with a 100% score. Even some of the permanent workers didn't score that high. Babe, I could barely speak, because I was trying to contain the sobs in my throat that I knew he could hear in my voice.

This man listened quietly as I babbled on, and then do you know what he said? He said, "We are not obligated to hire any of the temporary workers. We allowed you to take a week off to attend your class reunion and we held your position. We didn't have to do that." So, in other words, he didn't give a darn about what I've contributed to the company as an individual. He then clarified that he wasn't punishing me for attending my class reunion, because he wouldn't have missed his for the world. I didn't want to hear that shallow mess, so I just thanked him for his time and walked out.

I worked on the line for approximately 30 minutes more as I continued trying to contain those darn tears and justify continuing on there. When I couldn't endure it any longer, I walked off the line into the locker room, took off my hair net and lab coat, and marched the hell out of there without informing a soul. I've never quit a job before, and I didn't want to abandon that one, but I felt there was no way I could continue working a job everyday knowing in the back of my mind they refused to hire me for whatever reason, I don't know. I sort of felt it was a "black thing."

I was so upset that when I arrived home, I couldn't remove the key from the ignition. I was driving Henry's car and I just left it parked with the keys inside. Henry informed me afterward that I forgot to place the gear shaft in Park, which was why the key wouldn't disengage. After I shared my story, Henry said, "Don't worry about it. You don't have to tolerate that mess from anybody. I'll take care of you." I wonder why I couldn't get support like that from him when we were together.

Until next time.

With love,

Gwen

P.S. I'm sending you a $50 check because I left that money order that your sister sent in the car in Tennessee.

* * *

October 25, 1993

Dear Willie:

I'm going to begin this letter with this poem I wrote, and then I'm going to disclose the actual story.

The Mistake I Made
I made a mistake yesterday, I hurt someone I love
I know no matter what I say, I cannot rise above
The constant put up, let down, I always seem to give
The love and understanding you always seem to feel
This time I know that I'm wrong, wrong, wrong
And the love you feel is gone, gone, gone
I cut the communication wire which was the only closeness we had
I had to make a choice and I know now I chose bad
I gave up the one I cared about for the one I thought I needed
Now I need not, that's no doubt, my fears I have defeated
The blame upon myself, the bed I now shall lay
I'll carry to my death, the mistake I made yesterday
So Sweetheart, if I may, still call you this today
I'm sorry, oh so sorry, for my loss, I know I'll pay

I love you. Please forgive me for concealing the complete truth and what I'm about to reveal to you. I neglected to reveal to you that at some time between Henry's arrival and his departure, we indeed tried to make it work once again. I couldn't tell you because I didn't want it to appear as though I was switching back and forth between the two of you. I suppose I simply didn't want to hurt you, and I wanted my cake and to eat it, too.

The true story is that we were living here as man and wife. After a while it just resulted as such. I don't understand why I continuously grant second chances when he messes over me every time. I suppose I can't deny that I love him just that much to continue trying. I realize now that he only treats me with respect when he wants something in return. I'm so gullible that I fall for it every time.

He is presently living across the street with Roxanne, the girl he was cheating on me with. It is extremely difficult for me to handle this situation but more so to tell you. I don't want you to be in the dark about anything in my life anymore, so I will tell you the whole story regardless of the consequences.

You know how I take a lot of Henry's mess, right? Well, one day Henry informed me of plans to go to North Carolina for the weekend to get our furniture. He had driven down there once before on the weekend. I had asked him to bring my clothes and pictures that I had packed when I left him and that he promised to send but never did. I asked for the microwave oven, too, but he only brought the TV. He worked for a moving company and supposedly had access to the trucks after hours. I was hoping he would bring my things this time. He stayed the entire weekend and returned empty-handed. I questioned him, and he lied and said he had to leave our furniture in his job's storage area here in Tampa

He left his wallet at home one day and went to the pool. He was always at that pool, and I knew he was there with Roxanne, but I never checked on him. You do know how it's better to avoid looking for trouble or you just might find it, right? Well, I searched his wallet, looking for a storage ticket or anything that would substantiate that the furniture was in Tampa. As I searched, I feared he might walk in and catch me but I continued to look. I didn't locate a storage ticket, but I found four women's telephone numbers, including Roxanne's home and work numbers. I also found the receipt for my microwave that he pawned way before he even relocated to Florida. So I packed everything back inside his wallet and didn't utter a word about it. We were constantly arguing about Roxanne ever since she came to the house that day. He assured me nothing was going on between them; a likely story.

One day he said he was going to sit at the pool with a friend, and I instructed that if Roxanne came, he had better leave. He said, "Okay." I had no intentions of going to that pool, but I needed the keys to drive to the store and Henry had them. I walked to the pool; lo and behold, there they were, Henry, Henry's friend Fred, and Roxanne all sitting together at a table. When I spotted them, I stopped at a distance. "Henry, come here right now," I commanded in my nastiest tone. Instantly I realized how mean I must have sounded, so I corrected myself and said it again. This time I said "please" afterward.

If he would have come, I imagine I would have dismissed it all, but he tried to play hardball and responded, "You come to me; you are the one who wants me." I was so embarrassed, because by now we had the attention of the other people who were at the pool. Before I knew it I had screamed, "You're getting the hell out of my apartment, motherfucker!" I then went back to the apartment and started hurling his clothes out the front door. He did not follow me home but stayed at the pool the entire time I was throwing out his clothes. Later he attempted to enter the apartment using his key, but I place the deadbolt lock on the door. He picked up his clothes, came the next day to delivered his key, and left without saying anything.

Babe, after that I drifted into total depression, because I could not believe he didn't fight for me. For two days I couldn't sleep or eat, and I cried nonstop. I began praying to God to remove me from that condition, and I truly believe He was responsible for hindering my thoughts of extreme measures. I'd never experienced that state of mind before, and I don't ever want to encounter it again. As God is my witness, I will never permit that man back into my life.

I'll talk to you soon.

Love,

Gwen

* * *

October 29, 1993

Hey, hey:

You're messing up now. I'm getting too many letters here. I'm going to get spoiled in a minute. No, I'm just kidding, because hearing from you brings pure jubilation to my heart. You have nothing to be remorseful about, Babe. I know what type of person you are; how easy it is for you to forgive. I can also understand why you feel the compulsion to continue your attempt of reconstructing your marriage. It helps me to appreciate your determination to succeed, but in the end, I'm happy you made the right decision. I really loved that poem, too.

I hope you are doing fine and maintaining good health. It really hurts me to hear that you lost your job and were depending on him again. I really feel bad about sending that letter to you now that I know he was providing for you. I worry about you excessively when he's around and to hear that you revealed your feelings for me to him made me nervous. Were you entering into the "crazy zone" or what? I must admit I got a kick out of you telling him how you felt so candidly. I really think you deserve to be happy. I know you can be if you just search within yourself, because I see beauty that's locked inside of you.

That man was abusing you, and I don't think he even knew how he was sabotaging your mind. The physical part has ended, but the mental part still preserves scars that will only be observed by you, and only you can allow them to heal. I think you are beginning in the right direction. Don't ever go back to him, because he will never treat you the way you need to be treated. Even if he won 50 million dollars, he will continue his disrespectful treatment of you. I want you to understand that money isn't everything. That's why a number of ladies marry men who are rich and later divorce, because they discover their happiness means more than the money.

I'm glad that I am now the one who you compare everyone to. The things I do and say to you should be a basic standard for you to uphold for any man you allow into your life. You stated something to the effect that just because he displayed disrespect, it was not a basis for you to emulate his actions, and I presumed you were speaking in reference to corresponding with me. That is all a fragment of his abuse. There could never be anything wicked about you writing to me, because it makes you happy and feel good. We are only friends, although we both wish it could be much more. Still, now, that's all it is. I want to be the best friend that there could be for you. All of this time you have tolerated his girlfriends and you can't have a man friend, yet when you get one you have done something bad or dirty? That guy has more tricks up his sleeves than a barrel of monkeys. He will make you a promise in a second, knowing he can't fulfill it, because he knows you trust him.

I must say that I am a changed man, because just like last time I would have said, "Well, I give up." Now, I am much stronger and can deal with situations like a man. So don't think I'm naïve, because I'm not. I just can understand things much better. I know I'm not in a position to support you, so I don't pretend as such. I must not tell a lie, it seemed as though you only involved yourself with me when things were going poorly between you and Henry. I know that's not the way it is, though. I must say that this has helped me to figure out some things about you that might be beneficial to us in the future, if we are to have a one.

So that's the reason you stopped writing? How many times do I have to tell you that you don't have to write lengthy letters to me? I have tried to tell you how to prevent him from finding your letters by obtaining a post office box, or by purchasing a postcard to send to me when you go to the store. You just don't know how much that would have meant to me. It would have affirmed that you thought enough to say hi.

I hope you find a job soon so you can maintain your car and your bills. I really enjoyed your letter about how hard you worked to get to see me. You came so far yet, fell so short. That was so touching. It made me feel so special when I read it. It's a shame that nobody would loan their car, and your aunt was full of it talking about the miles being a problem. I suppose it was a nice way to say no. Babe, I sure would have been surprised to see you, too, with your sexy butt. I think I would have kissed your pretty little nose. Hey,

I haven't seen you in over a year. Isn't that something? It's been a long time since I've tasted those sweet lips.

Take care and be happy.

Love, Willie

P.S. I was thinking about you last night and started to write, then I thought I'd better not because I was in a bad mood. This guy cut in front of me in the chow hall line, and I pushed him. The guard saw me push him and punished me by confining me to my room today. Your letter cheered me right up. Thanks for writing and making me feel good, making me understand, and just making my day.

P.P.S. I sense that there is still hurt and pain, so I won't comment on that last letter.

I love you.

* * *

November 9, 1993

Dear Willie:

First of all, I would like to say thank you for being you. Second, I would like to inform you that I found a permanent job. After quitting my last job, I worked a week here and there through this temporary agency. I left the apartment one day destined to find a permanent job, and I did just that. The man hired me on the spot. I believe he was impressed with me serving in the military because he's a veteran, also. I work as a data entry clerk for a company that does walk-a-thons for high school fund-raising. I love it.

With the little money I saved and what my daddy sent me, I got my car back. Babe, shortly after I found this job is when Henry and I split up. I started catching the bus again. That first time I caught the bus home, I got off about five blocks away from my apartment to make another connection. I decided to walk home instead of wait for the next bus, since I had no ideal how long it would be. On my way home, I saw Henry and Roxanne driving by. The bad part is they saw me, too, and I became so embarrassed about it. Just the other day he was taking me to work, and now they had the enjoyment of seeing me walk while they rode. Saving the money to get my car back became my main focus at that point. I mailed the money to Shala, and she picked the car up from Tennessee and drove it to Georgia to her house. I caught the bus to Georgia and drove it back here. I talked to the dealer, and we agreed to refinance the car. The money order that was in the car was not good. It read "void after 90 days," and that car has been sitting in Tennessee well over that. So I never cashed it, and you need to send my $50 back, Babe. (smile)

You know what, Babe, you were right. You didn't stick by me for long after I left for basic training. As I recall, I only received one letter from you and never heard from you again. If you had stuck it out with me, you and I would probably be together today. Oh, how I wish I had revealed my true feelings back then!

Before I close, I want to share something else with you. After Henry finally got all of his clothes out, I told Charlene that he wasn't allowed back into the apartment anymore. He came one day while I was at work, and naïve Charlene let him in. Anyhow, he had the TV completely disconnected and sitting on the floor when Charlene called the police on him. He didn't believe she would do it after she said she would. After Charlene blocked the door so he couldn't get out with it, he finally left. The police showed up after the fact. I was so mad with Charlene, because I'd told her not to let him in.

Love,

Gwen

* * *

November 12, 1993

Dear Sweetheart:

I feel bad that you received that nasty letter and didn't comment on the first letter I sent you that consisted of five pages, front and back, with two pictures enclosed. I hope you have received it by now. I would hate for you to think that I would write a letter like that after our long pause from communicating.

Girl, I received that envelope with the $50 deposit stamped on it and began thinking about buying shoes. I read the other letter and said, "Well easy come, easy go." I will return the money as soon as it's posted to my account, which may be next week. I don't think I'm allowed to mail money orders to nonfamily members. It's supposed to be a family-member-only privilege. If they deny my attempt, I'll send it to my mother and have her send it to you. So now you are going to have to be patient with me.

Well, well, well, I am delighted to hear that you have gotten your wheels back on the road. My Babe is riding high and on her way, too. "Get it, girl!" I am also happy that you were able to make arrangement to eradicate your delinquent payments so you can keep your car. It would have been unfortunate for you to have finally obtained the car only for the dealer to repossess it because of overdue payments.

That must be something, to constantly run into your ex with his girlfriend. Just hold your head up high and put it from your mind. Remember, he's the one who lost a good woman, and he will realize it eventually. I hope Charlene will listen to what you say the next time. He has no business coming in there without your permission, and she needs to respect that.

Lady, do you know that I can't remember what you feel like anymore? I do know one thing, though, it's a good feeling that I can't wait to refresh myself with.

I love you,

Willie

* * *

November 15, 1993

Dear Willie:

Hi. Now, those are the type of letters I prefer receiving from you! I understand you were infuriated, and you had every right to be. I won't object to your taking it out on me, since I'm the one who caused it.

So, tell me more about this trouble you got into. Will this create an extension to your original sentence, or what? I like the picture, but why were you standing in the sun, frowning and looking mean? Babe, please don't get too heavy, okay? Don't make me have to customize my preference as far as characteristics in a man. You know I don't like big men. I don't want to get pulverized by the one I love. I hope you understand my meaning.

Do you know what, Babe? I probably shouldn't talk about this to you, but after all, you are my friend first, right? I've started meeting people, and there are five guys who have remarkably entered my life. Babe, I can't locate a single person who I enjoy spending time with. The fact that individual traits don't match is definitely a problem. One is married, and that's a problem in itself, because I have never dated a married man before. Since you've been married, we've only kissed, so that doesn't count. Well, I don't really like him at all, but the fact that he wants to wine and dine me and take care of me sounds good. He wants a side lady, and I'm not into that kind of stuff. I hate for a man to constantly boast about his expertise in lovemaking. He always gazes at my breast as opposed to my face when we're talking. I mean, I don't even want this guy to touch me. I advised him that he shouldn't kiss anyone other than his wife, because I'm sure he has kissed her in more places than her lips. Shoot, I just point-blank told him I prefer not to play the kissing game.

Another guy was scoping me out at the club, and since he knew the girl I was talking to, he asked her to give me his phone number. I called, and he took me to the movies. We went out to eat another time. He spends time with Li'l Henry, because he's a big kid, himself. He's good-looking, but there's disfigurement about his mouth because he has a crooked smile. He never converses on a serious level with me and has never tried to kiss me. I had to smack him on the lips the last time I saw him, because I figured I should at least do that considering we had been out on a few times. He calls every now and then, but he hasn't visited in a while. I don't know what's up with him. Maybe he just wants a friend.

Then there's the mailman. When I met him, I didn't realize he was so small. He's just as small as I am. I knew we wouldn't work out after talking on the phone and noticing his high-pitched voice. I would love to create a friendship with him, because our conversation hit it off very well. When he came over and I observed his ladylike gestures, I definitely knew I wanted him as a friend only. He tried to kiss me, too. I had a time trying to hold him away from me.

Then there's this older guy who I've recently met. He appears to be pretty nice and he sings in a gospel choir. He wants to wine and dine me and buy nice things for me. He's not married, but, unfortunately, I haven't had an opportunity to get acquainted with him yet.

Last but by no means least, there's Terry. Perfect height and size, nice looks, stable, own house, nice car, staff sergeant in the military. However, he has too many obligations and limited time for me that's restricted to weekends only. He has not escorted me anywhere. He simply wants to lounge over here and cuddle, but only on the weekends, I say again. Now, he may have been Mr. Right, next to you, of course, but I refuse to sit in the house with a man weekend after weekend and never experience the exhilaration of being pursued by means of spending loads of money to win my affection.

So I've discovered that my best option is to be by my darn self until the deliverance of your body into my arms. Then and only then will I have the love that I long for. I'm not choosy; I just want someone like you, that's all. So would you prefer me to live alone, Willie? When are you getting out of there—and I don't want to hear your normal response of not knowing!

Charlene requested the hold to be reinstalled on the phone. We got into a big argument about it, too. I was upset because she neglected to tell me beforehand. I heard about it from Pam, when she called all the way from Michigan. This was around the time I started writing you again, so I was pretty upset. Her argument was that she is unable to refrain from accepting collect calls. We agreed that once you've mentioned calling, she'll get rid of the hold.

I'm going to end, so take care. I love you, and my thoughts are with you always.

Gwen

* * *

Chapter 6

November 20, 1993

My Sweet:

It sure was nice to hear from you. I really enjoyed the fragrance of your perfume. Please don't deny me that wonderful sweet smell of you in your future letters. I am really enjoying hearing from you on a regular basis. I am pleased that you have been taking the time to write me.

I see you have become curious about my release date. That's not implying that this is something that has recently come over you or anything. I want to tell you the truth, but then you'll say that same thing you've always said. "I don't know!" You asked me has the fight extended my sentence? Well, I'm sorry to say that yes, it has. I suppose that should be expected when you split a man's head open to the white flesh. I would like to narrate more about the fight, but what more can I tell you other than I had been tolerating this man's ridicule and intimidation tactics, or so he thought. I asked him once before if there was anything he needed to get off his chest, because I didn't particularly like the manner in which he spoke of me to people. I would say it was all about respect, and that's the bottom line. My out date could always be extended, depending on my conduct. I can come home earlier if they allow me to go to the YMCA. Then I would be released six months earlier. That fight cost me more than I would have thought was possible. I hate that it happened, but there was no way around it. He approached me, so a man has to do what a man has got to do.

Babe, you asked a question that's difficult for me to answer. First, I must say that I'm honored to be the man who you set your standards by for your happiness. Now, as a man I want you to be mine and all mine now and forever. I must also add that as a friend, I want you to be happy, and if that means having other men in your life, then so be it. You have sexual needs that I can't fulfill right now, so if you crave sex and companionship, you have my blessings. All I ask is that you be careful. I don't want you to catch something that you may not be able to get rid of, if you get my meaning.

Now let's get to the picture I sent. From my understanding, you didn't particularly like it, or am I perceiving something erroneously again? I will say on my behalf that I would like for you to look at the picture when months have passed without a word from you. That's how I'll feel. That's the look I've been walking around here with. I also want you to observe all that body that you haven't seen in such a long time.

I'm going to end on that, but remember my love for you is eternal.

Love,

Willie

* * *

November 23, 1993

Dear Willie:

How are you doing, Love, since the last time we talked? First I want to tell you that I consider spraying cologne on my letters to you every time I write, but I always feel that it's inappropriate, considering the issues I've written about lately. For instance, is it suitable to spray perfume on a letter that's relating to other men? I think not. Lately my letters have been explanations or discussions about other men. This one will be more appropriate, so I will spray some, as you call it, "smell good" on it.

I enjoyed your last letter very much. It's nice of you to answer all my questions. So what's up with that? Why do you make a point to answer every question? Don't misunderstand me, I definitely like it. Look, Babe, I have no other choice but to set my standards to you as far as men are concerned. You're the only man who has been a friend to me. Maybe I'm overrating your qualities slightly. I have to take into consideration that you are incarcerated, and that alone can generate certain actions, especially from loneliness and despair. Babe, you know that you were a bit impulsive in the past. The consideration, kindness, and understanding were all there, but not as sincere as it is now. I have faith and trust in you, Babe, but it's difficult to dismiss that thought from the back of my mind.

There was a guy in jail who Charlene corresponded with, and they made plans to get together afterwards. He got out and didn't have anything to say to Charlene. See, that's pretty hard to digest, you know. I'm not telling you this with expectations of an explanation, either. I will trust until I have reasons not to. I know that we haven't made any plans or promises for the future, but I would like to know that you will remember my name when you get out. Actually, I would love to be the first female you see when you get out of there.

Willie, I'm still shy in a lot of ways when it concerns being with someone new. I was unaware of this because the circumstances hadn't occurred until now. I'm still very quiet and can't really be myself. I will probably behave in this manner with you once I get a chance to really spend time with you. Don't let these letters fool you, because I've always been known to express myself better on paper. When it comes to the real deal, I'm just a little shy at heart. I wish I could be a talkative person and not let things embarrass me so much. I can't imagine not being comfortable with you after conversing so long on paper and the phone calls, and even my visits. If not that, especially after narrating my life story, but I don't know. Even when I came to visit you, I was always self-conscious about my looks and the possibility of running out of discussion topics. I was always nervous, but hopefully you didn't notice. Then again, maybe that's something to appreciate, Babe. Just think if I became cool, calm, and collected around you, it could indicate that my feelings are weakening for you, or something to that effect. Maybe if I ever felt comfortable around you or with you, it's a sign of becoming bored with it all. This may appear to be bizarre, but that's how it happened with Henry and me. Once you understand a person thoroughly, you're comfortable enough to get mad, argue, and talk smack. Do you understand what I'm saying?

So, Babe, I didn't really need to know about the fight, play by play. Not the combat portion anyway. Look, Babe, if you felt that's what you had to do, then I believe that's what you had to do. I know you're strong enough to prevent people from pushing you around, but I also know you're capable of walking away from a situation that's going to cost you extended time. Fighting is not always the best way to handle situations. I don't like to fight. You have decent morals, and I know you'll handle your remaining time honorably. After all, we must remember that you're not the only one anticipating your release. I am, as well, so if you don't think of yourself, please keep me in mind. Remember, I love you.

Take care,

Gwen

P.S. I have concluded my struggle, because my first check went to the car, my second went toward bills, and payday is two days from now. I suppose I can say don't worry about the money. Keep it as an early birthday gift, and get the tennis shoes.

Bye, Babe.

* * *

November 30, 1993

Dear Gwen:

Babe, where in the world are you? I wanted to talk to you on the phone so bad. I hate that I missed you all of those times I tried to call. I even feel worse because I haven't written back. I preferred to talk to you on the phone about some of the things you mentioned in your letter. The guy that had the three-way (as you can see, I'm speaking in past tense) is out of commission for now. I'm hoping he has a new phone by next week. I feel so bad that I haven't talked with you. You spoke of my responding to all of your questions. Well, I try my best, and I also remember you "checking" me once before about it when you were here in Michigan. I read your letters several times before writing back on the questions you asked. Now I think it's time to discuss some of the things you talked about in your last letter.

I think you have the wrong impression of the use of perfume. I want to be able to smell you each and every time I hear from you. I seldom get a chance to see you, so what I'm trying to do is develop a sense of smell of you regardless of whatever you talk about in your letters. You act like it should be a special occasion to spray some "smell good" on your letters. Well, I'll tell you a little secret. It is special every time I receive a letter from you. Hey, would you come to visit and not wear perfume or underarm deodorant? Well, that's what I'm talking about. Girl, give me all I've got coming regardless of the circumstance.

Lady, you are something else. How can you "fix your mouth" (say something) to degrade my sincerity? Hello, have you forgotten we didn't communicate for five years prior to my lock-up? Don't misunderstand me, I have changed significantly during my stay here, and I think it's for the better. I've learned to put the interest of others first instead of myself. How you concluded your theory on my sincerity after my release is beyond me. Why wouldn't I acknowledge you when I got out? If you can recall, I have always inquired about you and tried to keep in contact. I'm sure that will never change. Please try not to compare me with a guy who your sister met while he was in prison. I know if I met a lady who I didn't know prior to my being locked up and didn't have feelings for, I would lie to get whatever I could out of her just as he may have done to your sister. That's how most men behave, but it's not limited to men in prison alone. Men on the outside will utilize that same approach.

You must be delusional if you think I feel that you are not shy with me. If you weren't bashful, you would have stated your desire to be the first lady who I make love to instead of saying the first female I see when I get out. Just like that. So I know some things just don't change. I know you feel nervous when you're near me, but what you don't understand is that I have the same feelings, too. That's normal when you want to make a good impression.

I really don't want you to believe that once you get to know me to the point where you're comfortable; it will signify that the thrill is gone. The thrill will always be there as long as we work at having it. That special feeling that we have for one another comes from putting a smile on each other's faces. In other words, keeping one another happy. I would like to get flowers, gifts, and wrapped candy just like you. Those endowments would touch a special part in my heart as well. Those are the elements that shape and stimulate a relationship when it's not a holiday or birthday. You know what I mean? I think when you become relaxed around me, you will like what you have and then you'll want to be with me even more than ever. I think when a person is happy with someone, it brings along a bond that keeps them wanting more of that happiness.

Hey, what's up with you not getting the block off the phone so I can call you at anytime? Speaking of time, when are you at home so I'll know when to call you? It seems that you're a road runner.

Love,

Willie

P.S. Thank you for the money for the shoes. I really needed it. I am not doing so well here in the money department.

P.P.S. Make sure you spend quality time with your son.

* * *

December 5, 1993

Dear Willie:

Look, Babe, I've written two letters to you this past week and didn't get around to mailing either one. So I'm combining them into this letter, if that's all right with you. I have much to talk to you about. First of all, I want to announce that I found a part-time job at Montgomery Ward for the Christmas season. Babe, I messed up real bad, and I know you're going to say, "Dog girl, you need to stop that mess!" but I'll tell you anyway.

Over the previous month, I have lost almost $300 playing bingo. Look, my intentions were to win and make life easier. I had Christmas coming with a mere four checks remaining to earn beforehand. I had bills to pay, consisting of my car note and insurance, plus I needed more repairs done on the car. It needs front brakes and two tires, because I only bought three before and the treads on that used tired are completely gone. They also told me that the rear CV joints needed replacing. So I thought,

How can I accomplish all of this? I immediately thought of bingo, with aspirations of winning the money to at least eliminate half of my debt.

Babe, there was no way of achieving my goals by means of my paychecks alone. I began by losing $40, and then I continued losing more and more attempting to retrieve that original $40. Now, Babe, I realize the foolishness of it all, and you are the only one who knows how big a fool I've been. I've certainly learned my lesson. This time I'll give that game up entirely. I had submerged so far under, and that's the reason why I needed to get this part-time job. With this job, I think I can fulfill my Christmas responsibility to my son and pay my bills. Hopefully, the car will hold out until after Christmas.

I don't want to keep secrets from you, and I promise I won't anymore. Another thing I withheld from you, well, I wouldn't say withheld, I just didn't comment about it. Remember I told you Henry and Roxanne are living across the street? Well, I feel so awkward about this situation. He can actually see whoever comes into this apartment from his window. Roxanne comes over mostly when I'm not here to get Li'l Henry. One time while I was here she came to give Li'l Henry some new tennis shoes she had purchased, and I didn't say anything to her. I didn't exactly know what approach to use because I didn't exactly despise her, yet I couldn't respect her, either. I mean, she was aware of his marital status. On the other hand, she couldn't coerce Henry into infidelity. She and Charlene are pretty cool with each other, so I can't really demand that she leave. Besides, she's been very generous to Li'l Henry.

As a matter of fact, when I advised Henry to pay childcare every week in lieu of child support and he disagreed, she felt he should at least give $50 a week for his son. I filed for child support because he refused to assume the $35 a week childcare expense. The child support office contacted him at work about a week ago. Henry kept telephoning my job until I finally called him back. I notified the secretary not to transfer his calls, because every time he saw me with a man, he would call my job the next day. Well, he informed me that he was mad as hell.

It's funny, because earlier that day he had called me at home to disclose how much he missed me, which I thought was a joke. Now I'm sure he wishes he hadn't done that. He couldn't believe I initiated something like that, because I've been categorized as the softy, always taking his junk and never throwing any back out. He really thought my aunt had encouraged me, because she works for Social Services; but it really was of my own initiative. I've even written a poem about no-good dads that I'm enclosing in this letter. Maybe you'll get a kick out of it. Then, after discussing child support, he brought up the fact that this wouldn't be happening if I hadn't impetuously kicked him out. I told him that I kicked him out because he couldn't keep his penis in his pants and I wasn't going to allow him to have his cake and eat it, too. I couldn't refrain from criticizing his boldness to move right across the street, which triggered his usual response of not having anywhere else to go when I kicked him out.

Babe, Roxanne disclosed to Charlene that they were indeed together that weekend Henry supposedly had gone to retrieve the furniture the second time. I also found out that the paper with Roxanne's home and work numbers that I found in Henry's pocket that day was about a different girl. I finally got enough nerve to call her, and I figured out she was another Roxanne who lived in our apartment complex, too. This man is something else. I don't want to go in to detail, because there's so much going on. When I get my income tax, I'm getting a divorce; and when the lease expires, I'm moving the hell away from here. I do enjoy being single, but I get lonely sometimes because I don't have anyone steady in my life besides you, of course. On the other hand, I like being able to do what I want, when I want, without someone developing animosity.

I've changed a lot, Babe. Maybe you haven't noticed it through my letters, but I have. I don't sit around the house anymore on the weekends. I've been going to this club quite often, and lately I've been going alone. Charlene is eight months pregnant and is too big to go anywhere. I don't have any friends my age who I can go out with, so I go alone and have a nice time. I dance, and I've even gotten to the point where I'm comfortable to move in ways that I'm capable of in the presence of people. I used to feel self-conscious about people watching me, so I barely moved, but now I'm developing my self-esteem and I'm shaking my booty a little bit more. I've asked guys to dance, and you know that's something I've never done. Babe, I've got to get with the '90s. I'm tired of living my boring life, sitting around crocheting and never participating. I have to enjoy life, because it is too short.

I'm so sorry I missed your call. I'm glad that we are writing each other on a regular basis. I very much enjoy hearing from you, and I especially enjoyed this last letter. It put a smile on my face a mile long. I want to see you so bad. I think after I get myself straight, I could get the car fixed and perhaps make that trip one more time, so I can see my Baby. I am long overdue for my "fix" and you know I'll do it, too. I miss you, Babe.

Guess what? When I picked the car up from Shala's house in Atlanta, your name came up when we were talking. She knows you. She lived around the block from you in Saginaw. Her name is Shala Myers. I imagine you must know her, also, right? Well anyway, your wife and kids are living in the same complex that she lives in now in Atlanta. She knows them, and I gather she's been over there a few times to visit. She asked if I wanted her to get pictures of your kids to send to you. So I'm asking you, and I apologize for the delay, but I just remembered to ask. So let me know something.

I'm going to end on that. I'll write again soon.

Gwen

Daddy No Good
Special tests to become a dad
Ninety percent walked out mad
Men with children had to pass or pay ten thousand dollars in cash
Jobless men were penalized
To jail you'll go, the officer advised
You divorce your wife, not your child
This crime is punishable without trial
One hundred percent was the passing score
The entire place was in an uproar

"Calm down, Beastleman," said a very loud voice
What were we to do, you gave us no choice
You can't create a life then leave it astray
You bond with your child, that's the American way
Just think if mothers behaved as you do
To whom in the world could a child turn to?
To be born, whose choice was that to be?
Not one of a child, obviously
So Beastleman, I say, I call you that today
It takes a beast to treat a child in this deranged way
So stand in line, take the test, and pass it if you can
Take a chance to show the world you are a better man!

* * *

December 9, 1993

Hi Babe:

I love you. I just had to say that right off, because those words were just dancing around in my head and I thought you should know. I was thinking about how much you care about me and how there's nothing you wouldn't do for me within your means. That thought amplified today when I went to the property to get my shoes. I must say thank you once again.

I'm presently on this basketball team, and we had a game the other day. Babe, I played terrible and, hey, I can only place the blame on the shoes. Well, I won't have that excuse anymore because I now have some new Nikes.

Hey, I knew something was wrong. I don't have my picture sitting next to me. Okay, now everything is in order. Your pretty legs on this picture look so good. I mean they look so luscious that it seems as if I were to hold them ever so tenderly in my hands that juice would come oozing out feeling so warm and soothing. Oh well, there I go again. I'm going to have to cut that out, huh?

There is something that you mentioned in your last letter that I didn't address because I was in a hurry to mail my letter. I don't believe this. You know Shala? Isn't that something? I have known her since she was about seven years old. She used to live across the street from me back in the day when I stayed on Fifth Street. Then we moved to Janes Street, and then a few years later they moved around the block. I appreciate the kindness and her generosity, but that's okay. I have gotten pictures of my kids from my sister. As a matter of fact, my middle daughter is in Saginaw, because she didn't do well academically in school in Atlanta last year. She was enrolled at the middle of the school year and couldn't adjust to the school's curriculum. As smart as she is, they wanted to hold her back, so her grandmother registered her in a private school that placed her in her correct grade. I hope my sister brings her to see me before the school year is over. Then again, my sister has only come to see me three times this year. I have my fingers crossed. I got the pictures that I've always wanted: their school pictures.

Now, speaking of pictures, we can get Polaroid pictures again, so send some of you at the nightclubs. I want to see just how jazzy you are out there asking those guys to dance. Girl, you are something else.

Babe, I showed your poem to my bunkie, and he couldn't believe you didn't get it from a book. He was so impressed by it that he copied it for himself. I really enjoyed that poem, too. It made me laugh to think how you feel about no-good dads.

Hey, Babe, I was in the weight pit working my "home boy" to death one day. He weighs about 220 and is very weak for his size. He says he can't lift heavier because of an injury that he has. Oh, and by the way, what are you talking about you hope I don't get big? I want to let you know one thing, I'm jealous of those shoulders you have on you. I think I'll close on that. Peace!

Love,

Willie

* * *

December 14, 1993

Dear Babe:

I was just sitting here feeling sort of lonely today. I began thinking about us, and it seems as though our telephone conversations are off course a bit. They're not as intimate as they once were. It's as if we're just casually talking to each other. What do you think is going on here? Maybe I shouldn't have written that letter about the men. Am I making a mistake in thinking something is awkward? Maybe you're being more cautious because of the time when I stopped writing. Maybe you don't really understand like you said. I just don't want to do anything that will cause your feelings to change for me or to mess things up. If it's anything that I'm doing that you disagree with, by all means tell me, because I don't like feeling this way.

Well, that's about it. Hopefully we'll get to talk soon. I really do need to talk to you.

I love you,

Gwen

* * *

December 17, 1993

Dear Gwen:

I hope you are doing fine. I can see that working all those hours has gotten you stressed out, or did I miss something in your last letter? I don't understand what you mean by saying our conversation aren't intimate anymore. I thought that last conversation was pretty hot. Well hell, I know I felt pretty heated. I don't know what mistakes you're talking about. I am starting to wonder if you were drinking when you wrote this letter. If you were, don't do that anymore.

I have always hoped you would believe that I am an understanding person. I have not thought about the last time our communication broke down. I told you that I would understand if I didn't get a chance to hear from you because you're working. Like when you said you were making those quilts. I trust you when you say that you're busy and don't have much time to write. Now, if you have time to go out and shake your butt or go out on dates, then I think you have time to write me. It all boils down to how you choose to spend your spare time. I'm not saying don't have a good time, but, then again, I feel your writing me is one of the best forms of enjoyment that you can have.

Babe, my feelings for you have not changed since I saw you in those white jeans with the stripes. I wanted you then and I want you even more now, so don't question my love for you anymore. I'm going to end this letter so I can put this in the mail today. I'll write again this weekend. I want to make sure you get this before Christmas. I must admit that I'm guilty of loving you, and I can't wait to prove my love for you

Loving you always,

Willie

* * *

December 20, 1993

Hey, hey:

It's me again. I love you. I am still puzzled over your last letter. I hope I can better understand where you're coming from in your next letter. I really need to talk to you on the phone if that last letter didn't clear things up about my feelings for you. It has been very difficult to use a three-way phone lately. Now, the only time I'm able to make calls are 1:00 PM, and then I can't afford to pay most times. Now don't misunderstand me, I will pay it, because there is nothing more important to me than to hear your voice. I must say I do have to play hardball with them, because I don't want word to get out that I'm a sucker. Then I won't get any respect if I want a deal the next time.

Gwen, my bunkie just pissed me off. I told him I was going to inform you so that if you see him on a visit, you can kick his butt. He said he didn't care if I told my woman. He's mad with me because I asked him to assist me in adjusting my bed. Well, I won't go into detail on what my intentions were, but he would not cooperate with me. He refused to lie on the floor, because he had recently taken his shower. I needed him to lie underneath the bed to hold the bar while I moved the mattress. I was only trying to adjust my bed, and I didn't think I was asking too much by requesting that he lie on the floor. He pissed me off by not helping at all. Oh, and he also misplaced a pair of my socks—another reason to be mad. Well, I must say on his behalf that he did find my socks.

Babe, we have a basketball game scheduled for tomorrow. The first game we played, I didn't get to play much. I assumed the coach didn't think I could play, and it pissed me off. I was only able to play five minutes, and the bad part about it was that we lost. Now, you know I don't like to lose. He wouldn't even put me in, but he allowed those "bombs" to play. The events that had taken place since then have changed his mind about me. There was a tryout for varsity (that's where the best players are chosen to play the teams from the outside world), and I had a point to prove. At first I really didn't want to play, but I made a lot of heads turn at that tryout. I must say, I didn't think I had a chance in the world, especially against all of those big guys who could stand under the rim and jump to dunk the ball. They were the best group of guys that I've ever played with, so I felt the need to prove my skills so I could play. Lo and behold, I made the team. I know those guys were thinking to themselves, How in the hell did he make the team? I must assert, I think it was the shoes (smile), because before I always played in those state-issued low-tops. Now the coach is going to start me in the game tomorrow, so I have to show him "what time it is." I think that tryout brought a lot of my game back to form.

Babe, I'm trying to gain some weight, and I'm having a hard time because of the running and playing basketball. I try to eat as much as possible, but it's just not enough. I guess my problem originates from the fact that I'm unable to eat in the chow hall when spicy food is served. Spicy food seems to trigger a burning sensation in my rectum during defecation. I think I have hemorrhoids, because I'm beginning to see blood. Ooh, I told you something private about myself. I hope you will still respect me in the morning. (smile) I know you will. I'm just being silly, but because of that I don't eat as I would like to. Some people take protein and substances for their body, but I can't afford that. Then again, I don't want to take pills and drink those powders.

Excuse me, but I have been thinking about something that's totally out of context with this letter. Now, I want to know if you can relate to this, so don't forget to write back and share your feelings about it.

All right, hold your horses: I'm going to tell you what I'm talking about. I want to know if you sometimes daydream about when you and I grow old together and some of the things we might do. Better yet, things you think we will do together when I get out. I was thinking of you, and I thought of you doing something sweet. For instance, we're driving down the highway and you grab my hand, kiss me on the cheek, and tell me how much you love me while holding on as if you were grasping for dear life. I squeeze back as if to say, I'll always be here for you. Another thought is you wanting to argue, and I tell you to come to me so I can kiss you and tell you how much I love you. If you have thoughts like that, please share them with me. I want to hear about it.

Love,

Willie

P.S. I hope the New Year brings you happiness and much closer to me because I am your happiness.

* * *

January 1, 1994

Dear Willie:

Happy New Year, Baby!

First of all, I want to say thank you for being you. You know, Babe, those last two letters I received—I really needed them. Sometimes I get into moods where I suppose you might say I want reassurance. Sometimes I develop a disposition where I yearn for more attention than I ordinarily receive. Is it ever like that with you? I wasn't drunk, I just felt something slipping there for a moment, but everything is back on course in my mind once again. You've made it right and thank you. But I must warn you that from time to time I develop these types of temperaments when I just want to be loved. I won't forewarn you about my emotions. I suppose I just want you to automatically know. That's vicious, isn't it? I don't want to be cruel, it's just that I like to show love and receive love all the time and not restrict it to special occasions.

I love to cuddle all the time. Of course, I fantasize about us being together. Willie, when we used to go over to your sister's house in Flint and lie in her nice bed, I would fantasize then about us being married. I thought about either you or me washing dishes and the other coming up from behind, holding the other around the waist real snug and bestowing soft kisses on the neck while whispering, "I love you" in an ear. I think about learning the two-step dance with you, creating our own special technique and style. I think about us lying in the bed talking, smiling, and laughing about old times. I think that if we were to ever get together, we could have a happy life. I think that with you, I could finally have that fairy-tale relationship I've always dreamed of. Well, so darn close to it, it'll probably seem fictitious. Sometimes, Babe, when I think of us together, I just smile because I know you will be all the man I will ever need.

Since you're playing basketball now, I suspect you won't be able to write as much, right? It sounds like you're really enjoying yourself with the games and everything. The degree of intensity in your words builds contentment within me to know that your spare time is spent enjoyably. *Why do you want to gain more weight, Babe?* Tell that bunkie of yours, if he knows what's best for him, he'd better stop upsetting you or he'll have to answer to me.

Look Babe, Charlene is supposed to take the hold off of the phone Monday. I would like for you to call me Saturday, if you can. Let's say somewhere around noon.

Love,

Gwen

* * *

January 10, 1994

Hi, Babe:

I love you. I was just sitting back thinking about how lucky I am to have you in my corner. If you by chance don't know, it means a lot to me to know I have you there for me, even though you are thousands of miles away. I must be truthful in saying when you told me you wanted more than a friendship three years ago, I thought it would never last this long. Hell, at that time, I thought you were insane for wanting to have anything to do with me, considering the situation I was in. Now, when I reminisce about it, you were that special someone I needed to help conserve my sanity by knowing somebody loved me. I know now that if you could have taken me home, you would have loved me and held me tight and close to your heart. I like the nice little love cuddling that you talked about. Those are little things that make a relationship grow into something very special. I sometimes think about massaging your feet after a long day at work, just to soothe your tension and give you some time to relax. I guess I have turned into a softy, because the only thing I desire is to make my woman feel loved and appreciated.

Baby, I want to gain more weight because I only weight 150 right now. I would like to reach and maintain my previous weight of 165. I have lost a lot of fat that I would like to replace with 15 pounds of muscle. I just feel light in the butt, and I can get pushed around easily. I want to be solid as a rock; an unmovable object.

I don't like it when you permit thoughts to penetrate your mind about me thinking of you as anything less than the most important person in my life. Basketball can never coerce neglect concerning you. I can only say I will never decrease my quantity or quality of letters to you because of it. I will make sure I keep some special thoughts in reserve for my Baby, because I can see you need some special loving sent your way.

I'm going to end now.

Love ya,

Willie

P.S. Make sure you tell your son that you love him at least three times a day.

* * *

January 24, 1994

I feel good!

Girl, you just don't know how good it was hearing your voice on the phone. I mean, your voice made me feel so loved and cared for. Babe, you are the only lady that can make me feel this way. I just love it when you call me your Baby. It just does something that's unexplainable. The only way I can describe it is to say you make chills flow through my body.

Did it seem like we had talked for a half hour to you? Maybe I was just hypnotized by the sound of hearing your voice, and time just seemed to stand still. Did it seem that way for you? I mean, it was as though you had just started talking. I am supposed to get connected with a three-way telephone sometime soon. Then I'll be able to talk to you a little while longer. They usually allow us to talk between 10 and 15 minutes at a time. I will be happy with that until I can find another way to call you. I try to work my magic as much as possible, because you know if there is a way; I will make it possible to call my Baby. Now, if I could only find a way to get you up here to see me. Well, I think I should leave that one to fate. That subject hurts to think about, and that's why I ask for so many pictures of you. I want to see the changes you go through. I truly believe you can only look better with time. I think I'll take a picture this week and send it to you.

I don't know why every time you refer to Henry's departing, I think he's leaving the state, or is that true? I am glad to hear that he is trying to do the right thing with respect to his son. I also want to state on paper that I think it is generous of you to take $50 a week instead of the court-ordered amount of $75. You are a very good person. I want you to know that, just in case you haven't heard it from anyone lately.

Life in here has made me think about my health and how important it is. There are a lot of foods you can eat that will cause a feeling of fullness, but your body is sometimes tired and sluggish. It's telling you that you're not getting the nutrients you need. If you are not eating properly, you should take some vitamins to supplement the energy your body may need. I think you should give your son those Flintstone vitamins. I didn't know that a person should eat fruit everyday, but that old saying is true about an apple a day will keep the doctor away.

I used to think plain water wasn't good for anything. I can remember my father's wife telling me to drink eight glasses of water per day. I looked at her like she was crazy, but now I know what she was talking about. Water is good for flushing your system. I hope you start to take the things I say to heart in terms of the advice I give. For instance, the baking soda in your laundry; try it and see for yourself how bright your whites become.

That's a wrap for this one. I'll write back soon.

Love ya,

Willie

* * *

February 25, 1994

Dear Babe:

Lately I've been thinking about you so much that I haven't been able to do much of anything else. I've noticed you haven't written lately, and you're never home when I call. Now, the last time I called, your sister said something I didn't think she meant to say, and it's got me sort of bothered. Now, don't go questioning her, because this doesn't have anything to do with her. I just have a feeling you may have met someone. Maybe this someone is good for you, and if so, then I'm happy. Unless you tell me otherwise, I'm going to step aside so there won't be any pressure for you. There won't be any hard feelings, Babe, because I'll always have the time we shared together, the visits, the phone calls, and the many letters to furnish me with enough joy to last a lifetime. Just remember, don't settle for less than you deserve. You are a queen, and don't let anyone treat you any less than that. Remember you'll always hold a special place in my heart. I love you always, my Babe.

Willie

P.S. I can say one thing: Your sister is right about there is no perfect man. There is a phrase, "a man that makes you happy." So don't let her talk you into getting a man who doesn't have your happiness in mind. I must say you are choosy, but I will also add that you have a right to be because it's your life.

PART IV
GRAND RAPIDS, MICHIGAN

$$\mathcal{C}hapter \; 1$$

August 15, 1996 (Two years later)

Hello, Love:

I assume when you see my name on this envelope, you'll stop in your tracks. This is not a mirage; it's really me, a ghost from your past. I was released only two days ago, and after seeing my mother, my sister, and my kids, you were the next on my list. I went over to your sister's house, and they supplied me with your home and work numbers and your address. They were very surprised to see me. Diane gave me a big hug and said you were not going to believe I was out of prison. I also saw your son, and he has really grown. He didn't remember me, though.

Well, I called all night long, and you were not at home. In between calls, I began writing this letter to you. I was so anxious to get in touch with you some kind of way, any kind of way, that I couldn't sleep at all. I left my mother's and sister's numbers with your sister, just in case.

Oh, how I have missed you! There wasn't a second, minute, hour, or day that passed these last two years I didn't have warm and loving thoughts of you. I prayed you were not married and that one day we could reunite. I don't know what's happening in your life, or who's happening for that matter, but I know within my heart I won't be able to rest until I give us one last try.

Oh, I have so much to tell you. This has truly been the longest two years of my life without communicating with you. I kept thinking, hoping, and praying that a letter would come, but it never did. Not in my wildest dreams would I have ever thought we would lose contact.

I will continue to call until I reach you.

Signed,

Still in love

* * *

August 20, 1996

Dear Willie:

I'm in a daze. I still can't believe I talked to you on the phone. When Diane called me at work and asked me to guess who came over there, your name never entered my mind. When she said your name, I told her she was lying. She said you were still looking good and smelling good, too. So, you know when I left work today, I had to call you. I star-69'd the phone, and sure enough your telephone number was there, but Diane had already given it to me. The impassivity of our phone conversation made it seem as though the feelings were gone away. You didn't give me any kind of clue that you still felt the same.

A lot has changed with me. I am a different person from that girl you used to know. I've done a lot of growing up these past two years. Like I told you over the phone, I'm living alone with my son and have been for the past year. You remember how I was always afraid of making that move on my own? Well, now I don't know what the heck I was afraid of. Henry and I never got back together after that last time. We're not divorced yet, but I'm working on that. I'm going to school part-time at night, working full-time at a medical clinic, and also part-time at a hotel on the weekends. I am a busy girl. I do have someone who I spend time with, but it's not a relationship or anything like that.

So, you've met my son, huh? I let him spend his summer vacation in Michigan. Pam is watching him in order to help me out while I'm going to school. He's coming home this weekend because school for him starts here in two weeks. I'm glad because I'm really missing my baby. Li'l Henry will be in the fourth grade; he's my little man. I was coming to Michigan for Christmas, and then I changed my mind. Now that you are there, I guess I'll have to go back to my original plans and price those round trip tickets from Florida to Michigan for Li'l Henry and me.

You know, Willie, I did write you one last time, but I didn't mail it. I remembered writing the letter and putting in my desk drawer at work. After I got off the phone with Diane, I searched for that letter, and there it was, right where I'd left it two years ago. I'm sending it to you now, basically, so you can understand what went on and how I felt at that time.

I'll talk to you soon.

Love,

Gwen

September 15, 1994 (Two years ago)

Hello, Love:

I know I am a stranger in your book right about now, and I am aware that I should have written to you a long time ago. Believe me, I wanted to, but I couldn't because of a certain situation I put myself in with you and I was unable to keep my end of the bargain. I reneged on our promise to one day be together, and I was ashamed. I know you don't understand what the heck I'm talking about, but I will explain it to you before I end this letter.

First, I would like to tell you how I've been doing these last few months in case you're wondering. I've moved and am now living with a guy named David and have been for the last five months. David is a man of every woman's dreams. He takes good care of me and tries to please me in every possible way he can. I couldn't pass this man up. I know you made it clear that you were fine with me dating other men. You said you would always be there, as long as I dropped a postcard every now and then. I stopped writing to you shortly after I met him, because I knew I could never be true to the both of you. I didn't know what to say to you anymore. I felt it was impossible for me to concentrate on two men at the same time. Even though we both agreed and talked about if this ever happened that we would remain friends, I still couldn't bring myself to write and tell you what was going on.

It got to the point where I was embarrassed about not writing for such a long period of time again. Nevertheless, I felt you deserved an explanation, so I wrote this letter. I just procrastinated and procrastinated on mailing it until time convinced me that it was best to never contact you again. I know I promised I would never do that and it was very unfair to you, but what can I say, I was just a chicken. I didn't want to tell you I found someone else. I really felt that the best way to deal with that and my feelings was to avoid it, and that is exactly what I did.

Now, I guess I've gotten to the point where I'm feeling very irritated with myself for leaving you hanging in such a way. It's wearing on my mind, and I'm feeling very bad about it. Despite my better judgment, which is not a good one at all, I've decided you have the right to know what's going on because I made promises to you that I know I destroyed by not communicating with you. I'm sorry, Willie, for being the person I know you thought I could never be.

I also promised some money to you before I stopped writing, and that too I didn't do. At the time I promised it, I had every intention of giving it to you. Situations came up and I had to do a priority thing. I know you had stressed to me how much you needed it, and I was ashamed that I had promised it to you and couldn't come through. I would think, "Well, next check I'll give it to him," and every time the next check came, I needed it for something else. I also told myself I wasn't going to write until I had it to give, so that was another reason why I put off writing you. How could I possibly write and not have the money in the envelope? Of course, you would have expected it in the next letter because that is what I promised. It wasn't because of Bingo this time, either. I didn't have time for bingo, because if you recall, at that time I was working two jobs. It was just needed in other areas. How could I tell you every single time I had something else to do with my money? So I just avoided it by not writing.

Willie, I don't expect you to forgive me for this, only to understand what went on. I know that it's probably approaching the time for you to leave there, so this is the best time for me to explain. Babe, I didn't mean to hurt you in any way. I'm very sorry. You can write me if you want, it's your option.

This person I'm living with, I'm not in love with. I once loved him. We are presently together, so I try to do the right thing by him. David doesn't trust me when I'm around men, and he makes me feel guilty if I want to be somewhere other than with him. He smothers me, and I imagine that's why my feelings changed. I want to ask him to leave, but I don't want to hurt his feelings. I do care about him very much, yet I just feel numb inside knowing he's in love with me and thinking I feel the same way about him.

David is in the National Guard and has a full-time job. I suggested he get another part-time job, since he was having such a problem with me working two. He did just that. He was recently hired at the detention center for the State, making a lot more money, and still has his part-time job. He gives me both of his checks and leaves it in my hands to handle the bills. His National Guard check, he has directly deposited into my bank account every month. He goes out of his way and does really nice things for me. Every single ring that I wear on my fingers, he bought. He treats me like a queen. That's why I stopped writing you shortly after I met him, because he is definitely a Romeo. It's just that I have to put up with a lot of extra stuff.

He's the baby of his family, and he really likes to be pampered, which was okay until my feelings changed. He gets an attitude, and he just wants to have his way. He doesn't really want me out of his sight. When he's at work and I'm at home, he calls continuously, and it's beginning to get on my nerves. I thought it would be nice to know that someone loves me, wants to spend every single minute with me, and puts my best interests before his own, especially after being in a marriage where my husband didn't give a damn. However, I've learned that's not for me, either. So right now I guess you could say I'm in a confused state of mind.

I do miss talking to you, but I guess that's something you prefer not to hear right now. Well, take care, stay well, and I really do hope I hear from you again.

Love,

Gwen

* * *

September 15, 1996

Dear Baby:

What's up? Me in your book, I hope. I've just decided I'll write instead of calling collect. Even though I can talk to you all night long, I must realize that time talked is money. I can adopt our old habits.

Well, I'm happy to hear you're not attached, but I am very curious to know about that someone in that letter you wrote that I never got. Could David also be that someone who kept you out all night when I tried to call that first time? You see, I know how hard it is for you to just let things go, especially when you've been in a relationship for a long time. Even with these kinds of thoughts flashing through my head, I have no other choice but to trust your word. I'm trying to get reacquainted with you and hopefully become a part of your life once again if at all possible. I have never stopped loving you, yet somehow I feel like the feelings are not mutual. I presume you're going to make me ask the question. Do you still love me? Do you have any feelings at all for me? I need to know this, Babe. Please don't make me wait too long on an answer.

I moved to Grand Rapids, Michigan, with my aunt. I figured this would be the best place to seek a decent-paying job. I figured correctly, because I started working this past Monday. Jobs are easy to find here, even if you are an ex-con. I don't like to consider myself as that, because it makes me seem like a bad person and I'm not. I figured I'll start saving a little money and get myself together.

I am delighted to hear you will be coming home for Christmas. I must have read that part over and over about 50 times. I must be someone special to travel all these miles for. My first thought when I got out was to come to Florida to live after I knew you were there. My kids are in Saginaw, and I really don't want to reenter into their lives only to leave again. I was sort of hoping I could talk you into moving back home. Well, I'll end on that note.

Love ya,

Willie

P.S. You are still my Baby.

* * *

October 10, 1996

Dear Willie:

I hope this letter reaches you in the best of health. At first I suppose I sort of blocked our past out of my mind, but now I think it's coming back fresh. You see, I have a hard heart now, and nobody has been able to penetrate it since Henry. That relationship that I wrote about to you lasted a little over a year, and like I said he was very good to me. I think he was a once-in-a-lifetime deal, because I don't think I'll ever find anyone else like him. I loved him at first, but my feelings slowly disappeared. That love was never anything like what I felt for Henry and you. There was another guy (and I think I mentioned him in one of my past letters to you) who I thought had a chance of stealing my heart, but he didn't seem to want it. Now it seems as though no one can come close to what I know to be real love. Lately I have longed for that special feeling in my heart that I used to feel when I know I'm in love. I am so hoping that you and I can rekindle the magic we once shared. Maybe you are the one I've been saving myself for all of this time. I do love you, Willie. What we had was something special, and how can I ever forget that?

Love,

Gwen

P.S. It's been said that employers don't hire people who have been in prison, but I knew you would prove that myth to be wrong. You go, Boy!

* * *

October 29, 1996

Dear Gwen:

It really feels good to feel you're opening up to me again. Just like old times. Do you know what? I am the man you've been waiting for. There is no doubt in my mind, especially after coming back into your life and discovering you are not in a relationship. The three words at the end of your letter, I've been longing to hear.

I noticed you didn't answer the other question pertaining to moving back to Michigan. It's sort of premature, but I know in my heart you are the woman I need to spend the rest of my life with. Whether the answer is positive or negative, please tell me how you feel about the chances of that happening.

They've let me go at the job. That's the bad news. The good news is I've got another job making $8.50 an hour. I relocated here to Grand Rapids because these jobs pay $7 per hour. The jobs I've been getting lately have been temporaries, yet they are long-term assignments. I like the job I have now because it's pretty easy. I work on an assembly line that welds automobile parts. Right now I'm only examining the parts for defects, but I was told if I stay 90 days and get hired on, I could get trained as a welder. That also comes with a pay increase. As you know, I have never worked for anyone before, because I've always had my own business. This job will have to work for right now so I can get back on my feet. I did have aspirations of reopening the plastic covering business, until I discovered the taxes went unpaid on my house.

Oh, I didn't tell you I got a divorce while I was in prison. Yes, I've been a single man now for over a year. My ex-wife is living in the house with her boyfriend and our kids. They are living there rent free, and all I requested of them is they pay the property taxes. I've got until the first of February to pay or I'll lose the house. So I'm going to Saginaw on my day off to talk to my ex-wife, because somebody has got to pay those taxes.

Babe, I'm going to call you this weekend. I'll call Saturday around 5:00 PM. You see, now I am able to give you some money for the telephone bill. I can't wait to hear your voice.

Love always,

Willie

P.S. Who keeps your son while you are at school?

* * *

November 8, 1996

Dear Willie:

I can't really answer your question right now regarding relocating to Michigan. I think maybe we should at least see each other first before we discuss a major deal like that. We need to know how we are together and if we can rebuild that bond we once had. It has been a long time. So, tell me how can you ask me something like that without even seeing me first or touching me, for that matter? I understand you don't want to leave your kids and I respect you for that, but let's just play this by ear, okay?

I'm sorry to hear about your house. I didn't know that they were still living there, but I'm glad to hear you finally got a divorce. So you were still able to keep the house after the divorce even though she has the children? I remember when you told me how you used to ride past that house as a kid and wish it was yours. It would be a shame to just lose it to taxes after all this time, especially since the mortgage note is paid off.

Babe, I was going through my papers and I found some of your old letters. I saved the ones you've written since I've lived in Florida. I also have all the ones from Michigan, but they are stored in Diane's garage where I left them a long time ago. When I read these letters, it surely brought back old memories. How in the world could I have forgotten that you really did love me? I know now for sure you are indeed the man I've been waiting for. When I get to Michigan, you better not prove me wrong. We only have a month and a half to wait, and I will be there for 12 long days.

Talk later,

Gwen

P.S. David, the guy I spoke about in the letter, watches my son while I'm in school. We are still good friends. Yes, he is also the guy I stayed with that night you first tried to contact me, but you have to understand our relationship. We have an understanding with no strings attached.

* * *

November 15, 1996

Dear Babe:

How are you doing? I hope you are fine and in good spirits. I hope this letter unfolds in your ever-loving arms only to bring you joy, to warm your heart, and to put a big smile on your face as it was intended. I hope this card I'm enclosing helps in letting you know someone loves you very much and that someone is me. I know you don't think you can truly love again. I am asking, no I'm begging you to just give love another try. I promise I won't hurt you. I will only show you the love and attention you have longed for from the day you were born. I know your heart is hard and cold right now when it comes to love. All I am asking for is a chance; the opportunity I have waited so many years for. Let me show you how I can use my hands to massage your hard heart and make it feel soft as cotton again. Let me use my arms to hold you tight every night, and I guarantee I will warm your heart like never before. Believe in us and you will have all the love you ever dreamed of. I promise.

Love always,

Willie

P.S. Before I got a divorce, I sold my house to my sister for $1 so my ex-wife was not able to take it.

* * *

November 27, 1996

Dearest Willie:

That was a beautiful card, and you always say such nice things to me. I've forgotten how nice and special I felt after getting letters from you, and this brought back old memories. Your way of writing is beyond words. It makes me really believe you love and care for me, it really does. That card made me feel so special. You can tell someone you love them all day long, but it really doesn't sink in until you actually do something to prove it. Now I feel it has really sunk in my mind that you do love me. See, we don't ever get serious when we're talking on the phone. So I guess that's why it's taking longer to soak into my mind. Maybe that's the reason I feel we really need to be face to face in order to make certain any decisions about us. Then we would feel comfortable enough to be serious with each other, even over the phone. By the way, if you haven't noticed yet, I am more of a serious person, but I do like to laugh sometimes. Can you make me laugh? That's the question.

Honey, I love you and I want to let you know before I end this letter. I guess that's something I'm really going to have to prove to you, because again just saying it is not enough. I do long to be near you again, and I just hope it's everything I imagine it to be. Well, I know it will be.

I have to go back to work. Thanks for taking care of me with the $50. I do appreciate it. I'm going to pay this month's telephone bill with it. I love you.

Gwen

* * *

December 3, 1996

Dear Sweetheart:

You have made me the happiest man in the world. I don't know why you decided you would move back to Michigan with me, but that doesn't really matter. It's the right decision. You mentioned your lease expiring in September of next year, but we overlooked the fact that school will start the month prior.

Well, I have good news and bad news again. My job dismissed me because the workload decreased and they didn't have anything else for me to do. The good news is that I bought a car. I bought it from an elderly couple, and they assured me they were the only owners. I was wondering what I was going to do when you got here as far as transportation goes. Now I've got wheels, and I can drive you wherever you want to go. I was also wondering if you were going to spend any time in Grand Rapids when you came. My intention is to await your arrival in Saginaw, but I was sort of hoping I could "abduct" you for a few days and keep you all to myself. I would also like for you to meet my aunt.

Hey, wait a minute. I am so overjoyed about your decision to relocate here I neglected the primary reason why I wrote this letter. After we finished our conversation on the phone, I began thinking that something was troubling you. Is everything all right, Baby? I'll call tomorrow at 5:00.

Signed: Happiest Man Alive

* * *

December 9, 1996

Dear Willie:

Listen, I didn't go into detail about this over the phone. I had to quit my part-time job because I haven't had an appetite lately. I've lost twelve pounds (six in one weekend). I began experiencing fatigue, and I talked to Dr. Kelly, the doctor who works here at the clinic. He advised me to take a blood test. He discovered that I was anemic, which I already knew. He prescribed some iron pills and instructed me to quit my part-time job since it was contributing to this sudden change in my body chemistry. He asked how I was losing all of this blood which frightened the hell out of me. When my cycle came, I could hear his words asking, "Well, Gwen, how are you losing all of this blood?" I'm stressed out because too many thoughts are floating around in my mind. Li'l Henry isn't doing well in school academically, and I was paranoid as hell about leaving him alone a couple of nights while I attend school. I didn't have a babysitter. I know it was crazy to leave a fourth-grader home alone, but he promised he wouldn't open the door. I have to take my lunch hour at 4:00 PM to drive him from the park to the apartment and fight that late-hour traffic to return to work for only one more hour because no one else wants to work until close at 6:00 PM.

This job is getting on my nerves, and the patients are irritating me by asking for this and requesting that. I now wear a size three, and I'm uneasy about my appearance. I'm convinced that everyone thinks I'm on crack or something. I feel aches and pains in areas I've never felt before, and I'm continuously crying because I think something detrimental is about to happen to me. I'm worried about the well-being of my son if something does.

I had thoughts of admitting myself in a crazy home, because sometimes my mind races. The only thing preventing me for doing that is I have only two more months remaining to finish my schooling and then whose going to take care of my baby. I am so weak it's a struggle to climb the stairs to my apartment. My typing speed has decreased at work and at school, tremendously, and my accuracy is embarrassing. When I tried to read to Li'l Henry the other day, I stuttered over my words as if I couldn't read at all. I'm sluggish and cold all the time. I actually fell asleep in class last night. Babe, something is not right.

Gwen

* * *

December 15, 1996

Dear Baby:

How are you since we talked yesterday? Fine and in the best of health, I hope. I'm happy to hear that your appetite is regular again. You really gave me a scare with that last letter. I thought I had found you only to lose you again from the way you were talking. I'm glad you decided not to take those NoDoz pills because, Babe, every time I think about people who take pills I think of addiction. I know the purpose of those pills is to maintain vigilance, but it's unnatural.

The countdown has officially begun. We have exactly one week remaining before I can hold you in my arms again. I'm nervous and on edge, yet I'm excited and thrilled all at the same time. Did I tell you today that I love you? If not then, I'm telling you now.

I think the taxes on the house will be resolved around March, and I could maybe get a two-bedroom apartment to await your arrival. See, I've already initiated plans, because I have confidence in us without seeing you first. You are the love of my life, and it doesn't matter how you look or behave because I'll only see you with my heart. I've got 12 undivided days to infiltrate your heart with the intensity of love I possess for you. We've been through so much together, Girl ,and now here comes the reward: the life that we've always dreamed of and talked about in our letters. I'll never disappoint you, not in a million years.

Babe, try to take it easy and not carry more than you can handle. Pretty soon I'll be able to lift that burden, because we are going to be together; that is a promise.

Signed, Your Baby,

Willie

* * *

December 20, 1996

Hi Babe:

Everything is fine now. I've gained two more pounds and school is out for the next three weeks. I thought I would never see that last day before Christmas break.

Guess what happened when I got home from school that last night? I was locked out of my apartment! Somebody had severed half a key into the lock of my front door. When I attempted to insert my key, I shoved it deeper into the keyhole. I was locked out of the apartment for nearly two hours while the maintenance man endeavored to pry his way in through the bedroom window. After a lengthy attempt, another maintenance man finally entered through the sliding glass door. Luckily, I didn't have that bar on the door or he wouldn't have succeeded that way, either.

Remember I told you my spare key was missing? Well, David was the only person who knew where it was. After I informed him we were not going to see each other anymore, he didn't handle it as well as I'd anticipated, so I replaced my lock on the front door to be on the safe side.

Maybe I should just start from when he discovered you and I were communicating again. Of course he was upset, because even though he agreed to our maintaining a semiplatonic relationship, he hoped conditions would change to how they once were. After I revealed to him I wanted to give you and me a chance, he insisted we remain friends; strictly platonic, of course. I skeptically agreed, and I began lessening our proximity by forbidding him to babysit while I attended school at night. I figured we were seeing too much of each other, and I didn't want to convey any mixed signals.

We continued to talk on the phone, and he visited sometimes. He displayed true companionship when I went through that ordeal when I got sick and lost the weight. He made sure I ate, gave me encouragement, and got me out of the house. He was real sweet, and I'll always remember what he did for me. He knew all about us getting back together and that I was coming to see you for Christmas.

He accompanied me when I went to collect my Christmas layaway one day. I had two large bags to carry, and he volunteered to tote one of them. I wanted to exchange the size small bra and panty sets that I bought, because when I put them on layaway, I had just lost all of that weight. Now, since I've gained weight, I wanted to exchange them for a medium. I asked David to look around while I made the exchange. He left but went somewhere where he was able to observe me. He then approached me and said I never bought lingerie like that when he and I were together. I strangely looked at him because I didn't believe he was going there with me, especially after he claimed to be okay with us. I chose to act dumbfounded and asked what was he insinuating? He flat-out answered, "You're buying sexy lingerie for that man in Michigan!" I corrected him in a patronizing voice. "No, David, I am buying underwear for myself."

I couldn't believe we started arguing, and afterward he refused to tote my other bag. I carried both of them to the car and drove his butt straight home. He called later at night, and that's when I informed him I didn't want anything else to do with him. He implied something threatening to me, so at that point I decided to get the lock changed. I didn't confront him, because I didn't have any sound evidence that he had taken the key. He called again and apologized for his behavior, but I wonder what he would have done if he had gotten in the house. I suppose I'll never know.

Four more days and counting.

Love,

Gwen

* * *

Chapter 2

January 10, 1997

Dear Willie:

I told you I wasn't angry when I left there; only disappointed with your current affairs concerning your ex-wife and the way in which you were handling them. For the record, I would like to say you really did show me a good time during my stay there in Michigan. Now I can honestly believe you love me. It's been a long time since I had someone spend every single minute of every single day with me. I hope I didn't offend you when I asked for a little space. I want to apologize again if I made you feel bad, but you've got to understand my last relationship was exactly that way. I carried a shadow around with me everywhere I went, and I don't ever want to live a life like that again. After reflecting on the visit, I realized that I shouldn't have said anything, because it wasn't as if I would be there forever. I just feel it's important to let you know up front about situations that bother me, and I expect the same from you. With this, we'll know and can avoid them or try to in the future.

Now back to your current affairs with your ex-wife. I kept quiet about a lot of situations, because I didn't want to spoil our time together and I wanted everything to be good between us while I was there. I also needed time to rethink these thoughts before I opened my mouth to speak on them. Now I think it's time to share these thoughts with you. First, I want to tell you there are certain rules I've established for myself which I feel I'm bending for you. It's okay because I love you, and that's why I choose to do it. However, the reality is if I'm ever in a bind, I can't really turn to you for financial support. That's not really what I look for in a relationship, but it does play a major part. I'm not worried about it because I knew your financial circumstances and I chose to be with you and allow us to prosper together.

My major concern is I'm not going to begin a relationship with a man who's still allowing his ex-wife to control his life. I feel if that is not put into prospective right now, there will be no future for us. I know you love your kids, but if she's going to use them against you to make you jump through hoops, then maybe you need to refrain from portraying that love so intensely in her presence. If you don't put your foot down, she will continue to manipulate your life and eventually get you back into hers. Now, I'm not being jealous or anything like that. I just can't see myself with a man whose ex-wife can call up anytime she feels the urge, children-related or not, and have you stop in the middle of whatever you may be doing to cater to her needs or she's not going to let you see the kids. What kind of mess is that? What right does she have to become angry and use your kids as a weapon against you because she knows I'm in town?

I also didn't like that I didn't get an opportunity to meet your kids because of her. I also don't like that you've got to pay child support while she, her husband, and your kids are all living in your house, rent-free. I don't expect you to kick them out, but dog, they need to pay all the taxes. It's not fair for you to pay half the taxes on the house that they have lived in rent-free for over two years. You are not ever going to get your life straight, financially or any other way. Why would you want to bring me into a situation like that?

I love you, Babe, with all my heart, but a jealous ex-wife I will not tolerate. Also, I have something else to tell you. I've changed my mind about moving there. This is crazy for me to even consider quitting my job, packing up, and moving there. You don't even have a job right now, and if your wife won't let you see the kids because of me, what do you think will happen if I moved there? The bottom line is I just don't want to come back there and live and deal with another woman's venom. Anyway, it's so cold in Michigan and I had truly forgotten how chilly it used to be until I felt it again. It's not just that because when I said yes, I was at a very low point in my life. I had an issue with my health, and I thought something was going to happen to me. To be honest, I just needed someone to be a part of my life that I loved and who loved me. The bottom line is, I really don't want to quit my job and go to a cold place and most of all deal with an ex-wife. I don't want you to feel as though I'm toying with you because I'm not. I really do want to be with you and spend the rest of my life with you, but I don't want to live in Michigan.

Take care, Babe.

Love,

Gwen

P.S. By the way, I really enjoyed the three days we stayed at your aunt's house in Grand Rapids. You are indeed my kind of man, and please don't be mad.

* * *

January 17, 1997

Dear Gwen:

Girl, that letter was deep. I can understand your position in this situation. First, I want to say I feel much honored that you have bent your rules for me. I don't expect you to tolerate a jealous ex-wife, and I'm definitely not going to continue living my life at her beck and call. As a matter of fact, I informed her she will have to come up with all of the taxes, and she finally agreed to my terms. Hell, she has a husband who works, so it shouldn't be a problem. We agreed she would start paying rent. Since my wages are not being garnished for child support, I am going to pay $100 to her per month until the arrearages are current. I'm charging them $250 per month for rent, so that's a total of $350 toward back child support. Once the arrearages are current, she's going to keep the $250 per month for child support.

Babe, all I was trying to do was be able to spend time with my girls. I couldn't let you meet them, because I knew that if my ex-wife learned you were here, she wouldn't allow me to see them. It was true because that night I spent over at my mother's house, because you needed space, I had Cynthia, my youngest daughter. That was also the night I told my ex-wife you were in town visiting and also when I learned she was married. I told her you were here because I just thought she would find out from your cousin's friend, since that's how she'd gotten information about you in the past.

Needless to say, my ex-wife came and took Cynthia after finding out about you, and she didn't let her spend the night with me. See, I know how she operates, and I was only trying to keep the peace so they would uphold their part of the bargain in regard to paying at least half of the taxes, which we had agreed on at the time.

Babe, I'm not oblivious to what my ex-wife is attempting to do, and I've realized I can't live a lonely life because of my kids. I never planned to live in Michigan forever, because I don't like the cold, either. I dreamed of living in a place where the climate is warm most of the year. My choices were Arizona, California, or Florida. I presume my choice has been made, because I don't want to be anywhere anymore without you. I love you, Sweetheart, and there's no way that you can ever say you don't believe that. I clung to you like white on rice when you were here. I just wanted to show you how much I really do love you. The fact that you needed space didn't make me feel sad, but only made me aware. I understand you didn't want your man in your face 24/7. I gather that when I come down there, I'll have to get Li'l Henry and go somewhere so we can give you a little space from time to time. It's going to be a while before I can come, because I don't want to transfer my parole down there. If I wait it out these next eight months, I'll come there a free man.

I want to let you know I enjoyed the time we stayed at my aunt's house, too. It was nice having some one-on-one time. Girl, you are something else. No, you are my Baby

I love you, Baby, and please don't give up on us.

Willie

P.S. I love you more than the air I breathe

* * *

January 22, 1997

Dear Babe:

How are you since we last talked? In the best of health, I hope. Well, I'd promised this will be a deep letter; one you can lose yourself into. I'm going to tell you all my thoughts, fears, and anything else that comes to mind while I'm in the process of sharing. Today, I am offering you, Steven Willie Johnson, a onetime free offer, nonrefundable certificate, redeemable for Gwen Morgan's thoughts only. Let me stress nonrefundable, because it simply refers to the possibility that if my thoughts are not by chance what you'd expected, you can't say, "I wish you never told me." Okay, so those are the stipulations.

Listen, Babe, I really love and care for you, but I have to admit, my feelings are not as deep as they once were. Maybe it has something to do with us not being together for so long. I am really hoping when we get together my feelings will grow as they once were, because I truly want to be in love with the person I choose to be with. In order to love someone else, I learned I had to first love myself. I think I am at a point where I am happy with myself and am able to share an unconditional love with someone. I want that someone to be you.

I'm not completely happy with my financial situation, but I feel I have the determination and the drive to alter that in a different direction. I would like to know that you and I at least think along the same lines when finances are involved. That's why when I was there I asked that question about how you pay your bills. Do you recall the question? I need to feel confident that bills are being paid and on time. There was a time when Henry would blow most of his paycheck. When the bills were due, I would use my credit cards until I eventually maxed them out. Now I have A-1 credit, and I worked hard to get that status again.

I see you and I handle issues differently. For instance, let's take how you handle your car. Whenever I get any notion something maybe malfunctioning on my car, it immediately becomes priority. I know now one mishap with a car can trigger another, and so on and so forth whenever a car is concerned. I postpone bills and anything else short of my son's health to keep my car running in perfect order. It's my only transportation to work, and it'll always be a priority. I can also understand your situation as far as procuring a lemon and preferring not to continuously put money into it, as opposed to just purchasing another car. I was in the same predicament a while ago. Everything that could have gone faulty with my car did. You do remember when my car broke down when I drove to Saginaw for the class reunion, don't you? Well, the car had a warped head and it cost $500 to fix. You better believe I raised that $500 and got my car. Since then, I've had to get a new clutch installed and CV joints and boots all around. Those are two expensive mechanical jobs, but I paid it and I continued to drive. Thank God for David, because he helped pay for the repairs, and I stressed the same fact to him that I'm emphasizing to you right now. If that's something you can't relate to, let me know. Share your pros and cons about it with me and help me to understand if your views are contrary to mine.

I would like to know how you feel about all things. What do you expect from me when we get together, and how do you feel about arguments? Do you normally walk away or do you argue until doomsday? Do you hold feelings inside and not talk about them, yet behave in a harsh way because of them? In other words, do you hold grudges? Do you trust me? How do you feel about friends coming over to visit? I feel that as far as being affectionate enough toward one another, we have mastered that feature. I would not like to think we couldn't progress in the future because we weren't able to agree on petty affairs like finances, priorities, or misunderstandings. I'm very flexible and always willing to compromise, if you can support your disagreement with logic. I don't like to enter a relationship not knowing what to expect. I know life is about taking chances, but I am content with my life the way it's flowing. I have learned that I can be happy alone. I get lonely sometimes, but I accept those lonely times to be occasions when I can sit and evaluate where I've been, what direction I am heading, and also to bond with God.

At one point in my life I felt there was no one else out there for me. I was in a marriage where my husband didn't respect me and put everyone else's feelings above mine. I then lived with a man who made me feel like I was a prisoner in my own home. Then, I met a man who I took a chance with my feelings and he proved to be unworthy. I had the notion that whoever I cared about didn't care about me, and vice versa.

Now, here I have a man who I very much care about and who does, as much as I can see, care very much about me. Can I let down this shield that I've held over my heart all these years so I can love him to the best of my ability? Can I do things for him I wouldn't normally do for a man and enjoy it? Will he be there for me when I need him most? Will he, sometimes, know that I need him even if I don't ask, or will he say something like, "I can't read minds, if you don't ask, I won't know." You are the person who I risked my marriage for, couldn't get enough of, and just had to have in my life, whether it was friends or lovers. You were the one who made me feel like I was special and able to be loved by a man. You made me feel worthy of a man's attention when I thought I wasn't. You were the one who comforted and consoled me through heartwarming letters and conversations and didn't want to see me hurt anymore in a failed marriage. Why should I question your love for me? Likewise, why should I question my love for you? There should be no ifs, ands, or buts about this, but I have some uncertainty, I'm sorry to say. Maybe you can clear that up when you respond to my letter. Maybe we can clear the air before we get together.

Well, I've saved the best for last. Sex! I know you really want to know my views on it. Before I arrived there, I had mixed feelings about you in this department. I felt you were a kinky person after you enlightened me with some of the things you liked. You scared me when you emphasized your feelings as far as if someone really cared about you, they would do anything within their power to try to please you sexually or something to that nature. I felt I had something to prove, and that was not a way to begin a relationship.

I feel that what you stated was correct to an extent. You know as well as I do that everyone was reared with certain morals and values. One of my morals is, I'm not going to do something I despise or simply just don't want to do, and I feel that I shouldn't have to. We both shared with one another the things we liked and disliked as far as sex is concerned, and from here on out I feel we already know. What we choose to do to one another from this day forward should be our choice to make. In other words, I prefer you not to ask for sexual favors. Yes, that's exactly what I feel it is when someone asks for it.

Now, I'm not going to totally withhold sexual pleasures from you, because I simply just don't want to do it, just postpone them until the time has come when I feel comfortable with it. I'm not ignorant or inexperienced with the "You must keep him happy so he won't go astray" mentality—but I won't continue to exercise something that doesn't stimulate you, because it would only bring my self-esteem down. Do you understand? I also feel if we could have a stable sexual relationship, a lot of the skepticism and anxiety in my mind would be eliminated as far as this letter is concerned.

I want to let you know I have never had my breast kissed in the way that you did. I really enjoyed your expertise, and I'm really looking forward to advancing in other sexual adventures with you. I'm certain that will happen.

All in all, I'm looking forward to sharing my life with you, Babe. I have grounds to believe that this relationship will be far more fulfilling and more story-book-like than any I've yet to experience. I know this because we have grown and learned so much apart that we can teach each other together. I'm so happy to have you back in my life once again, and I'm going to do all I can to make this work. Just promise one thing, okay: that you will never make me cry. I have not cried from the actions of a man since Henry. No one else has ever been able to do it. That is a promise I made to myself, to never allow it to happen again. Make me that promise, Babe, okay?

Well, I guess that's about it for now. Next time, it will cost you for my thoughts. Again I say this is a one-time free offer.

I love you,

Gwen

* * *

January 28, 1997

Dear Sweetheart:

I now have a new understanding of the saying, "There's no fun when the rabbit has the gun." I am referring to the way that I feel about you versus the way you feel about me. I have never cared so much for a woman who didn't feel as much or even more for me. It really hurts to know that a woman can make a grown man cry. I could sense your disturbance with me and your eagerness to board that plane and be rid of me. I knew it had something to do with my ex-wife. I was hurting so bad when you left here that it was painful to even breathe just thinking of the woman I love had just walked out of my life. I'm not going to ask you not to hurt me, because I know God won't give me any more pain than I can handle. All I ask is for you to give me a chance; a chance to make you happy, a chance for you to let your guard down and let me love you, and you me. I know you will enjoy being with me with all of your heavy shielded walls down, the ones you have carried around for so long.

I sometimes wonder if I'm the man you wanted yesterday. What I mean by that is I think I possess all of the qualities you want in a man and then some, but it's as if you don't want those things anymore. If you want turmoil and conflict, then you have a right to have doubts about me being the man for you. See, I have been there and done that. I feel I have been given a new chance at life, and I want to fill it with love and joy. The woman who I want to share this love and joy with is you. I openly express my feelings to you no matter how deep they are, no matter how much your answer may hurt me. I want you and only you as my woman for the rest of my life.

I see you are asking some questions that I have answered before. Well, allow me to speak on them again. Finances: I feel that bills come first. I also feel that something should be saved for tomorrow. I don't believe in, "Well, we'll save some, next year." I had $1,000 saved with my sister for when I got out, but she spent it. I was mad, but she never knew it. I think you have forgotten that I do have my priorities in order. My house comes first and then my car, because I can get a ride to work if needed. I can't get that house back if I don't pay those taxes. I have to take care of that business first. I hope you can see that as I do.

Arguments: I don't see much of that in my future anymore due to the fact I see you as my equal. I feel as you do. If your argument has bearing, there is nothing to argue about. I can admit when I'm wrong and we can move on. I sometimes think we have so many things in common that there isn't anything to fight about. There are no issues for us to iron out. I trust you more than I have ever trusted a woman. Now, don't get me wrong, I have my moments of doubt, but they quickly fade away. When you called and told me you never got on that plane and you had to stay another night because of the fog, I was so upset I couldn't spend that last night with you. I don't know why I, for just an instant, thought you may have been with someone else at your sister's house the night before you left. I think you will use good judgment in regard to having men friends over to visit. If you do love me, I don't think you will do anything that will put our love in jeopardy.

The things I expect from you are the things any man wants from his woman. I want your total commitment to what we have. I want you to be able to take into consideration the situations I have been through in my life. I want you to stand by me and be there for me. I expect for you to work with me on everything. I expect for you to trust and believe in me, that I will do the right thing for us at all times.

This is really hard on me, us being so far apart. I want to be near you so badly. I think about you every moment of the day and night. I can't believe how much I think about you. You are so far away but so close in my thoughts. I guess that's what immortality is.

Well, you know what I said when I saw the word "sex," right? Just in case you're wondering, I said, "Damn!" I am so glad that you can find a silver lining in the sex category. I hope your breasts are the stepping stone toward pleasing the rest of your body. If I was kinky, you don't have to worry about that anymore, because I'm back to the basics again and I want to master that before I do anything else. Now, speaking of being scared, I'm afraid of you. As good as your love nest is, I think I will be content with that for many years to come. Believe me when I say I have never tried to please a woman as hard as I tried to please you while you were here. If I succeeded, then I imagine I'm just a natural. (smile)

I have to go to sleep now, so that will close this letter—but never my heart.

Willie

* * *

February 6, 1997

Hello, Baby:

Happy Valentine's Day! I hope I sent the card off in perfect time to reach you on V-Day. How are you? In the best of health since we last talked, I hope. Speaking of the last time we talked, I felt a warm feeling within when I hung up the receiver. I felt as though I was very much a part of your life, especially after you asked for my opinion on your choice about your employment directions. I felt there's no need to write to you about doubts anymore, because they've all been cleared up. In essence, all I really want to write about is the love I feel for you at this present time and the newfound light that I see in our future.

I would like for you to recall a certain statement you made in our last telephone conversation about me saying what you'd thought I would say. Isn't that such a great feeling for us to be in sync with one another? What's even better is for me to do something you'd thought I would do. Just think, somewhere within our inner-self, our spirits combined and thought the same thought at the exact same time. Sometimes you can hear the unsaid by listening inwardly with your heart, which in turn allows you to understand a person better and ask fewer questions of them. I would love to be able to bond with you in that sort of way.

With each disappointment, there's real temptation to stop opening your heart to love, and I fell right into that trap for so many years. I'm so happy you've held that key to my heart all of this time and did not throw it away. You were courageous enough to unlock it without fear of disappointment; just taking a chance at love. Now I'm able to love the way I want to love again. You spoke of my love for you as love of yesterday, and I spoke of its deepness. The best way that I can clarify that is to say: We all handle situations differently when we were young versus when we mature. Maybe the way we love goes through a maturing process, too. Just maybe the way we felt when we were young, however intense we thought it may have been, in reality is the same love we're experiencing now, but at a different magnitude because we are older. That's the explanation I'm going to accept for my feeling because I know how I feel for you now, and I remember how I felt then.

Listen, Babe, I hope you enjoyed your gift and candy. It's just a little something from the heart for our first official Valentine's Day together. Now you see, when I asked the question about your underwear, it was for a reason. I hope you like the red-and-black bikini briefs. It was a choice between Reese's Peanut Butter Cups and Kisses. I pondered for a while as I weighed my choices. The Kisses won by a landslide, because that's what I want to give—a big, juicy kiss.

Take care, love ya,

Gwen

* * *

February 10, 1997

Dear Willie:

What's up? Hey, I'm sort of getting back in the habit of writing you again. Well, I've decided I'm going to do less calling and more writing from now on. I have been taking for granted being able to call you at liberty now, and I've forgotten the shock of receiving the telephone bill. Reminiscing over the time when writing letters was our only source of communication, it really wasn't bad at all. I do understand I won't be endowed with all of your attention like before, simply because you don't have the time to think of every special thing in the world to say to me. It's okay, though, I know you're busy, and I also know that you're on a mission and that's to get those taxes paid.

Me, I've finally finished school, quit my second job, and will have all the time in the world to write you as much as I like, as long as I like, and especially as passionately as I would like. I guess you're wondering why I quit my part-time job, right? Well, Babe, on two occasions I didn't show up for work. The second time, I had every intention of going because I had my uniform in the car when I took Li'l Henry to the State Fair. I'd already planned to be one hour late for work, but, when that time came, I wasn't ready to leave, and I knew Li'l Henry wasn't ready, either. I didn't even feel obligated to locate a telephone to call in.

When I start feeling that way about a job, something just isn't right anymore. When I begin placing my personal life above a job incessantly, I don't need to work there anymore. It's unfair to the employer, because they can't rely on me; to the employees, because they're left with more than their share of the work; and to me, because I feel guilty about causing all the turmoil. These thoughts were dancing around in my mind as I continued to enjoy the fair with my son. After leaving the fair, I thought about going in three hours late, but I really didn't want the inconvenience of dropping Li'l Henry off and then waking him up to take him home afterward. So I drove to the hotel and turned in my uniform. Of course, the boss wasn't there at that late hour, but my intentions were to call her the next day.

The boss and I missed each other's calls the next day. I've tried to quit before when I was sick, and she wouldn't allow it. She continued to call and call until I said yes. If that happens this time, I'll just work on an on-call basis only. Then I'll be able to say "No" if I'm doing something else.

Babe, I'm just tired. I have worked two and three jobs at a time, worked all day for days at a time, and I am sick of it. I am tired of working my life away. This world is passing me by, and I'm not playing my role in it because I'm too busy working. It's time to be more than a quarter-part of my son's life. It's a known fact that the more you make, the more you spend. I will learn to budget correctly and just make it work with what little I have, because I am ready to enjoy life. One job is enough. I just need to make this job pave the way. With time that's possible, and if not, I'll move on to bigger and better things because there's nowhere else for me to go but up.

Before I let go of this subject, I don't want you to feel like a blast from the past. And I'm talking about the fact that your ex-wife wanted you to work while she sat at home. I am an independent woman; always have been and always will be. I will never, ever, ever, totally depend on a man to take care of me. The reason for that, more so than the fact I want to be my own woman, is I want to control my own life. My outlook on life is by far broader than you know. As I'm watching it unfold, I see you as a man who has entered, yet is looking around in bewilderment. You have touched the surface, Babe, yet there is more to me to learn, experience, and understand. I will help guide you and even hold your hand along the way, because I want you to know me completely. I want you to understand me just as you do yourself, and vice versa, of course. At that point, you would know not to ask questions that would embarrass me. You would know to be considerate of that. Me, I suppose I would know that your prefer me to initiate self-enticing entertainment, rather than other means. In other words, use my sex toy for my sexual enlightenment (smile).

Well, anyway, I talked to the travel agent and I really didn't like the quotes. From Grand Rapids to Tampa is $266 round trip. This quote is for one week's stay, departing Wednesday, June 11, and returning Tuesday, June 17. She assured me that cheaper rates could become available as close as two weeks in advance. I'll just continue calling to find out when they will have something cheaper.

Take care,

Gwen

* * *

February 15, 1997

Dear Willie:

Presently it's 5:45 AM, February 15. I woke up about 45 minutes ago with you on my mind, and what I'm having are not good thoughts, I'm sorry to say. I tried not to show it, but I was upset on the phone yesterday and I know you could sense it. I didn't say anything because I felt I was being selfish for getting upset over something that possibly could be trivial to you. However, when it causes me to wake up at 5:00 in the morning with tears in my eyes, I think maybe it's not a selfish thing and not so trivial at all. I'm sure you already know what's up, because you're not stupid.

It has always been difficult for me to pretend. Didn't you notice how poorly I performed on the phone when we talked? I have a bad habit of trying to pretend I'm okay about something, because I fear someone might think what I really feel is stupid. Today I'm going to ignore those feelings and share what's on my mind with you.

I am upset because you didn't think enough of me to give me anything for Valentine's Day. I believe you weren't even going to call if I hadn't sent that gift. Allow me to give you a synopsis of my Valentine's Day history; beginning from high school. On Valentine's Day and Sweetest Day, people would walk into the classroom with roses purchased in advance by the guys who wanted to make their girl feel special. I wouldn't really be involved with anyone at the time, but oh man, I just felt so bad when I didn't get anything. Then I was involved with Henry in eleventh grade and I just knew for sure I would get one that year. But, guess what? I didn't. I thought to myself, Why do I always fall for the ones who don't give a damn! I think I received a rose in my twelfth-grade year, but it was from someone else who was attracted to me or something. It didn't count because it didn't come from someone I loved or who loved me. From then on, Henry and I were together and he never did anything for Valentine's Day. So, it was something I had to get accustomed to but I didn't like it.

Then David came along, and Valentine's Day was *the* day. He made me feel I was someone special, truly loved, and just queen for a day. And he did it every year, because he felt I was worth his effort. Speaking of David, he taught me a great deal about love and the many ways to express it. I mean, every day was special with him, and holidays were icing on the cake. That song, "Find One Hundred Ways" by James Ingram, was my reality when I was with him. Hell, I used to feel guilty about not thinking of ways to give it back to him, even though I didn't exactly feel about him as he felt about me, but it didn't matter to him. Please don't think I'm comparing you to someone else, because it's not about that. The bottom line is this, I've been spoiled. I've been spoiled rotten. And once you've been spoiled, it's hard to go back and accept the old ways you were treated.

Now, I tried very hard to believe you were not only saying and doing things to make me feel special because you were in jail and needed to have someone out here waiting for you. I said, "Nope, this is Willie, and he would never play with my feelings. He's still going to make me feel just as special when he gets out, and I know he won't take me for granted." But what other day is there to make me feel special, loved, and cared about than Valentine's Day?

So, I'm sitting here in the middle of the night trying to weigh the pros and cons and debating the issues. I have to understand you have higher concerns that require your attention—and your money, for that matter. I also know you do indeed know how to make me feel special, because I can recall the time when you were in jail and had a rose sent to me. I'm sure it took a lot of maneuvering to accomplish that from inside, and a hell of a lot more money, but you did it because you wanted to make your Baby feel special. Even though lately things have been going smoothly between us, this one action has made me second-guess your intentions. I'm thinking you feel you don't have to work hard at this relationship. Did you even think about how I would feel about you not even acknowledging Valentine's Day? I go to the malls and see all of these men hurrying around trying to find something nice for their loved one, and I'm sure you saw that, too. The bottom line is you can choose to do something or not. You didn't have to and I suppose I shouldn't have expected it, but I did, and I set myself up for disappointment.

What's sad about it is in the back of my mind I thought that you were not a Valentine's Day person, but I didn't really know. So I deliberately sent that letter to you with my work address on it, just hoping maybe you would catch the hint. You know, "work address, send rose to job." Don't think for a moment that I prefer to get upset after the fact, when I could have forewarned you of my feelings so you could have done the right thing. There's no fun in my telling you what to do in these situations. The beauty of it all is you knowing what to do without me opening my mouth. I mean, my goodness, this is a newfound love and a relationship that you and I have just discovered again. Pardon me for being sentimental, but what better way to set it off then to express it on our very first Valentine's Day? If you didn't do anything for future Valentine's Days, you definitely should have done something for this first one.

I know you may feel like I'm overdoing it and hitting the nail too far in the hole, but I can't help it and I want you to know exactly how this makes me feel. You need to know why I'm going to ask you to pull back, because I need time to rethink things, regroup, and make some decisions. Doubt is shooting me straight in the face right now. I feel like I'm going to expect things in the future, and you're not going to come through, and I'm going to be left feeling like I do today. I can't go back, Babe. I've been out there and I've been exposed to something good that I'm kind of thinking I'll never find again, and I can't go back to yesterday. If I can't have what I had or close to it, I don't want anything at all. I suppose that's the reason why I live alone, because I'm not settling for less. I have to realize that there's no sense in me asking you to be someone you're not, because even if you tried, it would only be you doing something for my benefit, and that charade cannot be played forever.

Baby, I also don't want you to feel I'm thinking this way because of one simple mistake and that I'm not giving you a chance. Get this into your head this time. I am constantly bending my rules for you. It's okay because I love you and I want to do it, but I'm not going to continue doing it. At some point I've got to say, "No, this is enough." I'm saying it now because I have found happiness within myself after being alone for so long; true happiness, and I'm not going to let someone come into my life and destroy that for me. I'm not going to live my life unhappy simply because you are the love of my life. *Unto thine own self be true.* And that's why I'm going to do. I'll be darned if you didn't do the very thing I'd asked you not to do (make me cry!).

Take care,

Gwen

* * *

February 18, 1997

Dear Sweetheart:

I've done something very bad and I don't know what I can do to make it right again but, I will try my best. I'm so sorry that my actions have caused you so much pain. Please believe me when I say I would never, ever do anything intentional that I felt would cause you sorrow or make you cry. Now that I'm looking back on the situation and your reaction, I realize I was stupid not to have known Valentine's Day would be important to you or any woman, for that matter. The truth is I was concentrating too much on getting those taxes paid on the house and finding a permanent job that it never crossed my mind. However, I know there is no excuse to have not displayed my love for you on Valentine's Day. I will say that I'm not the type of guy who waits for a day of the year to show the woman in my life that she is special. You are special to me every day and I tell you that through the words I share with you. I show you that whenever I take the time to carefully select the best greeting cards to send to you. I display my concern for your well being when I send money, not only to cover the telephone bill but, extra for other areas that you might need help with.

I'm not going to always know what to do to keep a smile on your face, but that doesn't mean I don't want to make you happy. Please forgive me for taking for granted that Valentine's Day didn't mean more to you than it did. I truly and wholeheartedly understand what it means to you now and this will never ever, ever, happen again. I promise your eyes will never be wet again because of me.

I love you yesterday, now, and forever more.

Willie

* * *

Chapter 3

February 20, 1997

Dear Babe:

Let me share with you what made me smile, laugh, or made my heart feel warm inside today. First was Li'l Henry wishing me a happy birthday. Then after I drove him to school, there was this duck on the curb trying to cross the street. The person coming in the opposite direction and I stopped to let him cross. That made me smile. Everyone at work remembered my birthday, and that made me smile. Charlene's boyfriend, William, came in with a birthday card and insisted that I open it while he watched, because he wanted to see my expression, and that made me laugh. Charlene called me at work and wished me a happy birthday. My hairdresser called and wished me one and volunteered to touch up my hair, free of charge. One of the patients remembered and wished me one. Most of all, what really put a smile on my face and a warm feeling within my heart today was when a lady walked through the door with a dozen long-stemmed red roses and a balloon saying, "I love you," from my Baby.

All of that was really nice. What really made me happy—truly happy—was to have seen another year. I can say I was able to take care of my son, provide for him, see him through another lesson learned, and watch him grow another year older. This year brought you back into my life and helped me to realize that there's someone out there to share love again with. Most of all, I was happy I was in good health to enjoy this day.

Babe, do you remember when you told me you were vulnerable because you've opened up to me and shared your real feelings? Well, I didn't believe you really felt that way about me. I didn't believe your feelings could be so deep for me after not being a part of my life for so long. It was hard to totally believe because I knew my feelings for you weren't as strong as they once were. At that point, I felt if anything bad would have happened between us, I could have walked away without a tear to shed.

Remember when you said you were beginning to feel I really loved you? When you were feeling it, it was really happening. Now comes the scary part for me, too, because I have indeed opened up my heart completely to you. That feeling I longed to feel and hadn't felt in such a long time, well, I feel it now. It's like butterflies or a fluttery feeling in my heart every time I think about you. It sort of hurts but in a good way. Do you know how they say it "hurts so good?" Well, that's what I'm experiencing.

I am so happy I found someone (well, I know you found me) who loves me just as much as I love him. After Henry, I wanted to be with someone who loved me more. My theory was women are more sensitive to needs than men are. Most times when a woman doesn't love a man as much, she will present the love that she does feel as more than it really is and make that man feel she loves him just as much because of that sensitivity. Men can't really magnify their feelings in that way or, shall I say, show more affection than they really feel. Anyway, I thought that would be good for me. In the long run, I ended up feeling empty inside, that it wasn't right, and missing the hell out of that feeling in my heart that I used to feel.

I can't wait until you come to visit. I am going to show you all of these feelings that I'm experiencing right now. I probably won't be able to tell you better than I can show you.

All my love, and thank you very much.

Gwen

* * *

February 25, 1997

Hi, Babe:

I must be a woman in love, because I haven't done this much writing since I was a woman in love. From the time I stopped writing you until now, I had really lost my desire to write. There were a few friends from my military days whom I've wished I had kept in contact with, but I always made an excuse when it came to writing. It just didn't do anything for me anymore after you.

Speaking of military, there is a secret that I'm going to share with you. I guess I was too embarrassed to tell you up to this point. Believe me, I would have taken this secret to my grave, not even my mother knows. Remember when I told you about me being stationed over in Germany, and that's where I got out of the military? Well, I didn't exactly get out in Germany; I just got away from there.

After I went on my 30-day leave before I was to report to Germany, I was staying with Henry because he was in the Marines at the time. We had already had Li'l Henry. When the time came to leave, I didn't want to go so, I fabricated a story about not having anyone to keep my son. I was able to delay going for about a week. When the week was over, I tried to lie again, and the man on the phone said something that scared the hell out of me. "If we find out you're lying and interfering in military orders, you could be court-martialed," he said. I heard him loud and clear and I wasn't about to risk being reduced in rank or have money taken out of my paycheck. So I agreed to leave the very next day. Babe, I had never cried so hard in my entire life, because I was to leave my son for two years.

The reason I reenlisted to go to Germany was because I wanted to go somewhere my family could go, too. I had been in the Army for over two years, stationed at the same duty place, so I felt that sooner or later I would get orders to go someplace. I didn't want to go somewhere like Korea, where I wouldn't have the option of taking my family, so that's how I decided to reenlist for Germany. Henry wasn't in the military when I made the decision to reenlist. He was staying with me in Fayetteville but, enlisted back into the Marines shortly after.

After I reenlisted, I wasn't due to go until three months up the road. Henry was trying to get into the Army, but to no avail. Things got tight, and it became more difficult to make ends meet since he wasn't working. Henry then reenlisted in the Marines after the Army kept giving him the runaround.

When my orders came, they read "Unaccompanied Tour"—and I was devastated. All I could think of was I couldn't take my son, no way, no how. So I moved all the furniture down to Jacksonville where Henry was stationed, and we agreed he would keep Li'l Henry. We convinced my sister Pam to relocate to Jacksonville to help take care of him.

When I got to Germany, it was terrible. No one was there to meet me at the airport. I walked around among all those foreigners in a place I knew nothing about. After a while, I finally saw an information booth and the lady spoke English. She gave me a telephone number and pointed me in the direction of a bank that was inside the airport. She said I needed to transfer my American money to marks (German money) in order to make the phone call.

Babe, I only had $6 in my pocket at the time. Imagine traveling all the way to a foreign country with only $6 in your pocket!

I made the call and was informed I would be picked up shortly. I walked around the airport in search of a place to eat that I could afford, but to no avail. I had arrived in Germany in the early morning, and would you believe I didn't get picked up until 7:00 PM. I was miserable, I was hungry, and I was mad because I didn't want to be there.

A German man finally came to pick me up, and he didn't speak a lick of English. We rode to the Army post in complete silence. It was the longest ride ever from the airport to the barracks, because I kept feeling I should say something, so I couldn't get relaxed. We had to stop at the gate, where there were two German soldiers standing on guard. Imagine them guarding our military post. Their uniforms were faded gray with one-button-flap closure on four pockets: two on each side of the chest, and the others at the hips. High above their waist like, Pee-wee Herman, and on top of their uniform jacket, they wore a black, thick leather belt with a large buckle. The hard hats on their heads looked like they were on backwards. We had to show our IDs in order to be allowed into the base. I thought they were going to extend their right arms like I remember seeing in those Adolf Hitler movies, but they saluted the same as we did.

I finally got something to eat when I got to the barracks. I checked in, took a shower, and went straight to bed, because it was 10:00 PM in Germany but 10:00 AM in the United States. Jet lag was kicking in. Saturday, the next day, I ate breakfast, lunch, and dinner all alone, and I didn't have a roommate, either. The barracks did not have a day room where soldiers usually gather for entertainment. There was nowhere to watch TV, socialize, or play pool, nothing. So I stayed in my room most of the day, watching the four walls. Finally when I couldn't take anymore solitude, I went out of my room to ask the soldier, who was in charge of quarters, a question. "Could you tell me how to make a telephone call to the States?"

Just as I was asking, lo and behold, this guy was passing by and he stopped. "Oh, I'll take care of that for you, Roberts," he immediately butted in. "My name is John and everybody calls me

Trainer," he said as he pointed to his name tag located above his upper right pocket on his uniform. "What's your name?"

"I'm Specialist Morgan," I said as I shook his hand. "I'm just arriving from the States."

"Oh, okay, so you're a newbie, huh? Come on, the pay phone is right around the corner and I'll show you how to make the call."

Trainer seemed pretty friendly, and we hit it off very well. He introduced me to some people, and I spent all of my time with him from that point on. We went out to the noncommissioned officers club and even to a couple of spots outside of the gate. Trainer took me over to a friend's house to play cards and socialize. His friend was also in the Army but lived on the economy, which is what everyone calls housing area outside the military gate. The house entry doors opened to the outside instead of the inside, which is common in the United States. There McDonald's had beer on the menu, and it was also a selection in the vending machines.

Trainer taught me how to catch the bus to town and even introduced me to the slot machines. They had many different models right there on the post: one-, three-, and even nine-way chances to win a straight line. They even had nickel machines, and I won instantly on the first try, which had me hooked. I found out Bingo was played every Tuesday night, so I was in heaven. Trainer and I ate together, and I was happy to have found a friend. He never even tried to hit on me until the very end, but even if I'd wanted to, it was too late because by then I had accepted him as a friend. That decision was confirmed in my mind right after he took me into a room full of men to play cards when we first met. I was convinced that if he was trying to get with me, he wouldn't have done any mess like that. He was light-skinned, chunky, and only a foot taller than me, so he wasn't my type. Anyhow, it really was too late, because Trainer had only had three weeks left before he was to return to the States. So I was thankful that he'd helped me to get acclimated while lessening my loneliness, yet it didn't take away the yearning for my son, whom I missed very much. Li'l Henry couldn't even say "Mama" before I left him. I would sit in my room and write poems about him all the time. Unfortunately, I lost all but one of them.

Well, anyway, I ended up working in the Personnel Administration Center again, and I asked the NCOIC about taking leave for Christmas. Now, I had only gotten there a little before Thanksgiving, but I couldn't imagine spending Christmas away from my son. Thank God the NCOIC said, "It should be okay, but we would have to see." Boy, was I excited then.

I met this lady during our in-processing who was just getting there, too. It was nice to have a female to talk to, and she lived right down the hall from me. I used to go to her room and sit with her until she met someone, fell in love, and was never there anymore. Nevertheless, things in Germany were beginning to work themselves out. I met a few people, I wasn't eating alone as much anymore, and I was even learning German. "Guten Morgen" means "good morning" in German. Everyone was automatically enrolled into this German course when we first arrived there.

Physical training was done in the early mornings, the same as in the States. Everyone had to fall into PT formation around 5:00 AM. We ran in formation around the post, and I even volunteered to be the road guard. The road guard wears a bright orange vest and is responsible for stopping the cars as the formation crosses intersections. I would run ahead of the formation and relieve the road guard who was previously holding off the traffic. He or she would sprint to the next intersection, and I would stop traffic until the entire formation had crossed. Upon reaching the intersection, I would extend my arm out and place my hand in the stop position while the other was held behind my back. Even though I still had to jog in place, it sort of felt like a break from the constant running. I never volunteered for road guard in the States, but I felt really happy. Everything was looking up, especially after I knew I was going home for Christmas to see my Li'l Henry, which was all I wanted.

On Thanksgiving, military people who were living on the economy came to pick up those soldiers who lived in the barracks and took them to their houses for Thanksgiving dinner. It wasn't a mandatory thing; you had an option to go or eat dinner in the mess hall. By this time Trainer had left, so I went with one of the families and had a decent time. We watched movies, ate dinner, and they brought us back to the barracks. Right after Trainer left, a lot of times I had to eat alone again, so I was kind of happy to go. As you can see, I didn't care much for eating alone. Just imagining myself sitting at a table all alone in a mess hall full of people was just embarrassing for me. I felt like people pitied me for not having at least one friend to eat with.

At that time, overseas had a deferred payment program. It's in the States now but wasn't then. I was excited about it because I had plans to purchase a TV and VCR and start fixing up my room. I wanted to try to make it feel lived in. Burger King was right across the street and the only restaurant on the entire post. I was going to put in an application there to work part-time so I could fill up some of the free time I had to think about Li'l Henry. I was on a roll then, planning out my stay there. They even told me I could bring my son down, but it would take a year to get on-post housing. If I brought him down, I would have to increase my tour to three years instead of two, which I didn't want to do. So I figured I'd just take leave every so often to see my son, and everything would work itself out. They have military hops where you can catch a flight back to the States for as cheap as $10. I figured by having that luxury available to me, two years would be over in no time.

So it started getting close to the time to submit my leave form. I typed it out and took it to the NCOIC with the big ole smile on my face. "Here's my leave form for you to sign," I said as I dropped it into his in-box. He then said something that wiped that smile right off of my face quicker than a rabbit making a dash for a suspended carrot. He said, "We're not going to be able to let you take leave for Christmas."

"Why not?" I asked

"Well, first of all, we are short staffed. Second, you haven't been here very long and other soldiers have seniority."

"Okay," was all I could muster up in response. I tried to say it in my most convincing voice, to make him believe I was really okay with his decision. I turned and walked out thinking I'd handled his response very well, but, boy, was I wrong. When I got outside his office, the tears from deep within began to build inside my eyes. Try as I might to contain them, I couldn't hold them back any longer, so I went to the bathroom and cried like a baby. I felt like I couldn't breathe without my son. I didn't want to live if he couldn't be with me.

I endured at least 10 minutes of bawling before I made up my mind that it was silly to continue. Once I made that decision, I didn't feel like crying anymore. What gave me a calm sense of being was an inner voice assuring me that I had full control over my reactions as well as my attitude. I could choose to view this situation as the end of the world, or I could find a positive outlook. After realizing I had that option and choosing to see the positive side, I was absolutely fine.

When I returned to the work area, the girls in the office were having a discussion about my taking leave for Christmas. They felt the NCOIC could have let me go. They were all explaining how the office could be run during the Christmas break. They felt the soldiers who weren't going home for leave could handle the extra workload. I looked at them and I said, "I'll go AWOL." Everybody immediately stop talking. They all looked at me and started laughing. I laughed along with them, but I was as serious as a heart attack about going absent without leave if that's what I needed to do.

My plans began by sending boxes of clothes home in the mail. I didn't see the need to continue studying German because I knew I would not be there to take that first exam. It was amazing how my interest in learning German quickly disappeared when the possibility of going home became my pursuit. After finding a flight to the States with several open seats, I began planning how I would make my escape. I would take the bus to the train station, and then railways would deliver me to my final destination, the big "A." Thank God for Trainer, because I never would have known how to catch the bus into town if he hadn't shown me.

Satisfied with all of my planning, the only thing I had left to do was wait for the money. My mom and dad who were now back together again and, who knew nothing about my plans, were sending the money. It was my Christmas present from both of them. As far as they knew, I was going home on leave for Christmas.

I was scheduled to leave in two days, and the money still hadn't arrived. I began to panic. I called my mother and I begged, "Mama, could you please purchase the ticket in the States? I still have not received the money in the mail, and I'm afraid the flight will book up. Please, Mama, I don't want to risk not being able to come home for Christmas."

"What about the $585 I've already sent for the ticket?" my mother asked.

"There's still a couple more days to get that in the mail. I'll bring it with me when I come and mail it back to you, okay?"

"Okay," was my mom's reply, so now all I had to do was pick up my ticket at the airport.

Normally, my mother would not have extra money to give to me at will. Fortunately, she had just hit the lottery for a large sum, and she divided a portion of her winnings between her six daughters. She wanted to do something nice for all of us for Christmas, and I was very thankful for the financial help she was giving me.

Unfortunately, the $585 was sent in cash at my request. I didn't want to deal with the hassle of trying to cash a check or money order. I wasn't about to leave without it, so I made several trips to the mail room only to continuously hear, "No mail." Even when I checked the day before, the money still had not come. "What the hell is going on?" I said to the mail clerk. "Are you positive it's not here? Because it was mailed well over a week ago!"

The mail clerk checked a second time and discovered the letter was misfiled in the letter "G" box for Gwen instead of "M" for Moore. It probably had been there several days ago, but I didn't care. I was so glad he found it. I had to wipe the sweat off of my forehead, because that very thing could have destroyed all of my plans, considering the flight had been scheduled for the very next day.

I decided not to take my large suitcases, because I didn't want to look suspicious. I took a small suitcase, a box, and a big bag that

I was able to fit the rest of my civilian clothes into. To hell with those military clothes, I thought as I left them all behind.

Six o'clock that next morning, I walked out of my room, asked the person who was in charge of quarters to keep my room key until I returned, as I often did. I walked out of the building and headed toward the bus station across the street. I had the small suitcase in one hand and the box and bag in the other. When I got to the bus stop, I realized I didn't have any change. The smallest bill I had was $20, and Burger King wasn't open for business yet. After the bus arrived, I walked up the steps and reached out to hand the bus my $20. Boy, was I hoping he could make change! He looked at me dumbfounded and said, "I need the correct change, Ma'am." I had to turn around and get right back off the bus.

I was beginning to feel like the odds were working against me. Nothing seemed to be going as planned, even after all of my careful preparation. Thank God I had a Plan B, which was to get started six hours before my flight was due to leave. I made sure I had plenty of time to compensate for any setbacks.

I sat there at the bus stop for a short while and waited for Burger King to open. I went inside and ordered a breakfast sandwich so I would have the change I needed. I had no idea when the next bus would arrive so, I decided to catch a cab instead. "Do you know the telephone number to call a cab?" I asked the lady who had taken my order. She wrote it down for me and I used the pay phone in Burger King to call.

"Guten Morgen," I said to the cab driver as he got out to grab my bags. He smiled and he also said good morning in German. When I was riding in the back of the cab, I kept trying to rehearse in my mind what I would say in German to the cab driver when I paid him. I remembered how to count to twenty. I also remembered the word "how" was "wie" and the word "much" was "viel" in German. Even though he was a complete stranger, I wanted to impress him with what I had learned. "Wie viel?" I asked as I opened my wallet. "Zehn," he answered which meant $10. I knew that in German money, two marks was the same as one American dollar. I handed him $6. "Danke schön," he said, thanking me as he handed my bags to me and returned to the cab.

As I waited for the next train to arrive, I saw some people I remembered seeing in my German class. They asked where was I going. I told them I was going to Frankfurt, Germany, to visit a friend. They made some cracks about it looking as though I was leaving Germany with the suitcase. We all laughed together. Little did they know, my laughter represented something totally different than theirs. I rode on the train thinking it would take me all the way to the airport. Unfortunately, my stop was two miles from the airport, and I had to catch another cab the rest of the way. The cab driver cheated me out of some money and I knew it, but I didn't care because I was one step closer to seeing my Li'l Henry, and that was all that mattered to me.

I checked in at the check-in counter and had the ticket in my hand when the attendant asked to see my leave form. I didn't really know that the airlines required a leave form to take leave. Hell, they never asked for one when I traveled on leave in the States. I didn't know what made me keep that leave from I typed, but I did and had it right in my pocket. I'd even signed my NCOIC's signature on it, just in case. As I handed it over to the attendant, I remember thinking how finally something worked out for the good of my careful planning.

The man reviewed my leave form then took my suitcase and sat it on the baggage belt. I walked onto the plane without a care in the world. I was on my way home for Christmas to see my baby, and after all of the setbacks, I was now confident it was going to happen. Not a soul knew of my plans at that point, not even Henry. When I think about that time in my life, what comes to mind is, I bet all of those people whom I mentioned AWOL to, and even the ones who saw me at the train station, said, "Doggone it, she really did it!"

That journey taught me a lot about myself. I learned if there's something I really, truly want, I'm going to get it, do it, and be it and I'm not going to let anyone say I can't. I don't see myself breaking any laws in the future, but the words "I can't" will never pass my lips again.

Now I'm going to ask you to answer some questions for me, either on the phone or in a return letter. Was my story about Germany interesting? Did you, at any part, feel anxious to read on? Was it suspenseful—meaning, did you want to know what happened next? Were you only interested because you believed this really happened to me? Please answer these questions, because it's for a good reason. I'm not going to tell you yet, but I have an idea. I love you Baby.

Until next time,

Gwen

* * *

March 2, 1997

Dear Love:

Well, it sure feels good to be bombarded with letters from you. This is just like the old days, but it seems we have switched places. I see you made reference to the possibility of my not being able to put as much feeling into my letters now that I am not in prison. Please understand you will get my all no matter where I am, because my feelings are real and they are constant. I can't and I don't turn them on and off.

Now I'll answer all of your questions. I am going to begin with the last letter I received. I thought your Germany story was very interesting and heartbreaking as well as eye-opening. I was anxious to read on; however, I am still looking for the missing pieces. I think I would want to read it whether it was a true story or not, simply because it came from you. If it is true, I have questions I would like to ask.

In this story it appeared as though you didn't care for your husband. I was waiting to hear something confirming how you felt about him, and I don't know why it was edited out. Then there was the part about the man who showed you how to catch the bus. I was shocked to hear you might have given him a chance if he had tried to hit on you before you knew he was going back to the States. It sounds as though you didn't miss or love your husband at all.

Now I am wondering, Is this the short version of a new best-seller short story entitled, "The Love of My Life"? I hope only I can be thought of in such a loving way through your eyes. I want to be longed for by the woman I love in that capacity. I want you to feel as though you can't breathe without me, because that's the way I feel about you. My hands feel so empty now that I can't feel the touch of yours warming me up through and through.

I really did enjoy your letter on happiness. I once said to you I could live without everything as long as I am with you. When you told me the jobs in Florida only pay $5 an hour and asked was it okay with me, I felt the need to revert the question back to you (and I didn't get an answer, either). You see, I understand that amount of money won't get me far. By the same token, I'm not trying to go anywhere except by your side, so how little I make will never be an issue for me. I have truly realized that money can't make me happy. Yes, it will come and go, but I know that being with you can make me rich beyond my wildest dreams. Again, the real question is, Can you deal with loving a man who brings in less money than you?

That reminds me of the conversation you and your sister Diane were having about her relationship. She has not found the type of happiness in her life that we have. It seems as though she is still looking for a fairy-tale love. She was talking about how she would do this or that and have dinner on the table everyday if she didn't have to work. A man bringing in less money would be unacceptable to her. I feel love should never be about how much a person makes but the contents of what is given toward happiness. I was in a marriage with someone who seemed to only care about how much I brought home. That along with other problems made me hate to go home, and I will never be like that again. There are three essential parts to a relationship: communication, sex, and money. As long as there is an understanding about these issues, especially money, everything else will work itself out.

I am so glad this birthday was a special one you will remember for a long, long time to come. Even more important is I will be a significant person in your fond memory. I think this is a scenario when you are in love; so many little things start to take on a much bigger form. It is as though you can smell the wonderful scents of the fresh-cut grass you have been walking on for so long, and now you can finally take joy in the oxygen it provides.

Your birthday may have had more meaning to the people in your life this year because of the way you feel so content with yourself. I hope I can continue to be a part of the happiness that makes you feel butterflies and a fluttery feeling in your heart. I don't ever want you to lose that special spark that you feel in your heart when I come to mind. Like I said, I am sorry I made you cry for Valentine's Day, but I am glad to have reached a part of your heart that so few have had the pleasure of captivating. I hope this is not the tip of the iceberg of the depths that we can reach. I want you to want me more than a fish wants to be in water, because I already want you that much.

I met this guy who I used to play ball against in high school, and he is really nice. I haven't met his wife yet, but from my understanding, his home is a happy one. He and his wife don't have much and money has never been a problem, because they are rich in heart. It seems as though they have a strong togetherness, and there are no problems they cannot face and conquer. That is what makes a strong relationship. As a matter of fact, he took me to Saginaw to pay my taxes last month. I was so thankful, because he saved me from having to catch the bus. Now I'm happy to say I have the taxes under control somewhat. I paid more than I expected, but I'll find a way to get my money back.

My friend also knows a guy who works as a travel agent. He can get me a ticket to Florida for $212. The only thing is I have to get the ticket before the end of the month, because he will no longer be working at that job. I don't want you to worry, because I can get it. Now, I don't want to buy this ticket and you flip out on me and not want me to come for some ungodly reason. I have not called, because I am afraid you might be on a down and say some stuff about us breaking up again. The last conversation was a good one, and I don't want to say or do anything to crack or break your soft shell.

I guess I should stop being so insecure, because I love talking to you. I am going to end this letter, but never my pursuit to make you the happiest woman on this earth. I can't wait to see you again, because I'm dying to know how you are going to exhibit all of these feelings you are experiencing. I can't wait!

Love,

Willie

P.S. Tell Li'l Henry I said hi.

P.P.S. Did you ever turn yourself in after going AWOL?

* * *

March 10, 1997

Hello, Sweetheart:

Well, well, well, what a beautiful letter! And very well written, I must add. You must have really sat yourself down and given me a part of you in that letter, and I am definitely going to savor it.

When I first met you, I was nervous about taking a chance with you because you spoke very intelligently. It frightened me, because I felt you were going to speak on issues I wouldn't understand. Luckily, that never happened, because back then it didn't take much to embarrass me. I don't feel that way anymore ,because I'm more knowledgeable and a lot fewer things embarrasses me now. I do have one fear, though, and I'm going to share it with you. I think I'm less than the average girl when it comes to sex. Over the years, I have been set in my ways. In other words, I didn't please my man to the best of my ability. I took sex to a deeper level only on special occasions or very seldom, and I've gotten by with that thus far. For some strange reason, I feel that's not going to work with you. I feel you are going to be the one who's not going to be content with my subtle ways. By saying that I'm referring to the fact that I've always preferred one position during sexual intercourse. I think I will be more than willing to experience new positions with you, yet I think there will be some that I'm going to flat out not want to even try. I'm talking about it now because I think it may be a problem for us in the future. Believe me, I do want to please you in every possible way, but I can't shake this fear.

To answer your question about my love for my husband in the story: I did love him, and I didn't go to Germany looking for someone to have a relationship or fling with. As a matter of fact, I had no interest in that guy whatsoever. Yet, if I had met someone I grew to like, care about, or whatever, I wouldn't have fought the feeling simply because I had been hurt too many times trying to do the right thing. In my mind, doing the right thing was as right as doing the wrong thing. I was taught that very thing by my dear old husband. Why would you question that, anyway, considering it was cheating on my husband all the time I was writing you under his nose? We may have been thousands of miles apart and couldn't share in intimacy but the way I felt about you was definitely cheating.

You know I would never commit a crime as severe as going AWOL and not turn myself in. The question I feel you should have asked was, Did I really go AWOL?

I don't recall you asking about the money thing, but I'm glad you asked a second time. I really don't want you to feel it's such a big issue with me when it's not. I guess you're probably concern about that, because I spoke of certain ways I had gotten accustomed to being treated by the man in my life. Expecting to be taken care of by my man was just the way I learned to live my life after my breakup with Henry. It was instilled and rammed in my head by Charlene and my aunt in an attempt to lift my spirits.

"You're a pretty girl with a lot going for yourself. You can have any man you want, so you better pick one who's going to take care of you," my aunt would always say to me. She said it so often that I began to believe that if a man couldn't do anything for me, then he didn't deserve to have me. In time, I realized I'd rather be moneyless and happy than to be unhappy with all the money in the world. Like I said before, I truly thought I could not fall in love again, but you proved me wrong because you have indeed won my heart once again. You didn't get it by wining and dining me, buying me expensive gifts, or even by taking care of me. All you did was present yourself to me as the real you with true feelings, and that's all it took. I feel that's good enough for me to make that change and adopt my old ways of accepting a person for who he is, rather than for what he can do for me. I realize that when you get here, you're going to have to pretty much start from scratch. I am ready, willing, and able to deal with anything that it takes so we can be together.

Love you,

Gwen

P.S. Thank you for answering my questions about the story. I'm going to write a book!

* * *

March 31, 1997

Hello, Babe:

I enjoyed our phone call today, but some things are bothering me that I would like to share with you. Now, I know after you read this letter you are going to feel like I'm Dr. Jekyll and Mr. Hyde, but what can I do? Do I keep these feelings bottled up inside and just pretend they don't exist? You already know I'm not good at that, and I don't want to start a relationship knowing that at anytime I could explode about something I've been harboring. I try not to make a big deal out of everything, but some things I just can't help. I've got to let you know how I feel about issues that bother me, and I want to discuss them before I get upset about them.

I feel as though you didn't handle the situation very well about David financially helping me out. There was a time, if you can remember, when I told you he was helping me out financially and you didn't have a problem with it. I understood then because we had just gotten back in touch with each other, and you really didn't have a right to comment on my life.

Now that you and I are closer, I don't feel at ease accepting financial support from him, especially when you are supposed to be my man.

The fact that you and I are close again did not stop David from wanting to take care of me, so of course he continued to offer. As a matter of fact, he offered for a long time before I finally accepted his help, and that was because I really needed it. I shared it with you because I didn't want to have any secrets between us. For you to not have a problem with it now implies to me that you don't care about me as much as I thought. Why would you allow another man to take care of your woman?

Lately I've been feeling there's nothing special about our relationship at all. We call each other once a week and casually talk, that's it. We don't ask each other how we are doing or discuss exciting parts of our day, nothing. We only talk about what we did and what we have to do. The only feelings that we share with each other lately is saying, "I love you," and it's beginning to sound robotic. What the hell is going on? We can say those words all day long and not even mean it. This is a long-distance relationship, and we've got to give this more than we're giving. It's as if we're doing just enough to get by. If we were to become committed to doing or saying something, just anything special once a week to make one another happy or smile, there wouldn't be any room for negative thoughts.

Babe, we just can't say we care; we've got to show we do. I'm not trying to make this difficult; I'm just trying to make it good. I want to be in a relationship that I feel good about every day. Remember when you shared with me how you were making your eggs the way that I like them for future purposes, and when you were concerned about my weight loss? Remember when you told me you didn't care what it took for you to come to see me in June? I feel it takes me to write a letter like this one in order for you to open up a little about us.

Babe, I am such a sentimental person, but you should already know that. Why do you think I have always talked about that fairy-tale relationship and how important it is that I don't have to tell you what to do to make me happy? I feel I have a lot more than I'm giving this relationship right now, but I'm purposely holding back just checking you out. I'm not going to pour out my all to you, and then you laugh at me or joke or not make a comment at all about it. Just like how you don't make any comments when I talk about my book. Don't you think I've noticed that? As a matter of fact, I have noticed it so much that I've decided not to mention it to you ever again. This is something that's very exciting and important in my life right now and I want to share it with you, but if you choose not to comment on it, then I choose not to share it with you anymore.

Babe, the bottom line is this: I have had a rough life in the relationship department. I have lived unhappy for many reasons, but there's one in particular that I would like to share with you. I sacrificed my happiness because I felt that I owed someone for being good to me. I don't like to hurt people, and I have always felt that men are very vulnerable when they've taken a chance with their hearts. So in other words, I'm sensitive to that so much so that I have lived unhappy in order for someone else to be happy. What I'm saying to you is if you were to come all the way down here and things didn't work out, I would never ask you to leave because I would feel I was obligated to stand by your side. I would definitely live unhappy again for that reason. That is why it is so important I know for sure your feelings are real and you really want this, because I do not want to live that way again

I want you to read my letters and really read them and think about this for a while. Ask yourself if you can really make me happy. If you feel like you can, then, Babe, you need to find a way to show me you care. Care enough to make that effort more often than not, because relationships are a lot of work. I'm willing to work hard, and I expect the same from you. If you can't make me happy, then let me go. I love you very much, and I have told you so many times how I haven't felt this way in my heart since Henry. It's scary, because you could not love me as much as I love you. I want a 50/50 love. You see, I know the limits I would go for you.

Take care,

Gwen

* * *

April 10, 1997

Dear Gwen:

Listen, I love you, and the only thing I want to do is make you happy. I know you've had a rough life. Hell, I lived your life through your letters, so I know better than anybody what not to do. Babe, I'm sorry I can't read minds. If you need financial help, you're going to have to let me know. Come straight out and just tell me as simple as that. There is nothing going on in my life so important that I can't help you when you need it. Now, what you're going to have to do is open your mouth and stop being so insecure about us, or you're going to hurt us. You've got to trust that we love each other, and you've got to believe that it's a 50/50 love or you'll never feel it. If you feel like we should do other things to enhance our relationship, then you should initiate it. I'm sure I know how to follow your lead.

So, you're holding back on me? So, in other words, you're saying you're not going to give me your all unless you see that I'm giving mine? If that's what you're doing, then you need to check your quality of love for me, because real love is unconditional. Look, Babe, I want all I've got coming to me. I am more than willing to exercise better tactics to make our relationship less boring, as you say, but I will not do it alone. Before I end this letter, I want to say something else. You made reference to the fact that you would live unhappy if things didn't work once I got down there. I want you to know I would have done the same thing if the situation was reversed. We both must understand that when it comes to relationships, there are no guarantees. We just have to take the chance. If you fail, so what! I know I would feel satisfaction in at least knowing I tried. How about you?

I'll call Saturday, and we'll talk about this more in depth. I love you, Babe.

Love,

Willie

* * *

Chapter 9

May 15, 1997

Dear Gwen:

Babe, why didn't you tell me you were losing weight again? I thought we weren't going to keep secrets from one another. Now I understand why you feel compelled to write letters about us going our separate ways. Nothing is going to happen to you. As soon as you see the doctor and figure out why you keep periodically losing the weight, the better we can figure out what we need to do. I hate to hear you talk like something is going to happen to you. Nothing is going to happen to you. We've been through this before, and remember after a while you started gaining the weight back? Well, that's what's going to happen this time. You're just trying to take on too many responsibilities again. Two more months, Babe, and I'll be there forever.

* * *

(Two years later)

Dear Sweetheart:

First of all, I would like to say Happy Anniversary, Father's Day, New Year's Eve, and every holiday I won't be able to share with you in body. In spirit I will always be with you and you must remember that. I wanted to leave you something in remembrance of me, and I thought that the chance to open one last letter of memoir would be the most precious gift I could give to you. It's not that we don't do a good job in person, but I really do miss expressing ourselves on paper the way that we used to. I want to thank you for pursuing me when we first met, and for opening my eyes to the true meaning of togetherness. Thank you for holding on tight, yet allowing enough space for me to make mistakes and learn from them. Thank you for being my friend first, standing by my side through thick and thin, and being understanding in every situation that I failed. Thank you for being my comforter, my savior, and my soul mate when I needed a shoulder to cry on. Thank you for never giving up on me when you knew at times I had. Thanks for finding me again and helping me to remember that you were and always had been the love of my life. Most of all, Baby, thank you for making these past two years the happiest ones of my life.

Babe, I've come to terms with this disease called cancer by viewing it as one of the many ways God has placed his calling. I know that my illness was not a part of our plans nor our happiness, but we must always remember that life is not always a bed of roses and unto it some tears must fall. Some dreams won't be fulfilled and plans won't be carried out. As we walked down that isle to matrimony, only God knew how long we would share in love together. I am forever grateful to him for at least allowing us two years of bliss, and it was truly delightful to live out our dreams of togetherness that we worked so hard to claim. I am also grateful to Him for giving my son a father. You're more of a daddy to him than his biological father could ever be, and I feel at ease in leaving him in your care. I know you will raise him to be a fine young man. Let him know that I'll always love him, and make sure you give him the box I prepared for him. It contains all the letters that you and I have ever written to each other. Through those letters, I hope he will understand my life completely and ask fewer questions of you, although I know you wouldn't mind answering them. I know the letters will teach him what he needs to know. Now last but by all means not least, I would like to give both of you this poem:

When I think of you, my darlings
It's so simple for me to know
How much I love you dearly
How much I'll miss you so
I'm going to be with angels
A place I've longed to see
Where all around me dangles
My wings of destiny
Although I've ended this tiresome race
It's so hard to say good-bye
Anguish tears, please don't waste
And please don't question why
My love for you will never end
So stand up tall with lifted chins
Surely, time will one day send
Happiness into your lives again

Gloria F. Martin

All my love,

Your loving wife and mother,

Gwen

PART V
SAGINAW, MICHIGAN

Chapter 1

2005: "Good morning, Mr. Johnson."

"Now Brenda, I've asked you time and time again to call me Willie. I know I'm an old man, but do you have to remind me? Come on in, Henry's in the family room," said Willie, laughing. "Go on back."

"Thanks, Willie," said Brenda as she headed for the family room.

"Hey, Baby, who are you talking to?" Brenda asked as she entered the family room and saw me on the telephone. I was sitting on the sofa with my legs propped up on the coffee table with a smile on my face that I'm sure she saw. Her voice startled me, so I jumped. "Listen, I'll call you back. Okay, later."

When I hung up the phone, I knew I had some explaining to do, because she knew I wasn't talking to a man. There's a certain mannerism that can distinguish the difference between talking to a man or a woman. For instance, you wouldn't smile on the phone if you were talking to a man. You also wouldn't talk in low tones to a man unless you're gay. I was guilty of smiling and talking low; heaven help me.

This wasn't the first time that Brenda, my girlfriend of one year, walked in and caught me talking on the telephone to a woman. I think my daddy purposely sends her back without announcing her beforehand, to irk the hell out of me. He thinks I'm a womanizer, but I'm just a nice guy. I can't help if women throw their telephone numbers at me. Hell, I don't ask for it. On the other hand, just because I have a girlfriend does not mean I can't have girls as friends.

"That was Sheila calling to see if we're going to the Homecoming game tonight," I answered.

"And what did you tell this Sheila?"

"I told her, yeah. Aren't we going together, Babe?"

"You know what, Henry? I am so sick and tired of your talking to all of these girls, disrespecting me. You're supposed to be my man, and I keep hearing about you talking to this girl and that girl. What's up with that?"

"Why you sweating me like that, Brenda? You know Sheila is nothing but a friend, so stop tripping."

"You've got life wrong if you think I don't know that you're messing around with those girls. I have put up with this mess for the last three months, and I'm not doing it anymore. I'm not going to the game or anywhere else with you until you figure out which girl you want to be with."

"Baby, you know I want to be with you. Why you tripping like that?"

"Look Henry, I care a whole lot about you, but if you want to continue being my man, you better get one thing straight. It's either going to be my way or the highway. I'm not taking this mess anymore. Henry, I love you with all of my heart, but I also love you enough to let you go. You treat me like I don't matter, like I don't have a say, like you're calling all of the shots. I hope you don't think you can have me and everybody else you may be dealing with. Believe me, you are not all that."

After speaking her piece, she stormed out with her head bent down. I couldn't tell if she was crying or not. She was definitely mad as hell at me this time. I'll give her a little time to cool off, and then I'll call her, I thought. I wasn't going to chase behind her. If she still has this attitude after she thinks about his, she can get in the wind. It won't be hard to find somebody else who wants to be with me.

When my daddy stepped in to the room, I knew he had heard the argument between Brenda and me, because he just shook his head. He has always preached to me about fidelity and chivalry and how important it is in a relationship, so I knew that was exactly what he was thinking.

"Henry, you are acting more and more like your father. Your mother would turn in her grave if she knew you were treating someone you cared about in this manner."

"Listen Dad, I'm getting good grades like my mama wanted, right? I'm going to school every day and I'm going to graduate on time next year."

"Son, is that all you can remember about your mother?"

After that, we both just stood still without saying a word, as if we were in a moment of silence for my mother.

I suppose I could never tame that raging curiosity to know the kind of life my mother lived. She died when I was eleven years old, and although some things are vivid in my mind, I've always felt that never-ending need to know more. I can still remember how she looked, talked, and walked; how she laughed, cried, and lived life without a worry. My mother loved me so much, and we had a close relationship. I remember her always trying to make sure I had everything I needed. We communicated very well and I could tell her everything that wasn't related to me liking girls. I never really remember her smiling until after she left my father.

Being a single parent, she was always up to the challenge and never, under any circumstance, would she surrender to defeat. She was very strict when it came to me. Education always came first, because as far as she was concerned, her son was going to be somebody. She was never too busy to sit down and help me with homework or just explain something I was curious about. She always stressed how knowledge was power, and the more I knew, the less likely I would surrender to defeat.

She really had her act together; her life perfectly planned out. Anything that could have happened, you better believe my mom was prepared for it. So, I suppose you could say, I wasn't all too surprised when my stepfather walked into my room later that night after my argument with Brenda. He had a pained expression on his face. "Sit down, son, so we can have a man-to-man chat."

I sat down on the bed. He said, "Son, I have always tried to be the best daddy in the world for you. I've tried to raise you as I felt your mother would have, had she the chance. She knew you would have questions one day, so she asked me to give you something. Now that you're 17 years old, I feel you are able to really understand what went on in our lives and maybe learn from it. Your mother made me promise to give you this box of letters she saved. Through these letters, she felt you could better understand the life she lived."

After saying that, a tear rolled down his cheek. He had a huge box in his hand and he handed it to me. "Son, these are the letters your mother and I wrote to one another before we got married. They have a story to tell, and it needs to be told to you. I'm sure there's puzzlement inside your mind that has been there for quite some time. Now all of that can be erased if you just take the time to read and understand every letter in the box. I've sorted them in order by the post date."

When my daddy left my room, I found myself wiping tears from my eyes that I didn't even know were there. I placed the box on the foot of my bed, removed the lid, and grabbed the first letter. I felt eager to know, yet frightened that it may contain something I didn't want to learn. I took a deep breath, opened that first letter and began reading.

* * *

I locked myself in my bedroom for the entire weekend and believe it or not, I finished reading all of the letters. The only times I left my room were to eat, take a shower, and of course, relieve my bladder. Even then I took a letter with me. When I took my shower I could not wash my body fast enough to satisfy that aching desire to return to the letters. I never did find an ending place where I was actually able to sit the letters down in order to take a break. I suppose that subconsciously I didn't want a break. I craved to know my mother completely, just like a baby would crave for a bottle.

After reading the last letter with my mother's poem to us, tears began to flow from my eyes. Although I had been eleven years old, I remember when my mother died very well. I remember going to the hospital every day with my daddy. We saw her transform from a semi-healthy woman into a person who was too weak to lift her arms in order to embrace her only son. I watched her hair fall out, facial and that on top of her head, strand by strand, and her already petite body rapidly lose its weight, pound by pound. I remember her last words to my dad and me as clear as the sun is shining outside today. She asked, "Do you see the rainbow?" Then she named the seven colors: violet, indigo, blue, green, yellow, red, and orange. My daddy and I looked at one another and then thoroughly around the room, but we never saw it. Later my daddy told me how the rainbow represented God's promise to the world to never flood the earth again. We both just assumed the rainbow was God's reassurance to my mom that her family would be well taken care of after she was gone. She died the next day.

I was so engrossed and eager to discover everything about my mother. What made her strong, weak, fight, hold her tongue, what made her mad, sad, or happy. Then to feel how she felt after being finally rescued and given the kind of happiness she so longed for her entire life. After reading the letters, a lot of things seemed clear to me, especially her being such a strong woman.

I don't remember my father putting her through so much, but I was too young to know. No wonder I never heard from him again after he and my mother divorced. How could he face me after not giving 100% of himself to my mother and me? He never even tried to contact me after my mother's death. Since I was adopted by my daddy, I saw no reason to find him, either, or have him become a part of my life. If I were to ever come face to face with him, I would respectfully and tactfully tell him exactly how I feel about him. That I could never love him because of the pain he caused my mother. Never giving our family a chance at happiness together, which was all my mother ever wanted. Always putting those women in the street before our happiness, concerns, and needs that we had to make our lives complete. I would say just enough to give him something to think about. I wouldn't be vindictive, because I know that whatever come around, goes around to the originator.

My mother worked one, two, and sometimes three jobs at a time, cooked, cleaned, did laundry, and made sure everybody had clothes on their backs. It's unbelievable how much of herself she willingly and unconditionally gave to me and anybody else she loved. In so knowing this, how could my father just walk all over her and abandon me as if I never existed? My mother had to look outside our home for the love she craved for. Thank God my daddy satisfied her appetite for love by saying, doing, and being all the man that she could ever need. Giving her all the love she could ever wish for and a chance to feel real happiness. How effortless it was to give into love when you had a good woman to stand by your side. I don't understand why my father couldn't see it.

At that moment a bell begin ringing inside my ear. A light began to flash before my eyes. You stupid fool! You have just allowed the one woman who loves you to walk out of your life. At that moment I realized I was becoming my father all over again. I would never want to bring the pain, humiliation, nor all the tears that my mother had to shed into someone's else's life, especially someone who I love very much. I would not do that!

"Hello, is this Rosie's Flower Shop? Yes, I want to order a dozen of long-stemmed roses for my Baby. Yep, baby brush, Mylar balloons with 'I love you' written on them, the works. I want the card to read, 'To the love of my life. It wasn't until today I realized how much you really mean to me. If it takes all the tomorrows to come, I'll spend them proving that to you. I love you yesterday, today, and I will love you forever. Henry.'"

When I turned around I saw my father smiling. He looked up at the ceiling and said, "I think it worked, Babe."

Epilogue

"Brenda, you and Li'l Henry need to hurry up. My dad's going to kill me if I'm late. I'm only the best man."

"Chill out, Babe, I can't get Li'l Henry's tie straight."

I grabbed my two-year-old son and begin tying his tie. "Me no wanna wear stupid tie!" cried Li'l Henry.

"Henry Dewayne Johnson the third, how many times have I told you that women adore men who wear ties? Besides, this is a very special occasion. It's not every day that your old granddaddy gets married."

I couldn't believe my daddy was getting married. After 15 years, he's finally let my mother go and has gone on with his life. I'm sure her memories will last forever, because I still think about her from time to time. This is what she wanted, for us all to be happy. I couldn't be more happy than I am today. I have a wife of two years who loves me very much and a son who's the spitting image of me to carry on my name. A family who makes my life complete and happy beyond my wildest dreams. A family whom I vow to provide, love, and cherish and put first in my life after God. Now my daddy can taste some of this happiness, because life is about losses and gains, bitter and sweet, ups and down. We, ourselves, just have to find a way to live life as it comes and not let the sad times control us, but use them to our advantage. I allowed the death of my mother to control my way of thinking in regard to women. I've come to understand that we choose our own destiny, and our attitude determines whether it's good or bad. Thank you for helping me to become the man who I am and who you would be proud of today. I love you, Mama.